PUT OUT THE LIGHT

SARA WOODS
PUT OUT THE LIGHT

Put out the light, and then put out the light
Othello, Act V, scene ii

St. Martin's Press
New York

Library of Congress Cataloging-in-Publication Data

Woods, Sara, pseud.
    Put out the light.

    I. Title.
PR6073.063P88   1985   823'.914   85-18478
ISBN 0-312-65702-1

First published in Great Britain by Macmillan London Ltd.
First U.S. Edition
10 9 8 7 6 5 4 3 2 1

Cast of Characters

The household at Kempenfeldt Square
    Sir Nicholas Harding, QC
    Vera, Lady Harding, his wife
    Antony Maitland, QC
    Jenny Maitland, his wife
    Gibbs, Sir Nicholas's butler
    Mrs Stokes, Sir Nicholas's cook

People connected with the production of Crabbed Age and Youth *at the* *Cornmarket Theatre*
Cast, in order of appearance:

Sir Benjamin Oldfellow	Matthew Benbow
Becky, Lady Oldfellow	Margaret (Meg) Hamilton
Bess Brownlees, her maid	Amanda Chillingworth
Richard Twells, manservant to Gilbert Bold	Arthur Webb
Lucy Simpering, Becky's friend	Stella Hartley
Jack Bashful	Edward Brome
Gilbert Bold	Joseph Weatherly
Understudy to Miss Hamilton	Mary Russell
Understudy to Miss Hartley and Miss Chillingworth	Roberta Rowan
Understudy to Mr Benbow, Mr Brome, Mr Weatherly and Mr Webb	Mark Kenilworth

    Chester Cartwright, author/historian
    Jeremy Skelton, playwright
    Brian Barrington, director
    Hugh Clinton, stage manager
    'Miss Miggs', wardrobe mistress
    Tommy, prompter

The police (all of New Scotland Yard)
> Detective Superintendent Sykes
> Detective Chief Inspector Conway
> Detective Sergeant Porterhouse

Also appearing
> Roger Farrell, Meg's husband
> Geoffrey Horton, a solicitor
> Anne Skelton, Jeremy's wife
> Richard Trevor, drama critic of the *Courier*

Off-stage
> Sir Alfred Godalming, Assistant Commissioner (Crime) at
>   New Scotland Yard
> Sir John Cartwright, b1620, d1675

Michaelmas Term, 1975

Prologue

'Oh, no, darling, not this one,' said Meg Farrell earnestly. 'It's something *quite* different.' There was a moment's silence following this positive statement because both Antony and Jenny Maitland were perfectly well aware that it was something in the nature of a red herring drawn across the path of Antony's obvious distress.

They were close friends, these four; the Maitlands in whose living room they were gathered, and the Farrells, Roger and Meg. Maitland was a barrister, and before the new subject was introduced he had been explaining as briefly as Meg's curiosity would allow the outcome of a case, concluded earlier that day, on which he and his uncle, Sir Nicholas Harding, had worked together. Only a very insensitive person would have thought in this instance that their clients' acquittal was an unmixed blessing, and Antony, unfortunately for himself, was very far from that. Meg, who was better known by her stage name of Margaret Hamilton, had been resting – to her husband's great satisfaction – for rather longer than usual, and during the last few days had surrounded herself with such an aura of mystery that Jenny had felt could only foreshadow a new play, which might to some degree at least distract her husband. Meg, playing up nobly, had admitted that she was about to go to work again, but she still wasn't going to be done out of her meed of drama. 'It's still a deadly secret,' she went on, 'but of course Jeremy wouldn't mind my telling you.'

'He's decided to write another play? I could understand your being excited about the last one,' said Antony, 'because it was the kind of thing you'd never tried before. But it was a terrific success, and only came off about two minutes ago anyway. I can't see what's so special about his doing another.'

'I told you, darling, it's something different,' Meg insisted.

'So you did. You also told us it was confidential. But it's no good telling us to be discreet,' he added, 'unless you also tell us

9

what to be discreet about.'

'I was just going to do so,' said Meg, on her dignity. 'What do you know about the restoration dramatists?' she asked.

Antony thought about that for a moment. 'Enough to know they've nothing to do with anything Jeremy's likely to turn out,' he said at last. 'I've seen a few of the plays of course but it's not a subject I've ever studied. The theatre had been banned, and when Charles II came back everyone wanted to get in on the act. But –'

'Is it the tragedies you're interested in or the comedies?' said Jenny, seeing him momentarily – and most uncharacteristically, any of his friends would have told you – at a loss for words.

'The comedies. And interest isn't the right word really; I just wanted to find out whether you're capable of appreciating what I'm going to tell you.' Meg had decided to play the school ma'am, and was doing it very well as they both had to admit, but at that point Roger felt it expedient to take a hand, in the interests of getting the story told before midnight. He was that curious anomaly, a stockbroker who was by instinct a man of action, and to complete the paradox he had also a distinctly piratical look about him, which oddly enough had never proved to be a handicap when dealing with his clients.

'Who would you say is the father of the modern detective story?' he asked.

'If Jeremy's going to write a biography of Edgar Allan Poe,' said Antony, rather tartly, 'or even of Wilkie Collins, which might be more appropriate because he wrote full length novels while Poe, as well as being a journalist, confined himself mainly to short stories, I don't see what Meg is getting so worked up about.'

'Of course you don't,' Jenny agreed, 'and neither do I. You're being deliberately mysterious, Meg. Stop being enigmatic and tell us what this is all about.'

Meg relented, but only so far as to ask another question. 'Have either of you heard of Sir John Cartwright?'

Both Antony and Jenny started to say 'Yes, of course,' almost simultaneously, after which there was a moment's silence before Antony waved a hand to encourage his wife to continue. 'He's one of the most famous,' said Jenny. 'On a par with Congreve and Wycherley. And since you mention comedies I suppose that's what he wrote, though I'm afraid I thought that everybody did at

10

that time, and I don't remember ever having seen one of his plays.'

'There were some tragedies, too, but that's beside the point. You're quite right, Jenny, Sir John Cartwright did write comedies, and was noted for his wit.'

'What I don't see,' said Maitland thoughtfully (but it was obvious that his interest had now been caught), 'is what all this has to do with Jeremy.' He was a tall man with dark hair, a thin, intelligent face, and a humorous look that was generally very much in evidence, though that evening it had been conspicuous mainly by its absence.

'If Uncle Nick were here,' said Meg, 'he'd tell you that's something a lawyer should never do. Jump to conclusions,' she explained when she saw Antony's blank look.

'But you said —'

'There *is* a connection if you'll give me a chance to explain. There's been a good deal of argument on the subject of the origin of the detective story and some people have tried to introduce such extraneous matter as ghost stories or tales of witchcraft. But I'm speaking of the classic story, the pure puzzle.'

'And quoting Jeremy into the bargain,' Roger put in. 'Almost word for word,' he added.

'I've never had any difficulty remembering things,' said Meg, not at all abashed, 'and Jeremy has been studying the matter so he knows much more about it than I do. What would you say,' she added impressively, turning a little so that her remarks were now addressed to Antony and Jenny impartially, 'if I told you that the outline of a play with such a plot, written in Sir John Cartwright's own hand, has been discovered?'

'But nobody then —' This time Antony broke off without being interrupted, and looked from Jenny to Roger helplessly.

'I should say I'd need a good deal of convincing that it was genuine,' said Jenny. 'People in those days just didn't think that way, or so I've always believed.'

'It seems Cartwright did.'

'What was the name to be anyway?' asked Maitland.

'*Crabbed Age and Youth.* Not a good title,' said Meg consideringly, 'because nobody will know how to pronounce it, but descriptive in the manner of the age.' She sat back and sipped her cherry brandy, which Maitland kept under protest for her exclusive use. Apparently she had no more to say.

11

'But you can't leave it there,' Jenny protested, and Antony looked at her with amused affection. In any group she was generally the silent one, a better listener than a talker, and he was well enough aware that it was in his interests that she was rousing herself to insist on further clarification from Meg.

'I can quite understand your impatience, Jenny,' said Roger, though his amusement was more carefully concealed. 'I don't think Meg intends to leave it there, but if she does I'll tell you. It's worth waiting for as a matter of fact, because it happens to be an interesting story.'

'Did Jeremy discover this outline himself?' Antony asked.

'No, he didn't. Can you imagine Jeremy grubbing about in people's attics on the odd chance of making a discovery like that?' Meg enquired rather scornfully.

'I can't, but it's rather a pity he didn't. If this document is genuine it will make a tremendous sensation, both here and in America.'

'That's what I think, and what interests Jeremy so much.' Meg sounded complacent now. 'And if you'll give me half a chance I'll tell you. A man called Chester Cartwright –'

'A living man?'

'A man in his fifties, Jeremy says, but I haven't met him yet. He's connected with Sir John Cartwright's family or so he says. A maiden aunt of Chester's died, on his father's side –'

'That means she was a Cartwright too,' said Jenny to Antony. Where family relationships were concerned she had no faith at all in his ability to work them out.

'Exactly,' Meg concurred. 'As you'd say yourself, Antony, when you weren't parodying Uncle Nick.'

'Let's leave Uncle Nick out of it and get on with the story, *darling*,' Maitland exhorted her.

'As I was saying before you interrupted me, this aunt died, leaving Chester Cartwright as her executor and sole heir. When he was going through her things he came across this outline in the attic. As it happens, he's a scholarly sort of chap, or so Jeremy says, and the late seventeenth century's his period. In fact he's written several biographies, mainly of the playwrights of the period, and naturally he's particularly interested in Sir John so his life's among them. Of course his find was pretty exciting for him –'

'The first thing he should do is get it authenticated,' said

Maitland. 'With all the modern methods it's quite easy these days.'

This time Meg took the interruption without complaint. 'He's not willing to do that immediately and for a very good reason,' she said, but paused to direct a dagger-like glance at her husband who bore it with equanimity. 'I'm still quoting Jeremy, so you needn't interrupt again to tell them so. There'd been no attempt to keep it safely, it was just shoved in anyhow among some other documents, and by now it's in pretty poor condition. This Mr Cartwright – the one who's alive today – thinks the analysis, whatever it is they do, would finish it off altogether, so before that happens he wants to make something of a splash with it. I said he was a scholar, and I think more accurately I should have added the word impoverished to qualify that because his books haven't been very successful. But even so Jeremy doesn't think that the money there may be in it for him is his prime motive. It's the academic acclaim that would result.'

'You haven't explained,' said Antony sceptically, 'how he's going to make a splash with this outline if he won't let anyone see it.'

'He's shown it to Jeremy, and Jeremy is pretty excited about it, too, and you wouldn't call him particularly credulous,' said Meg. 'It's three sheets of paper, covered on both sides with very small handwriting, not at all easy for a layman to decipher. Mr Cartwright's got them between glass to preserve them. He also showed Jeremy an example of Sir John's handwriting, an illustration from his own book as a matter of fact, and even to a layman's eye Jeremy said it was obvious they were identical.'

'Well,' said Maitland, 'even if he won't have the ink and paper analysed, surely a handwriting expert could look at the outline without doing any further harm.'

'Without a really thorough examination his opinion wouldn't be worth much,' said Meg. 'That's what Jeremy says, and Roger agrees with him. Besides, Chester Cartwright's come up with this idea –'

'So you keep telling us,' said Antony, 'but you don't tell us what it is.'

'If you'll only have patience –' She broke off there, perhaps catching sight of her host's expression. 'He thought, why not have a play written, following the outline, and then launch it in a blaze of publicity? After that there'll be time enough to bring the experts into it. Well, he went to Jeremy –'

'As Jeremy so modestly puts it,' Roger couldn't resist interrupting again, 'as the greatest living exponent of the detective story.'

This was too much for Jenny. 'Aren't you forgetting –?' she began.

'The inestimable Agatha,' Roger finished for her. 'No, I'm not forgetting her, but she's written lots of plays to Jeremy's one, and perhaps Cartwright thought someone not quite so well known wouldn't steal so much of the limelight.'

'Don't let Jeremy hear you say that. Anyway, there are still any number of good women writers in the field,' said Jenny.

'My dear girl, I'd no idea you were an exponent of women's lib,' Roger teased her.

'I don't need liberating,' said Jenny crossly, but ill-temper was something she could never sustain for long. 'Does this mean Jeremy's going to write a play based on this – this outline?'

'It's already written.' It was, after all, Meg's story and she'd no intention of letting them forget it. 'He finished it before he spoke to me. He says – I'm quoting again, Roger – that he did nothing to spoil the original idea, just embellished it a little here and there. The original inclined to be somewhat sketchy, and he thinks he's improved on it a little.'

'I don't know that I like the sound of that,' Antony put in. 'Have you seen the play?'

'Not yet, I don't need to. A play by Sir John Cartwright and Jeremy Skelton; that's quite enough to ensure it a hearing. And if you're thinking Jeremy may have done a bad job of it, being used to modern dialogue, I think you're wrong. He says he'd been living and breathing Sir John's other plays for weeks before he ever started writing, and you know he's pretty good where words are concerned.'

'I'll take your word about that,' said Antony, 'but what about this mysterious outline – the one they won't have tested to prove its authenticity. Don't you find that rather suspicious?'

'Jeremy's met the man. He believed him.'

'That's just it, he wanted to believe him. Don't you think that might have made even Jeremy a little gullible?'

'No, I don't. He's good about people. You can't write novels unless you are.'

'But even if the paper is so fragile, a handwriting expert at least

14

could have looked at it.'

'Jeremy has, and he's satisfied. Besides, there's this thing about publicity. I think Mr Cartwright is probably right about that . . . it must be timed exactly. The play will make both their fortunes, you wait and see,' Meg said confidently.

'Well, I hope Jeremy's got an agreement properly drawn up. That's going to be pretty important.'

'He went to Geoffrey Horton.'

'That's all right, then. Has he got a cast put together yet? Besides you, I mean; I suppose all this excitement means you're playing the lead.'

'Yes, Jeremy says it's a marvellous part. But the rest of the cast isn't chosen yet.'

'Are they in town? Jeremy and Anne, I mean.'

'Yes, the flat they had before wasn't vacant so they're staying at Taylor's Hotel. I know he'll be getting in touch with you.'

'We must ask them to dinner,' said Jenny promptly. 'Does Jeremy know you've talked to us, Meg?'

'Yes, that's all right. At least, he knew I was going to, so you don't have to feign ignorance. And I really don't think Roger minds too much,' she added earnestly. 'There are lots of arrangements to make yet before we can even start rehearsing, so I'll be free for quite a long time.'

Maitland glanced at his friend. 'It had to happen sooner or later,' said Farrell. 'You can take it I'm reasonably resigned.'

Tuesday, 28th October

Antony and Jenny Maitland had their own quarters at the top of Sir Nicholas Harding's house in Kempenfeldt Square. Sir Nicholas was Antony's uncle, and the head of the chambers in the Inner Temple to which he belonged. It was a long time now since any of them had thought of the arrangement as anything but permanent, except for a brief period after Sir Nicholas's marriage a little over four years before to Miss Vera Langhorne, barrister-at-law, when Antony's scruples about possibly being in the way had almost got the better of him. Since then, however, the household had settled down even more comfortably than before; Sir Nicholas's staff approved of Vera, and even Gibbs, the elderly, disagreeable butler who had been inherited by Sir Nicholas along with the house, conducted himself in a slightly more reasonable fashion. In addition, the traditions that had grown up over the years were continued, among them being the fact that almost invariably the Hardings dined with the Maitlands on Tuesday evenings, except during the long vacation when all of them were generally away. It was Jenny's idea that on this particular Tuesday Jeremy and Anne Skelton should join the party, as they were all old friends, Jeremy having occasion to be grateful to Vera for having involved Sir Nicholas and Antony in his affairs some years before to his great advantage.

It was rather short notice, but Anne seized upon the invitation eagerly when Jenny phoned her, and when Antony and Sir Nicholas arrived home from chambers together that evening the rest of the party were already assembled in the big living room upstairs, which was comfortable if a trifle confusing to people who saw it for the first time, being almost entirely furnished by unwanted pieces donated by its owners' loving families, so that no article of furniture in any way matched another, with the exception of the two wing chairs that flanked

17

the fireplace.

Antony waited until the first greetings had been exchanged and then went across to the writing table where the drinks were set out. 'From what Meg says, you've a good deal to tell us, Jeremy,' he said, not looking round. 'I want to hear more about this latest project, but before we start I'd like your permission to tell Uncle Nick and Vera what Meg told us last night.'

'That's something you hardly needed to ask,' said Jeremy cheerfully. He was a big man, as tall as Maitland but very much more heftily built, his hair equally undisciplined but not quite so dark. He was also the possessor of a pleasant voice, a good share of self-confidence, and an enviable reputation as a writer of mysteries. A few years before he had made a success in another line, by converting one of them, *Done In By Daggers*, into a play which had met with a success not altogether attributable to the unpleasant events that had attended its opening night. It was this he was referring to obliquely as he went on, addressing Vera directly now, but with an occasional glance at Sir Nicholas. 'Anne tells me I shouldn't have anything to do with the theatre again after what happened, but I think I've made her see you can't run your life like that. After all, I make my living by writing, and if I'd given up mysteries after what happened in Chedcombe all those years ago where would we be now?'

'Yes, Jeremy, you've convinced me,' said Anne in her gentle way. Looking at her, Antony remembered very vividly the first time he had seen her – she had been Anne Fabyan then – and how her brown gold hair had reminded him of Jenny's in colour, though it was smooth and straight while Jenny's curled wildly. She had now, as she had had then, a trim figure, but there the resemblance between the two of them stopped. She was a little shorter than Jenny and lacked her serenity, though perhaps sometimes her very quietness could have again led you to a comparison between them. Jenny had grey eyes, while Anne's were more violet than blue, if that wasn't too imaginative a way of putting it. But Maitland had no time to pursue his thoughts further. 'You'd better let Antony tell Sir Nicholas and Lady Harding all about the play,' she reminded her husband now, 'or they'll be wondering what on earth we're talking about.'

'Well, I daresay he'll do that better than I should,' Jeremy admitted. 'Provided Meg didn't get it all wrong, of course. Go ahead,' he invited as Antony came back to the circle round the fire, first providing his uncle with sherry and then going back to fetch his own glass which he placed on the mantelshelf beside the clock.

Maitland was glad enough to oblige. The day hadn't been an easy one; there had been too many matters left over from the case that had just ended still to be dealt with, and now he was glad enough to turn his mind to a quite different subject, completely unconnected with law. And there was nobody here who would object if he took up his own favourite position on the hearthrug, a little to the left of the fire; not that he was restless particularly, but he was used to thinking on his feet, and generally did so except when it was likely to make his audience nervous. So he repeated what Meg had told them, in rather fewer words than had been exchanged the evening before. 'Have I got all that right?' he asked when he had finished.

'Yes, quite right,' Jeremy Skelton agreed. 'Meg will probably have read the thing by this time, and I hope she'll agree with me that it's turned out pretty well.'

'Are you sticking to the title Sir John Cartwright gave it?'

'It seemed the obvious thing to do. Suitable, and conveys the sense of period. What do you think of the idea?' he asked, looking around him, so that the question might have been addressed to any one of the company.

It was Sir Nicholas who answered. 'I'm sure it will turn out excellently,' he said. 'But a certain remark of Meg's that Antony repeated made me wonder . . . how does this Chester Cartwright like it now you've finished?'

Jeremy grinned. 'You mean because I said I'd improved it a little. I'm afraid my sense of humour got the better of me about that.'

'Better explain,' said Vera gruffly. They were all used to her elliptical way of speaking, which she abandoned only rarely, so none of them was at all surprised and when Jeremy turned to answer her he was still smiling.

'Well one of the characters, Sir Benjamin Oldfellow, the one who gets murdered, is always saying "Stap me vitals".'

'Why shouldn't he? Always understood some people said that every other word in those days, though why they should –'

'Yes, it was mentioned in the outline and that's why I included it.'

'Then why should Chester Cartwright object?' asked Vera,

who had an orderly mind, and liked to get everything straight.

'And where does your sense of humour come in?' Sir Nicholas demanded almost simultaneously.

'Because Sir Benjamin in the outline, in Sir John Cartwright's outline, was poisoned. But I couldn't resist having him run through with a rapier, a sort of dramatic irony I suppose you could call it. But Chester didn't like the idea.'

'Are you going to change it back, then?'

'Oh, I don't think so. I can be very stubborn, you know, when I set my mind on a thing.'

'Meg said Geoffrey drew up the agreement,' Antony put in. 'How was it worded?'

'As you'd expect. Chester Cartwright is supposed to approve the treatment of the outline. But as I said –'

'He isn't only stubborn, he can be very persuasive,' Anne interrupted. 'Jeremy pointed out that he had already found a director for it, and the financing was arranged – if Meg told you about that you forgot to mention it – and when Mr Cartwright heard that he soon changed his views.'

'I'm surprised at you, Anne. Such cynicism,' said Antony smiling. 'But no, Meg didn't tell us that.'

'Brian Barrington's going to direct. He seems to have fallen in love with the play,' said Anne.

'Barrington?' Maitland whistled, but broke off abruptly as he caught his uncle's eye. 'You've got yourself a big fish, haven't you? Is he going to take one of the parts himself?'

'No, you're a bit out of date, Antony.' That was Jeremy taking up the story. 'I admit I'd have liked that and he could quite easily have done both, but he's gone over completely to directing now. And he's got the backing, and he's even got the theatre picked out – the Cornmarket. I'm glad he didn't think of the Alhambra; that would have been altogether too much of a good thing.' (The Alhambra was the theatre in which Jeremy's previous play had started life.)

'Is there a very big cast to be put together?' The less any of them thought about that earlier production the better, Maitland considered.

'Not terribly. That's the next thing from what Brian Barrington says . . . to find people who can throw themselves into the spirit of the thing. It has to be played as a sort of a romp if it's to be at all true to what must have been Sir John Cartwright's

20

intention.'

'Yes, I understand that. Will the casting be done immediately?'

'As it happens, there's no great hurry. Barrington – he's an awfully nice chap by the way – is frightfully superstitious.'

'That can be said about quite a lot of actors, can't it? Though I must say Roger seems to have been able to keep Meg pretty well in check,' added Antony reflectively.

'Yes, but Barrington's superstition works in reverse,' Jeremy explained. 'He thinks what's unlucky for everyone else is lucky for him. So we can't open until February, Friday the thirteenth to be exact. It's not really very long to wait and it seemed worth humouring him.'

'Yes, but about the cast, how many people do you have to find?'

'There's the old man I told you about, the one who's murdered. His name's Sir Benjamin Oldfellow. And his wife, who of course is really very young, – hence the title – her name is Becky, and she's the only one already decided on because Meg can obviously do the part standing on her head. Naturally she has a maid, Bess Brownlees, and equally naturally the maid has a lover who happens to be the manservant of the hero. His name, the manservant's, I mean, is Richard Twells, and his employer is Gilbert Bold of all things.'

'That's five people already.'

'Only two more. Lucy Simpering – don't you love the name? – who is Becky's friend and confidante, and Jack Bashful who fulfils the same role for Gilbert Bold. We're making do with three understudies, one for Meg, one for the other two women, and only one for the four men, so it's to be hoped none of them falls sick.'

'And somebody runs Sir Benjamin through. Who is the dastardly villain?' asked Antony, entering into the spirit of the thing and twirling an imaginary moustache.

'I don't think I shall tell you that,' said Jeremy. 'Anne's hoping Jenny will come to some of the rehearsals with her, and you'll come to at least one I expect, Antony, unless you've less curiosity than I think you have.'

'I hope you're not casting me for the role of critic. I don't think I should shine at that at all.'

'You can represent the general public,' Jeremy told him. 'The man in the street.'

'That's better; the man on the Clapham omnibus,' said Antony, feeling that this role at least was well within his grasp.

'And of course,' said Anne in her gentle way to Vera, 'if you and Sir Nicholas would care to attend as well —'

Vera exchanged a glance with her husband. 'I think, my dear,' she said, 'we'd probably prefer to wait until the first night.'

'It won't . . . it won't be too reminiscent of the last time,' said Anne diffidently. Antony thought as she spoke that Jeremy wasn't altogether right in thinking she was completely reconciled to his taking on the role of dramatist again.

'Not a bit of it,' said Vera robustly. 'Different theatre, different cast, everything'll be fine, you'll see.'

And indeed it seemed as if she was right. During the next few weeks a cast was assembled, and Anne reported to Jenny that Mr Chester Cartwright had become quite reconciled to Jeremy Skelton's version of his relative's play, in fact extremely enthusiastic about the whole thing. 'And I don't know why he shouldn't be,' she added reflectively, 'I think he's going to make a lot of money out of it.'

Antony, when that was repeated to him, wasn't quite so sure. But it amused him to watch how the story unfolded during these weeks, from the first hint that the outline of a play by Sir John Cartwright had been discovered, to the rumour that its subject was unusual for the day in which he had been writing, and thence, by some devious route, to the final revelation that Mr Jeremy Skelton, that eminent mystery novelist, had undertaken to turn the bare bones of the outline into a complete work for the stage. By the time the name of the play and the complete cast had been announced, together with the opening date (as insisted on by Brian Barrington) everyone with the faintest interest in theatrical matters was in a state of simmering excitement. It was Jeremy's idea to stir the pot further by holding a small party in his hotel to celebrate the beginning of rehearsals, though this date was again chosen in deference to Barrington's wishes as Boxing Day happened that year to fall on a Friday. Antony and Jenny were invited, a fact that Jenny viewed with simple pleasure, while even her husband felt the affair might not be without its interest.

Christmas Vacation, 1975/76

Friday, 26th December

I

The party was to be held in a large room at Taylor's Hotel that
was available for such purposes. Anne had spoken of a small
gathering but to Antony, following his wife into the room, it
seemed very far from that. Later, talking it over with Jenny, he
attributed this to the feeling that not only was the cast of the play
present but also the characters they represented. And it was true
enough that the introductions (this is Arthur Webb, who is
playing Richard Twells) only added to the general confusion. In
addition to the members of the cast the three understudies were
present, as was the director and the stage manager of the
Cornmarket Theatre. Also, of course, Chester Cartwright, Roger
Farrell, and Jeremy and Anne Skelton in their capacity as hosts.

All this Antony had anticipated. What he hadn't expected was
that there would also be representatives from the four leading
Sunday newspapers, though naturally it didn't dawn on him at
first who they were. It wasn't until Jeremy, finding that Jenny
had been spirited away from Antony's side by Anne, took him
across the room to introduce him rather ceremoniously to Brian
Barrington and to the man the director was at the moment
talking to, Richard Trevor, from the *Courier*, that he realised this
was something he should have expected. But if he hoped for a
moment that a theatre critic would be above taking an interest in
the ordinary run of news he was quickly disillusioned. Trevor, a
short round man who looked as if he would have some difficulty
in fitting his bulk into an ordinary stall in the theatre, turned to
him eagerly. 'Antony Maitland?' he said. 'Oh, yes, you're the
chap who –' He broke off there and turned away, muttering.
'Sorry about that, thinking of somebody else.'

Jeremy had already left them. Antony and Brian Barrington
were left staring at each other with Antony only too well aware

that his expression must have betrayed him. In fact he had gone rather pale and Barrington eyed him with interest. 'I gather our friend put his foot in it,' he said. 'Tell me, Mr Maitland, did what he said disconcert you or make you angry?'

There was obviously no malice in the question, only a very genuine interest. Antony did his best to answer it in the spirit in which it had been asked. 'Both, I suppose,' he admitted. And then, confidingly, 'I wasn't counting on the press being here, which was rather naive of me, I suppose.'

'And you wish the whole lot of them to perdition? I can sympathise with that,' Barrington told him. 'You're a barrister, I believe?'

'And you've heard of me?' said Antony rather bitterly.

'Well, yes, I have to admit ... I was interested in the Alhambra Theatre business, of course. But you must realise that for theatre people publicity is meat and drink. I gather you're married to that charming girl who's talking to Anne Skelton now. Is that right?'

'Yes, that's quite right.' Antony couldn't be thankful enough for the change of subject. The man from the *Courier* might have been thinking of the Alhambra business, but there had been a case when one of his own colleagues ... 'Meg Farrell's a very old friend of ours, too. She's very excited about all this, you know.' He waved a hand vaguely to include the rest of the gathering.

'And quite rightly,' said Barrington with approval. 'Jeremy has done a first class piece of work and we've got together a first-rate cast to play it. Besides, you know, they're giving me my way about ... certain things.'

Since it was obvious from his expression that he hoped for further questions Antony had no scruples about continuing the subject. 'What sort of things?' he asked.

Barrington hesitated. He was a very tall man, one of the few people Maitland had to look up to when he wished to meet his eyes, and age had done nothing to lessen the rather spectacular good looks that had made him so popular in his younger days. Probably he was even better looking now, as the lines on his face had given it character. But his hair was grey, and certainly he didn't look like a youth any more. He laughed now in a self-deprecating way and said with a humorous inflection in his voice, 'We actors are a superstitious lot, you know.'

'Meg told me – or was it Jeremy? – that you wanted the

26

opening to be on Friday the thirteenth.'

'She's quite right, I did,' said Barrington as though he were proud of his decision.

'Most people who admit to being superstitious would think that was an unlucky day,' Antony protested.

'So they would. Friday on its own is supposed to be unlucky enough, that's why we chose it for this party. You see when I was very young I decided it was all nonsense so I did everything contrariwise. It took me some time to realise that was quite the right thing for me, because all the things that were supposed to be unlucky worked for me just the opposite way. So of course I've played it up like the dickens ever since.'

Antony smiled at him. 'But isn't that superstitious too?'

'Of course it is! I told you we were a superstitious lot. The thing is, you see,' he added earnestly, 'it works.'

'And you think it will ensure success for *Crabbed Age and Youth?*' He remembered what Meg had said, and was careful to pronounce it as she had told him.

'That and the cast were chosen,' Barrington affirmed. 'They're an excellent lot, as you'll see. Are you a theatre-goer, Mr Maitland?'

'Whenever I have time. And knowing Meg and Roger so well, that happens more often than I used to think possible.'

'Then I'm sure you'll enjoy this,' said Barrington confidently. 'Ah, here's Mr Cartwright. Do you know him?'

'Only by name.'

'Then let me introduce you.' He did so rather more formally than might have been considered necessary and Cartwright looked at Antony curiously but to his relief his name seemed to mean nothing to the other man. 'How are you, Chester?' Barrington went on. 'This is a good party, isn't it, a worthy send-off for the rehearsals?'

'And good publicity,' said Cartwright dryly. He was a much shorter man than either of his companions and very pale, with hair that grew well back from his forehead and straggled over his collar at the back. 'And I'm sure it's a good thing,' he added, 'for the cast to get to know each other before they start work.'

'My dear fellow, are you under the impression they don't know each other already? All stage people do,' said Barrington. 'We're a small community, you know, and none of these people' – he waved an explanatory hand towards the assembled company – 'is exactly an amateur.'

'No, I know that. I didn't realise though –'

'Well, take Amanda Chillingworth for instance, she's Mrs Arthur Webb in real life.' He turned again to Antony. 'The Webbs are playing the servants, which are quite large and important parts, and as they're unfashionable enough to be very much in love with each other that ought to help. Then there's Roberta Rowan; she's one of the understudies. She's engaged to Weatherly, or nearly engaged, I'm not sure which. He's our hero.'

'I hadn't realised that either,' said Antony. 'That there were so many inter-relationships, I mean.'

'Oh, well, I don't suppose you read the entertainment pages. But I haven't finished yet. I'll introduce them all to you in a moment and then you'll see. Matthew Benbow, our Sir Benjamin, is a widower of course. And Edward Brome and the men's understudy, Mark Kenilworth, are both young chaps not yet married. But Mary Russell, Meg's understudy, who is also unmarried, moved in with Stella Hartley after Stella's latest divorce, and even the single members of the cast all know each other at least slightly.'

'I haven't got them all sorted out yet,' said Chester Cartwright looking around him.

'Nor have I, of course,' Antony told him. 'But Mr Barrington has just been telling me what great hopes he has for the play.'

'We all agree with him,' said Cartwright enthusiastically. 'Jeremy has done an absolutely splendid job and I'm sure it can't have been easy.'

'For one thing,' said Barrington, 'he's managed to get the whole thing into one set, Lady Oldfellow's drawing room. That's a consideration these days.'

'I admit,' said Cartwright, who apparently hadn't been listening, 'that I was a little disappointed at first to find that the *modus operandi*, if I may call it so, had been altered, but then I realised that it was really more true to the spirit of the times than the one Uncle Jack had suggested. They didn't know much about poisons in those days and it might have been difficult to find a real one that acted in just the way he described. Besides, there's the question of the murderer having access to it. Jeremy says audiences – well, he said readers, actually – are much more particular about accuracy these days.'

'You talk about Uncle Jack,' said Antony tentatively. 'How close a relation was Sir John Cartwright to you?'

'My great uncle, if you like, though I don't know how many greats there should be in front of that. Do I seem to harp on the connection? He was a very great man, you know, and the continuing interest in his work is well deserved. I'm descended from a younger brother of his, a very obscure person. There was also a William Cartwright who was a playwright in the same century, though he died young in 1643 long before Sir John started to write. *He's* no relation at all.'

'Well, be that as it may,' said Barrington firmly – he could evidently recognise a hobby-horse when he saw one – 'it's high time you mingled with the rest of the guests. For myself I'm going to take Mr Maitland around and introduce him. The sooner he gets us all sorted out the better.'

Antony followed him obediently. He was naturally observant, as well as having the good memory that is *de rigueur* for a barrister, but in a crowd like this it wasn't as easy as all that to remember exactly who was who, and Meg was certain to demand his impressions of her new colleagues at the first opportunity. At the same time he found Brian Barrington slightly enigmatic; but he had taken an instinctive liking to the other man so perhaps the feeling was mutual and this was just Barrington's way of making him feel at ease. As they went Roger detached himself from a group across the room where Meg was holding court and joined them. He had obviously met Barrington before now, and equally obviously had seen him earlier that evening.

The first group they approached consisted of the elderly actor Antony had already recognised as Matthew Benbow; a small dark lively-looking woman in her thirties whom Barrington introduced as Amanda Chillingworth; a nondescript man perhaps a few years older who turned out to be her husband, Arthur Webb; and a young man, by far the youngest of the group, called Edward Brome. They all greeted Barrington with enthusiasm – 'we were just talking about you, B.B.' – and seemed to be equally ready to be pleased to make Antony's acquaintance, though it turned out a moment later that his name hadn't registered with any of them, except perhaps for Brome who had an enquiring look in his eye.

'Are you another of the chaps from the press?' he asked.

'Heaven forbid,' said Antony a little too emphatically. 'I'm –'

29

Meg came up at that moment, interrupting his self-introduction, and tucked her arm under Roger's. 'Mr Maitland is a barrister,' she said, 'and a great friend of Roger's and mine so you won't have to worry about saying anything you don't want to be reported.' But to Antony's discomfort a sudden silence fell over the group at the mention of his name; it was only too obvious that every one of them had heard it before. They'd naturally have been interested in the murder at the Alhambra Theatre, even if the rest of his career had passed by unnoticed, which in itself would have been a small miracle.

It was Barrington who broke the silence. 'So now we all know each other,' he said. 'But you'll have to satisfy my curiosity – what were you saying about me?'

'Matthew was saying something that was both sense and nonsense,' said Amanda and exchanged a grin with Arthur Webb. These were the two who were said to be very much in love, Antony remembered. Thinking of Meg and Roger he would have liked to ask them if the state of matrimony was easier or more difficult for theatre people when both were engaged in the profession; it was a pity he'd never know them well enough to put the question. Meanwhile Amanda seemed intent on tantalising, but Barrington was taking her teasing with his usual good humour.

'You're just making matters worse, my dear, but I suppose you know that,' he said.

'Let me satisfy that curiosity of yours, then,' said Benbow in the deep voice that Antony found he remembered quite well. 'I said, Sir Benjamin Oldfellow is a marvellous part even though he is cut off in his prime. But I didn't know why you wanted me when you could have done a better job of it yourself.'

'And direct as well? Oh, no, my acting days are over,' Barrington insisted. 'Anyway, Matthew, you mustn't grumble – you survive for a whole act and are on stage nearly all the time.'

'That's true, and I expect I shall find the experience rejuvenating,' said Benbow. 'There was quite a craze for these restoration comedies a little while ago; you young things wouldn't remember. I find myself very comfortable with the style of acting required and I'm glad to be doing it again.'

'And who'd have thought,' said Edward Brome languidly, 'that something quite new in this line would turn up.'

'A stroke of providence,' said Barrington easily.

'Probably due to your walking under a ladder the day Mr Cartwright found the manuscript,' said Meg gaily. 'Confess, B.B., wasn't it something like that?'

Barrington smiled at her. 'I spilled the salt at dinner and didn't toss it over my left shoulder.' Antony hadn't the faintest idea whether he was supposed to take that seriously or not. 'Anyway, Meg, it's given you what you told me is going to be a new experience and the rest of you good meaty parts in what may well prove to be a sensation. You should be grateful.'

It was Arthur Webb who answered that. 'Of course we are,' he said. 'Amanda and I particularly, perhaps, because it gives us a chance to work together. And the style – the particular style Matthew was mentioning – is exactly right for her. You may have a bit more trouble with me though. I haven't been so used to playing comedy.'

'Oh, I'm not worried about that. You see it's just as I told you, Mr Maitland, we've gathered together the perfect cast for the purpose. I don't know if Meg told you, but Edward here is playing Jack Bashful. As a matter of fact, it's a rather complicated part and I'm sure he'll do it to admiration.'

'Sinister,' said Brome. He had a rather light voice but allowed it to drop on the word. 'I'm the murderer,' he added in an explanatory aside to Antony.

'Oh, I see. Nobody would tell me that. The idea was that it should come as a surprise to me when I see the play.'

'Now there I don't agree,' said Brome emphatically. 'You wouldn't be able to appreciate the finer points of my acting unless you knew how it was going to turn out.'

'I'll bear that in mind,' said Antony seriously. He turned his head and found Barrington's eye fixed on him with an amused twinkle. 'As a matter of fact, I've heard enough about the play from Meg to raise my curiosity almost to fever pitch. Jeremy said I might attend a rehearsal if I liked, but I don't know if that's all right with you, Mr Barrington.'

'Why, certainly, I think we should all be glad to have an audience, even to our earliest efforts,' the director assured him. 'You may be interested in the way things are put together, the way order grows out of disorder.'

'Yes, of course, but I also find the background to this particular play intriguing. I know Jeremy has a way with words, but moving into a different century can't be easy.'

31

'He says the comedies were his bedtime reading for weeks before he started to write,' said Arthur Webb. He glanced across the room. 'Chester seems to be having a field-day with the press,' he added. 'I only hope he's saying the right things.'

'I don't see how he can go wrong,' said Amanda. 'We've got everything going for us. The right author –'

'How will that appear on the programme, by the way?' asked Roger.

'*Crabbed Age and Youth* by John Cartwright and Jeremy Skelton,' Barrington told him. 'But Amanda's quite right, we've got everything. The hint of a secret manuscript being discovered after so many years, Jeremy's name and Meg's. I mention her particularly,' he added to the others, ' 'because she's been associated with a play of Jeremy's before.'

'And your direction,' said Amanda cheekily. 'But I'm not altogether happy about this Friday the thirteenth opening, you know.'

'Now there I can't agree with you,' said Barrington. 'I admit I'd prefer it to be Friday the thirteenth of May, but that would be too much of a good thing, I suppose.'

'You needn't worry about it, my dear,' said Benbow, treating Amanda's comment with all seriousness. 'What's fortunate for B.B. is fortunate for the rest of us and that's all there is to it.'

'We have also,' said Brome, languidly now, 'the enchanting Stella. Who is no doubt occupying her leisure time at the moment in making a wax image of you, Meg, and sticking pins in it.'

'Don't be silly, darling,' said Meg roundly. 'Lucy Simpering is a very good part.'

'But she coveted Becky, and don't tell me she didn't,' Brome insisted. 'But if you don't like the idea,' he added, 'perhaps she's concentrating on one of the male characters, so that Mark can get a chance to appear on stage instead of just being an understudy.'

'Mark's not a bad chap,' said Benbow.

'Ambitious,' said Brome succinctly.

Jeremy Skelton came up at that moment with a waiter in tow to take orders for drinks. Barrington, whom Maitland suspected of drinking ginger ale, still had a full glass and Antony had hardly touched his Scotch. 'We'll leave the others to their tippling,' said Barrington cheerfully, 'and continue your education if you're ready.'

Meg gave Antony a radiant smile as they moved away, but he

noticed that her grip on Roger's arm had tightened and she had moved perhaps a little closer to her husband. 'That's Hugh Clinton, our stage manager, over there with Chester and the newspaper men,' Barrington said as they crossed the room. 'We'll leave him for later and join your wife if you like. She's with Anne Skelton, but of course you know Anne, and they're talking to Joseph Weatherly and Roberta Rowan.'

'Your leading man, if that's the right term, and one of the understudies,' said Antony not too positively. 'I'm trying to get them all sorted out,' he explained, 'because Meg is certain to ask me what I think of them the next time I see her.'

'Well, Weatherly certainly gets the lady in the end,' said Barrington, 'but when you see the play you'll recognise that every part is of equal importance. That's why it's so stupid of Edward to talk about jealousy. You know Meg better than I do – would it worry her?'

'I don't suppose she believes in witchcraft,' said Maitland, thinking his answer out as he went. 'She has her share of superstitions, at least she says she has; but I'm not quite sure, now I come to think of it, whether she's serious about that or not. But Roger's a very solid chap, he'll keep her feet on the ground.'

'Yes, I'd already got that impression. She's lucky, you know, it isn't easy being the other half of a theatrical marriage, but it strikes me he has the situation well in hand.'

'I'm sure he has.' (Though not without some occasional intervention from Jenny or me.) 'But you were telling me about the play, that each part in it carries almost equal weight.'

'I suppose that's a slight exaggeration, but not too much. It's rather light, airy stuff in spite of Sir Benjamin Oldfellow's death. Sir John Cartwright's outline called for three acts, but Jeremy has used the modern way and made it into two. Sir Benjamin is killed at the end of the first act and the second act is concerned with suspicion and elucidation. But in spite of that the mood is maintained throughout.' He paused a moment, obviously searching for the right word. 'Frothy stuff,' he said at last. 'I like it.'

'I expect I shall like it too,' said Antony sincerely. 'Do you think . . . I don't know whether to call her Miss Chillingworth or Mrs Webb.'

'Amanda will do.'

'All right, then. Do you think Amanda was really worried

about the opening date?'

'She's not one to take life too seriously,' Barrington assured him. 'On the other hand, you'll find we all have some queer ideas. I daresay you'll hear more on the subject before the evening is out.' They had come up with the new group now, who shifted their positions a little to make room for them.

'How are you getting on, Antony?' asked Jenny, giving him a look that contained what was perhaps an undue measure of anxiety. She didn't need to tell him that she was wondering about his reaction to the presence of the journalists.

'I'm broadening my education, love,' Antony assured her lightly. He had seen Anne earlier and contented himself with smiling at her. 'I'm out of my depth, of course, but extremely interested,' he added to the other two.

'This is my husband,' said Jenny and took over the introductions. Roberta Rowan was fair with straight hair cut short and a pair of very blue eyes. Weatherly was a well-set-up young man, not quite so strikingly handsome as Barrington had probably been in his youth but good looking enough all the same. He had dark hair and already to Antony's rather bemused eyes had acquired something of the swaggering air of the restoration and the costume or costumes he would eventually be wearing.

'I've no right to be here really,' said Roberta cheerfully. 'I'm only one of the understudies. All the same, B.B., I'm awfully glad you got Jeremy to ask me.'

'I think you have probably the most difficult part of all,' said Jenny. 'After all, you have to know every female part in the play by heart and think out how you'd play each character too if the occasion arose.'

'Only two parts,' Roberta corrected her. 'Mary Russell is understudying Meg. Anyway it's all good publicity,' she added, glancing across at the group that still contained the newspaper men, the stage manager, and Chester Cartwright. Jeremy Skelton had stayed with the people that Antony and Barrington had just left.

Perhaps reminded of the purpose of the party by Roberta's words, Barrington left them at that moment with a muttered excuse to cross the room again and join the drama critics.

'You'd get still more publicity out of it,' said Joseph Weatherly rather forcefully, 'if B.B. hadn't given Stella Hartley the part of Lucy Simpering.'

34

'But she's a marvellous actress,' Roberta protested.

'She ought to be declining gracefully into character parts by now,' said Weatherly not too kindly. 'She's far too old for the part. She's supposed to be a close friend of Meg's, which creates a supposition that they should be about the same age. Think of the title. Lady Oldfellow has to look like a young girl, which will be no trouble for Meg, but —'

'I don't agree with you at all,' Roberta interrupted him, looking quite cross. 'I know Stella's older, but that just means she has more experience. And she doesn't look anything like her age.' She broke off there and grinned. 'Whatever that may be,' she added. 'And when she's made up for the stage —'

'But B.B. doesn't even like her,' Weatherly interrupted in his turn. 'That makes it all the more extraordinary.'

'I don't think Mr Barrington would let his personal feelings influence him in a matter like that,' said Anne, obviously intent on pouring oil on troubled waters. 'Of course I'm sure you could do the part perfectly well, Roberta, but even being an understudy in a West End production must be a pretty good send-off I should think. Why, look at Mr Cartwright. The production has terrific possibilities for him as well as for the people more intimately involved.'

Weatherly seemed to find this point of view of interest. 'He'll gain financially, I suppose,' he said thoughtfully. (As Antony knew, if the play succeeded this was probably an understatement.) 'And I suppose he'll gain some academic kudos. But he has his writing, hasn't he, and his historical research? What more does he want?'

'A job, perhaps,' said Anne, and might have added if she had been less discreet, one that pays better than his books do.

'Well, perhaps he does want that, but will the play's success give it to him?'

'There's already some excitement about it,' Anne told him, 'about the discovery of the outline in Sir John Cartwright's own hand, I mean. Even here at home I should think it might help him, but Jeremy says the States are much more enthusiastic about that kind of thing and the feeling there is likely to reach fever pitch. I should think if he's right and if the play succeeds, Chester will have no difficulty in taking his choice of jobs.'

'Is that what he wants?'

'As a matter of fact it is. A good academic position in the

United States; he told Jeremy that himself.'

'He seems such a quiet man,' said Roberta.

'Yes, he is, but that doesn't mean he isn't ambitious.'

'Well, here's good luck to him and to the rest of us.' Weatherly raised his glass and the others followed suit immediately. 'Whatever complications Stella's presence may cause I'm glad to be working for B.B.,' he added, 'and glad you'll have the benefit of his guidance, Roberta, even if you never get before an audience this time.'

'I suppose it would be too unkind,' said Roberta, 'to hope that I do get a chance of taking over one of the parts.'

'I hope you do.' Weatherly was emphatic. 'For the sake of the production though it's to be hoped that nothing happens to any of the male members of the cast. I don't know if you've noticed but Mary's been looking daggers at Mark all the evening.'

'That's the understudy?' asked Antony. 'I haven't met him yet.' (But I'm already intrigued about him, he thought, by Brome's remarks.)

'Mark Kenilworth, yes.' But before Weatherly could continue with what Antony felt sure would have been another indiscretion Brian Barrington returned as suddenly as he had left them.

'It's time for another lot of introductions,' he said, disassociating Antony from the group with all the ease of a well-trained sheepdog. 'I said before, didn't I, that all the parts are more or less equally important? Edward was just talking nonsense about Stella being jealous of Meg. She's a star in her own right, but I expect you know that.' Perhaps it was because of what he had been hearing, or perhaps because Barrington had returned unnecessarily to a subject that should have been regarded as closed, but Antony immediately felt there was more than a little discomfort behind the words.

There were three people in the group they now joined. Undoubtedly the dominating personality was Stella Hartley, to whom Barrington introduced him first and who naturally he regarded with more than usual interest. Weatherly, he thought, had been less than fair to her. Even at close range and without stage make-up it wasn't too difficult to see her as a young girl, if that was the way she decided to play the part of Lucy Simpering. She was a redhead with the creamy complexion that goes with that colouring and the green eyes that also sometimes accompany it. Add to that classical features and a really beautiful figure and

36

you had someone who had no need to be jealous, even of Meg. Stella had been divorced, someone had said, and he wondered now how the husband had felt about it. He'd also been told that Mary Russell had moved in with her to keep her company after the divorce.

Barrington was introducing him to Mary now. She seemed to be keeping close beside her friend, almost as though on guard duty. In any other company she herself might have been regarded as a beauty, but her more conventional good looks and carefully tinted hair were insignificant beside the more glamorous Stella.

Mark Kenilworth, the men's understudy, was the third member of the group, and he too seemed to have difficulty in dragging his attention away from Stella Hartley. A casual description of Joseph Weatherly would have fitted him well enough, though there was actually no real resemblance between them. At present Antony had only Barrington's opinion to go by – that Weatherly was capable of projecting his personality across the footlights – but there could be no doubt, he thought, about Kenilworth. He was a fiery character, probably passionate, and if – as Brome had hinted – his feelings for Stella Hartley were prompted by ambition rather than love, he was also most likely an extremely competent actor. But Antony had no time to dwell upon this; Barrington had barely finished the introductions when Stella turned to him and said sweetly, 'Mr Maitland, how interesting. That nice Mr Trevor was telling me all about you.'

'Was he indeed?' said Antony rather grimly.

'The man who never loses a case,' said Stella, obviously quoting. 'You should be proud of your reputation, Mr Maitland,' she added, relishing his obvious discomfort.

'If that's my reputation someone's been making a big mistake,' said Antony, though he had heard the phrase often enough before and been equally annoyed by it. 'It's absolute nonsense, as anyone connected with my profession could tell you.'

'I'm sure you're just being modest. It must be so nice to be clever,' said Stella, looking up at him with rather overdone admiration.

'Come now, Stella.' There was no doubt about it, Barrington – whom at first glance Antony had put down as imperturbable – sounded definitely uneasy now.

'I'm sure it's true, and a compliment really,' she assured Antony. 'We're all practically morons.'

'I don't think,' said Antony, trying not to sound too much out of his depth, 'that any of you behave as if you are.'

'What do you feel about this find of Chester's?' Stella had had her fun, and this sounded like a serious question.

'I think the fact that Jeremy Skelton takes it seriously and that you're all here now speaks for itself,' said Antony. He still had his own doubts, but this didn't seem the time to air them.

Stella didn't look altogether satisfied by this answer but she let the subject drop. 'In any case it gives me rather a ghoulish feeling,' she said and shuddered elaborately. 'Like raking over dead bones.'

'What can you possibly know about such a gruesome occupation?' asked Kenilworth indulgently.

'It's just a manner of speaking,' said Stella with dignity. 'Sir John Cartwright has been dead for over three hundred years. Don't you think he ought to be left to rest in peace?'

'You've acted in restoration drama before,' said Mary Russell. 'You know you're particularly good at the comedies, and you didn't mind then that the authors were dead. In fact, I think you've probably acted in some of Sir John's plays before now.'

'Yes, I have, in one,' Stella admitted.

'And in several by other restoration dramatists,' Barrington put in, emphasising the point, perhaps rather heavily. 'That's why I wanted you so badly, Stella, I knew you could do it.' And perhaps, Antony thought, this was the simple truth and the talk about his not liking her was just gossip.

'That's too sweet of you, B.B., particularly when you'd already got Meg as a drawing card. And I wouldn't miss the opportunity for the world. All the same.' she added, and there was no doubt now that for once she was speaking sincerely, 'those other times were different. The play was already written, what the author left behind him was exactly as he wanted it. But for this play, all that we have is Sir John's outline of the plot.'

'Don't you like what Jeremy's done with it?' Barrington asked a little sharply.

'Oh, yes, it's good enough. I'm just saying it may not be what Sir John Cartwright wanted. And it was his idea that sparked it all off after all.'

'I'm afraid it's too late to do anything about it now,' Barrington pointed out. 'And you must admit,' he went on with an attempt at humour, 'that I'm doing my best to propitiate any evil spirits.'

'Yes, but your superstitions are all the wrong way round,' she objected. However, she left the subject and returned to the original point without pursuing the matter any further. 'It's a real trick, acting in comedy. Either you can do it or you can't. I can, and that's why dear B.B. wanted me to play Lucy Simpering, as he said, instead of giving the part to a sweet young thing like Roberta. And so can Mary, of course. Play comedy, I mean. It's a shame she won't get a chance unless one of us is ill.'

The compliment seemed to cause Mary Russell a little embarrassment. 'You wait till you see Stella as Lucy Simpering,' she said to Antony. 'But Chester's ancestor wasn't very original in the names he chose for his characters, was he?'

'Mr Cartwright says he isn't a direct descendant of Sir John,' said Maitland, wondering as he spoke whether that story changed from time to time.

'It comes to much the same thing.' Stella tucked her arm in Kenilworth's and looked up at him adoringly. 'And here's Mark,' she said, 'only wishing that poor Joseph would go down with scarlet fever so that he could play the lead. It would have been better still, of course, if that would have meant his playing my lover. We could have made beautiful music together, B.B.,' she added, surprising Antony who hadn't thought he'd ever hear anybody use that phrase. 'Why didn't you give us a chance?'

'It's too late now,' said Barrington. Antony thought he detected a certain relief in his tone. 'Jeremy had already spoken to Meg about playing Becky before I came on the scene. And it's no reflection on you, Mark, I think you're very capable or I wouldn't have taken you on, but you haven't had the experience yet.'

'I'm quite happy with the position,' said Kenilworth easily. But he added, looking down fondly at Stella, 'It's heavenly of you to care.'

'Well, I think we're all very well off as we are,' said Mary Russell, entering the conversation for only a second time since Barrington had performed the introductions. She cast an inimical look in Kenilworth's direction. 'Joseph will do very well in the part, and Lucy Simpering is almost as important to the play as Becky is.'

'I'm glad to have your endorsement of my opinion, of course,' said Barrington, with more sharpness than Maitland would have thought him capable. 'I think, however, we'll leave you to your discussion. Mr Maitland hasn't met Hugh yet, and I see he's alone with Jeremy now.' He guided Antony away with a hand on his arm but stopped halfway across the room. 'You mustn't take any notice of what they say, you know. It's all surface squabbling. They're really a very good team.'

'Yes, I'm sure they are,' Antony murmured meaninglessly. 'You know what "that nice Mr Trevor" told me, don't you?' he continued abruptly.

'More or less. You don't care for representatives of the press, do you?'

'Not much,' Maitland admitted. 'But at least,' he went on, smiling suddenly, 'nobody's said, "I've heard of you, Mr Maitland," except you, of course, and that was in answer to my own prompting. Not that it isn't bad enough when they just *look* it, because it always means, "I've heard nothing good." But when they say it as well it's awfully difficult to know how to reply.'

'Well, don't expect the company here tonight to take quite the same view that you do,' Barrington told him. 'Publicity is the breath of life to us,' he added briskly and started across the room again.

But he had done no more than effect an introduction to Hugh Clinton, a round rubber ball of a man with a cheerful expression, when the door of the big room opened slowly. Maitland, who was facing in that direction, expected that another waiter would appear. The service so far had been excellent, almost too excellent in that their glasses were kept constantly filled. But the door opened six inches and no more, not wide enough to admit a man. And it wasn't until his eyes dropped that he saw the black cat coming slowly across the floor towards them. Stella Hartley must have seen it at the same moment because she exclaimed excitedly, 'Just what we wanted, darlings, a black cat! You all know how lucky that is. Puss! Puss! Come here, pussy. Come to Stella.'

Everyone was looking at the animal now. It turned its course a little as Stella spoke, making its way towards her, and rubbed against her leg in an affectionate way, but there was definitely something very languid about its movements. Stella swooped to pick it up, and as she did so its mouth opened and a rather piteous meow emerged. Then it was up in her arms and she was cooing over it delightedly, but suddenly she screamed.

'It's ill! There's something wrong! Do something, somebody, please take it from me.'

And the body of the little black cat which had been limp in her arms gave one convulsive shudder and was still. Eerily in the background Mary Russell's voice could be heard intoning:

'Who's that ringing at the front door bell?
It's a little black cat and it isn't very well.
Rub your nose with a little mutton fat,
That's the best cure for a little black cat.'

Antony had time to wonder from what childhood memory she had dredged that piece of nonsense.

It was Hugh Clinton who took the animal from Stella. Perhaps it was to be expected that he would be of a practical turn of mind, and he was standing a good deal nearer to her than Roger was. 'I can't imagine where it came from,' he remarked as he did so. And then in an altered tone, 'It seems to be dead.'

Mary Russell said, 'What did I tell you? I knew as soon as I saw it – 'but Stella Hartley's comment was the more compelling.

She screamed once piercingly . . . like a banshee, Maitland thought, at least how he imagined a banshee must sound. And then said, still more shrilly, 'That's bad luck! You can't deny that's bad luck! It's because we've been meddling in the affairs of the dead.'

Hugh Clinton was still standing holding the dead. animal as though he had no idea what his next move should be. Brian Barrington was at his side in a moment and his voice had taken on a note of authority that Antony hadn't heard before.

'Nonsense! You all know that for me everything like that works in reverse.'

'But that's for you, B.B.' Stella was not to be silenced so easily. 'What about the rest of us?'

'I'm as much concerned with this production as anybody . . . more, perhaps. So what brings me good luck is bound to bring it for the rest of you.' They'd all fallen silent, but it was obvious that his calm tone had made an impression. 'A black cat crossing your path is good luck, so they say,' he went on. 'Well, for me it's just the opposite. Don't you see this is just about the best omen there could have been?'

41

II

The party didn't go on for very long after that; all the life seemed to have gone out of it. As soon as it showed signs of breaking up, Meg and Jenny got together and extricated their menfolk. Roger had the car, so he took the Maitlands to Kempenfeldt Square before going on to Chelsea. 'Come up for a few minutes,' Jenny suggested.

Roger smiled at her. 'So long as you didn't add, have a nightcap,' he said. 'After Jeremy's hospitality that would be altogether too much. But if you'd like to talk for a few minutes, Meg –'

'It's absolutely essential,' Meg said firmly, opening the car door and scrambling out on to the pavement. 'I know what you'll say, darling, stage people are all superstitious, but I'd like to know what Antony and Jenny think of what happened.'

As it was after ten o'clock Gibbs had already retired and they were able to make their way upstairs without disturbing anyone. 'I like your Mr Barrington,' said Maitland when they were all seated and he had refrained with some difficulty, from sheer force of habit, from offering unwanted drinks. 'I expect he's right when he says that any squabbling there is is only surface deep.' It occurred to him then that although he knew Meg so well he knew considerably less about Margaret Hamilton, who might have been upset about what had happened as well as by the remarks that Edward Brome had let fall so casually.

'Darling, Stella Hartley's well known for enjoying stirring up trouble,' said Meg, understanding him well enough and willing to put aside for a moment her well-known dislike of gossip to set his mind at rest, 'but even she would draw the line at witchcraft, I should think. No, I was thinking about B.B. and his reverse superstitions, and then that poor little cat.'

'Don't tell me you believe this Friday the thirteenth nonsense, Meg.'

'No, I don't exactly,' said Meg with a sideways look in Roger's direction. 'All the same,' she added more confidently, 'I do think it might be better to be on the safe side.'

'According to Brian Barrington it *is* the safe side,' Antony pointed out.

'Yes, I know, and that's what he said about the cat, too. But how did it get there?'

'Coincidence, obviously,' said Roger. 'Don't you agree with me, Jenny?'

'Of course I do. Even with nine lives cats have to die some time, and I expect when it felt itself ill it was attracted by the sound of voices.'

'Darling, animals don't do that. When they're dying they try to find somewhere to be by themselves. If it wasn't an omen, and I know you all think I'm being silly about that, tell me how it got there.'

'If you're thinking somebody deliberately introduced it into the room knowing its condition,' said Antony, 'I think you've also got to provide someone with a motive. You could say – though I think this would be stretching matters rather far even for you, Meg – that Brian Barrington wanted to reinforce his reverse superstitions.'

'He was in full view of the rest of us all the time, and if it was meant to be a good luck omen the same goes for everyone else with an interest in the play,' said Meg stubbornly.

'There are the people who are backing the production financially,' Roger pointed out, 'but they're all about a hundred and I can't imagine this is the sort of thing that would have occurred to any of them. And Jeremy and Anne are staying in the hotel, so you could say if you wanted that one of them bribed one of the waiters, but can you imagine either of them pulling a trick like that?'

'No, darling, I can't,' said Meg, but she sounded doubtful as she went on. 'I suppose you're all right and it was a coincidence.'

'But rather an unfortunate one,' said Roger, 'because it gave Stella Hartley a perfect opportunity for showing off. And I don't suppose every member of the cast is as level headed as you are, Meg.'

Antony had a smile – carefully concealed – for that bit of tact. 'That brings me to something that was puzzling me,' he said, seizing the excuse to change the subject. 'Do she and Brian Barrington really dislike each other, and if so why did he give her the part?'

'She's a very good actress,' said Meg pensively.

'Yes, *darling*, but that doesn't explain matters. There must be half a dozen other people who could have played what's-her-name just as well. After all, whatever anyone said tonight you've got the really important part.'

'I can explain that,' said Roger surprisingly. And added when they had all turned to look at him, 'Mr Tremlett is one of the backers –'

'No wonder you said they were all almost a hundred,' Antony put in.

' – and the gossip on the exchange is that she's been seen in his company more than once lately.'

'Darling, why didn't you tell me?' asked Meg reproachfully.

'Because it's only gossip and I know how you hate it,' said Roger. 'But I wouldn't be at all surprised if you find it's true all the same.'

'Well, she's a good actress,' said Meg again, 'and will play the part very well. And if no one is going to take what I say seriously we may as well go home. But I wouldn't be at all surprised if Stella was right and it's an unlucky play, and when something else happens you can remember I said so.'

Antony was laughing when he came back from letting the Farrells out. 'Meg's got the bit well between her teeth,' he said. 'She's enjoying herself thoroughly, but I don't think she believes a word of all this superstitious nonsense.'

'I don't believe so either,' said Jenny, but there was a tinge of doubt in her voice. 'Anyway, she'll soon be proved wrong when rehearsals start.'

'When is that exactly?'

'The end of next week, but Anne says they'll be doing no more than read their parts through. Jeremy wants to be at the rehearsals because he'd rather make any alterations then than lying under somebody's bed after a party on the first night, which I've always understood is the correct thing for a playwright to do.'

Antony grinned at the picture her words raised. 'It seems more reasonable this way,' he agreed. 'And Jeremy's far too hefty a chap to be really comfortable under anybody's bed. Does he want Anne along?'

'You know he can still hardly bear her out of his sight,' said Jenny, 'but she isn't quite so shy about going as she was over the first play. I offered to go along now and then but I think she saw I'd rather wait for the first night.'

'Just as you like,' said Antony, yawning. 'But don't get tied up with Anne until I'm back in chambers for the Hilary term. I like your company, love, just as much as Jeremy likes hers.'

44

Tuesday, 6th January

Neither of the households in Kempenfeldt Square had gone away for the Christmas vacation; it was a holiday they preferred to celebrate together. As custom dictated, Antony and Jenny had lunch with their uncle and aunt on the Saturday following the pre-rehearsal party, and had given between them a graphic description of the more dramatic events. The following Tuesday Sir Nicholas and Vera again dined upstairs, and none of them was surprised when Roger and Meg turned up when the meal was over. When Meg was working, Roger more often than not turned up in Kempenfeldt Square after he had left her at the theatre in the evening, and stayed until it was time to fetch her again. While she was rehearsing, of course, her working hours coincided more or less with his, so she was free to accompany him and their visits were almost as frequent.

It was immediately obvious that Meg had something to tell them, and as soon as the first greetings had been exchanged and they were all settled down again, she looked all round her, making sure she had her audience's attention, and then announced, 'You know, darlings, I never say I told you so, but this time I really did.'

Sir Nicholas, who had resumed his lounging position, remained unmoved by this statement. Jenny smiled but said nothing, while Antony and Roger exchanged a glance in which resignation was perhaps the dominant emotion. It was left to Vera to ask, 'What did you tell us, Meg?'

'Not you, darling, Antony and Jenny, and Roger too. They none of them believed me.'

This time Sir Nicholas roused himself. 'You're referring, I gather, to Skelton's new play which has now started rehearsals.'

'Of course I am, Uncle Nick,' said Meg. 'Surely Antony and Jenny told you what had happened at the party we had on Boxing

Day.'

'Said a cat died,' said Vera succinctly.

'Yes, well, I said it wouldn't be the end of things and it wasn't.'

'If you're going to tell us, Meg, get on with it,' Antony urged. 'Or perhaps Roger –'

'Roger thinks it's funny,' said Meg blisteringly. 'And so will you I expect, but it wasn't!'

'*What* wasn't funny?' asked Antony with exaggerated patience.

'I'm telling you. Everything was quiet yesterday, which was the first proper rehearsal. I knew my part, of course, we'd had the whole weekend to get word-perfect, but among the others only Matthew Benbow and Arthur Webb were ready to do without their scripts. I think B.B. got a little impatient, but nothing out of the way. But it was a different story today.'

'You're trying to tell us that something happened at the rehearsal.'

'Not exactly at the rehearsal – in my dressing room. Somebody wrote in lipstick on my mirror while I was on stage. What do you think of that?'

'A good luck message?' Antony asked hopefully.

'Nothing of the sort. It said quite clearly, *This is no play of mine.* What do you think of that?'

'Did you recognise the handwriting?'

'Of course I didn't. We don't spend our time writing notes to each other. In any case I don't think it can be very easy to write on a mirror. The message was quite clear to read, but just a scrawl.'

'Then I should say that probably Miss Hartley really does covet your part and is hoping to persuade you to retire from the play because Sir John Cartwright doesn't approve of it.'

'That's just like a lawyer. You would come up with something completely reasonable,' Meg complained.

'At least you agree it *is* reasonable.'

'If it wasn't for the other thing that happened –'

'What other thing?'

'Somebody put flour in the powder bowl in Stella's dressing room. She used it just before we left the theatre, and I think she must have frightened herself with the dead white face in the mirror because she came out into the corridor yelling blue murder and certainly she didn't look at all like herself.'

'Well, that one at least is obvious. I should say somebody

46

doesn't like the lady, and remembering her remarks at the party decided to play a trick on her.'

'What remarks?'

'I don't think you were there at the time, but she's probably said something very much the same to you since. She said she felt ghoulish to be acting in this particular play.'

'She's done lots of restoration work before,' said Meg doubtfully.

'Yes, exactly. But she said this is different because the other plays were exactly as their creator had envisaged them, while this one had actually been written by somebody else.'

'You can't have it both ways, darling. Someone gunning for Stella,' (Sir Nicholas uttered a faint moan) 'and Stella wanting to scare me off.'

'Quite right, Meg, but the explanation might be the right one,' said Vera. 'Could someone have mistaken your dressing room, Meg? It occurs to me that the message on your mirror might have been aimed at your colleague too.'

'I don't think –' said Meg doubtfully. 'But of course I can't be sure about that at this stage.'

'Well then! It seems to me a very likely explanation,' said Antony.

'If it was a joke I think it was one in extremely bad taste,' said Meg crushingly. 'Besides upsetting everybody, not just Stella.'

'Wasn't Mr Barrington able to soothe them down this time?'

'It wasn't exactly superstition,' said Meg; 'not the same as the cat – something he could twist around to his own point of view.'

'If you're trying to tell us it was Sir John Cartwright's ghost I'd call that superstition of the first order,' Antony maintained.

'I have heard,' said Sir Nicholas, 'that members of your profession, Meg, are not at all averse to publicity.'

'Uncle Nick, that's very unfair. Who would do a thing like that?'

'We're all familiar enough with Jeremy Skelton's work to know that he has a sense of humour.'

'I just don't believe it.'

'Well, perhaps not. I don't think,' said Sir Nicholas thoughtfully, 'that there's an ounce of malice in him. But what about this man Chester Cartwright? He's said to be very keen on the play being a success.'

'I don't suppose the press will ever hear about it anyway,' said

47

Meg. (She was wrong about that; there was a short but rather prominent paragraph in most of the papers the following day.)

'Well, was Mr Cartwright at the rehearsals, for instance?' Antony asked.

'Oh, yes, he's been haunting the place. The play's success really means a lot to him, and that's why that idea must be wrong, Uncle Nick. Even if it is a publicity stunt, it would be an awfully silly idea to upset everyone so much.'

'I think perhaps if Mr Cartwright is responsible, there might be an answer to that,' said Antony. 'He's the one person concerned who really wouldn't realise how superstitious you all are. After his previous experience Jeremy would know quite well, and so would all the members of the cast and all the people who are connected with the theatre in any way. But perhaps not Chester Cartwright.'

'Do you think anything else will happen?' asked Jenny uneasily, concerned for her friend.

'How can I possibly know, love? If it's spite against Stella Hartley, or if it's publicity, whoever is doing it may think it's gone far enough.'

'Well I think it's quite obvious,' said Roger firmly. 'I wouldn't blame anyone for disliking that Hartley woman, but publicity is a lot more likely. If anyone plays any more tricks, I think I'll just have a word with this Mr Cartwright.'

'Not unless I come with you,' said Antony, and Roger grinned in agreement.

As Meg was rehearsing they left rather early and Vera reverted to the subject as soon as they had gone. 'Do you really think Meg believes the theatre's haunted?' she demanded.

'Certainly not the theatre, she's played at the Cornmarket often enough. As for Sir John Cartwright trying to stop his play being put on, she's just enjoying getting as much drama as she can out of the situation,' Antony assured her. 'It's second nature to her. You'll never change her, and it won't matter in the slightest, unless she gets Roger worked up about it.'

'Too much sense for that,' said Vera shaking her head. And on the whole, on the evidence then before them, they all agreed with her conclusion.

Wednesday and Thursday, 7th and 8th January

Meg telephoned the following morning, just as Jenny was putting lunch on the table. Antony answered the phone and needed no telling who was on the other end of the line. 'It didn't stop,' said Meg in a rather distraught way. 'There was a bird in the theatre this morning!'

'Now really, Meg,' said Maitland, exasperated, 'you're as bad as the rest of them, and you know you don't really believe all this superstitious nonsense. Birds get into all sorts of places, there's nothing in the least frightening about that.'

'A magpie!' said Meg tragically. 'How on earth could a magpie get into a London theatre I'd like to know? Somebody must have caught it in the country and brought it up deliberately and let it go.'

'I admit that is rather queer.' He was aware that Jenny was still now, and listening to the conversation.

'It's more than queer,' said Meg firmly. 'Rehearsals had to break off while we tried to lure the poor thing outside. And all anyone could talk about was the jingle that starts, *One for sorrow, two for joy*. It was just *one* bird that came in.'

'Are you still rehearsing?'

'No, B.B. said we'd take a long lunch break and then perhaps things would have calmed down.'

'Then get in a taxi and come and have lunch with us,' said Antony. He turned and looked at Jenny who nodded vigorously. 'Jenny thinks that would be a good idea,' he added, 'so come right away.'

A quiet luncheon with her friends seemed to do something to restore Meg's morale, but Antony had an uncomfortable feeling that she now thought the position was getting too serious for what he would have referred to as her Mrs Siddons act. When she and Roger came round that evening there were no further stories to

49

relate, but there were signs of nervousness among the cast, and the afternoon's rehearsal had not gone too well. But there was plenty of time to remedy that, and if nothing else happened . . .

The following afternoon, however, Meg telephoned again, catching Antony and Jenny just as they had arrived home from a shopping expedition. 'Brian wants to talk to you,' she told Antony, making it sound rather like a royal command. 'He wants to take us all out to dinner and suggested drinks at his flat first.'

'Does that mean something else has happened?' asked Maitland suspiciously.

'Well, yes, it does. I think it will be better if we tell you when we see you,' said Meg, which might be a deliberate attempt to rouse his curiosity, or just mean that the matter was complicated. She then gave an address in Belgravia that made him reflect that Brian Barrington must have taken no decrease in income when he changed from acting to directing, if, indeed, he wasn't finding directing even more profitable. 'Will you and Jenny be there at about six-thirty?' Meg went on, 'I should think Roger will have finished work and arrived by then.'

Jenny hadn't even started dinner preparations yet and he was pretty sure without even consulting her that she'd enjoy the change. As for himself, he wasn't too sure. 'Yes, if you like, but you've made me curious,' said Antony. 'But I expect that's exactly what you meant to do.'

'It is,' said Meg and chuckled, so that he had to hold the receiver away from his ear for a moment and let her amusement run its course. 'But that doesn't mean it isn't serious, darling, so come as promptly as you can.'

True to Meg's prediction the other three had already arrived at Barrington's flat by the time Antony and Jenny got there. Maitland had been meditating on the journey, though without much success, on what fresh thing could have gone wrong. A useless speculation, but perhaps in some way self-protective, because, though he had no idea what the director of Jeremy Skelton's play could want with him, he had a very strong feeling that he would rather not find out.

The flat was every bit as comfortable as his imagination had painted it and Barrington favoured the same brand of Scotch as he did himself whenever he could afford it. 'No talk until we're all comfortably settled,' Barrington decreed, but as Meg and Roger were certainly comfortable already Antony wondered if perhaps his host also was unwilling to get to the point. At last, however, it could no longer be avoided.

'One of you had better tell me,' said Maitland, 'before Jenny and I die of curiosity. Did something else happen at the theatre today?'

'I should think it did,' said Barrington emphatically. He glanced at Meg as though for confirmation. She nodded, though without showing any sign of wanting to join in the explanation, which was so uncharacteristic that it gave Antony a fresh qualm of uneasiness.

'Meg says she's told you about the other things.'

'Everything, I think. First there was the black cat, we saw that for ourselves. Then there was the lipstick message, which I gather was supposed to be a disclaimer by Sir John Cartwright of any part in the play Jeremy Skelton wrote from his outline. After that the rather harmless prank of substituting flour for face powder on Miss Hartley's dressing table, and then – which must have been the most difficult to achieve – the introduction of a single magpie into the theatre.'

'Yes, that's quite right. They may not sound serious to you, Mr Maitland, but I assure you that to a parcel of actors these incidents prove, to say the least of it, exciting. I myself –'

'You're not going to tell me, Mr Barrington, that you agree with Miss Hartley in thinking it ghoulish to perform in a play that was outlined by a man now dead but not written by him?'

'No, I wouldn't say that.' Barrington sounded a little hesitant. 'What I am trying to say is that it never occurred to me, but the others seem to believe it might have seemed that way to Sir John Cartwright.'

'You too, Meg?'

'Of course she doesn't believe it,' said Roger. 'A lot of playwrights are dead. You might just as well say it was ghoulish to appear in Shakespeare.'

'Not quite the same thing, darling,' Meg pointed out. 'All the same, I'm beginning to agree with you and Roger, Antony, it may be spite or it may be a publicity stunt but it's nothing to do with the supernatural.'

Which being translated, as the three of them who knew her best realised, meant that the situation had grown too serious for any more play-acting, outside the theatre at least. 'Good,' said

51

Antony. 'And that reminds me of something I never asked you, Meg. What was Jeremy's reaction to that lipstick message? *This is no play of mine.*'

Meg just shook her head and it was Barrington who answered. He was obviously in a serious mood but in spite of that he smiled. 'It was perfectly typical,' he said. 'Stella was carrying on like anything, even though it was Meg if anyone who should have been upset, and all Jeremy would say was, "Nonsense, I'm quite sure he's honoured to be collaborating with me."'

'All right then, we'd better get on with what happened today.'

'Another message,' said Barrington. 'This time it was in red paint, one of those aerosol cans. We found it later on among the rubbish.'

'Was the message in one of the dressing rooms again?'

'No, on the wall in the greenroom. It wasn't a very long quotation. It just said, *Present fears are less than horrible imaginings.*'

'That doesn't sound very terrible,' said Maitland, unimpressed.

'No, but don't you see for the audience for which it was intended it couldn't have been worse?'

'Where does the quotation come from? It sounds familiar.'

'I should hope it is,' said Meg. 'It's from the Scottish play.'

'For heaven's sake! You mean *M*–'

'Yes, of course I do, but naming it outright would just make it worse,' said Meg crossly.

'And nobody's supposed to quote from – from that play off-stage,' said Antony slowly. 'That's what you mean, isn't it?'

'It certainly is. And if that wasn't bad enough – though I can assure you, darling, it was enough to send the whole cast into a panic – the way the quotation goes on just makes things worse because we all know it, of course.'

'I'm afraid I can't remember how it goes on.'

'*Present fears*,' said Barrington – he was acting unashamedly now, no longer quoting from something that had been written on a wall – '*Present fears are less than horrible imaginings; my thought, whose murder yet is but fantastical, shakes so my single state of man that function is smother'd in surmise, and nothing is but what is not.* What do you think of that?' he added in his normal voice.

'You're taking it as a threat.'

'Wouldn't you?'

'It's . . . horribly suggestive,' said Jenny. Antony turned his

52

head to smile at her.

'But that's the whole idea, isn't it, love? When Meg first told us what was happening I did wonder, as I told you, whether someone had a grudge against Stella Hartley, but my second thought was better I think . . . that it was a publicity stunt. The other things all got into the newspapers, didn't they?'

'They certainly did, and though I've asked everybody, no one will admit having told them. In any case, what's the use of publicising a play that's going to fail because the cast is completely demoralised?'

'It might have been done by somebody who didn't realise that, or who thought that when the incidents ceased the trouble would pass over. In that case anyone interested in the play's success might be responsible.'

'You're still thinking about Chester Cartwright,' said Meg. 'He stands to lose money if the play fails. Well, not that exactly, but he stands not to gain what might be a considerable sum if we have a long run.'

'Somebody told me – I think it was Anne – that he was more concerned with a possible appointment in the academic world, perhaps in America.'

'That's true, I've heard him say so too. But I can't believe he's responsible.'

'Bless you, Meg; to admit that would be as bad as gossiping, wouldn't it?' asked Antony, smiling at her. 'Has he been attending rehearsals?'

'Oh, yes, quite faithfully.' Meg sounded reluctant.

'Well, Mr Barrington, do you think anybody from outside could have got into the theatre and done all these things?'

'No, I don't,' said Barrington bluntly. 'That's one of the things that worry me most.'

'There must be more people who have business in the theatre than . . . well than those who attended the party, for instance.'

'Dozens of them, and in a week or two the whole place will be humming. But so far there's been nobody else around who could have been responsible for all the tricks. The dressers aren't in attendance yet, though the prompter is, a lad called Tommy. But I assure you he'd be quickly missed if he was missing from his place.'

'The question then remains, what do you want with me? I'm sorry about your predicament, of course,' said Antony rather perfunctorily, 'but I don't see what I can do about it.'

'Don't you?' Barrington was quizzical now. 'I'm quite aware of your dislike of being reminded of it, but you have something of a reputation, you know.'

'But this is something quite different,' Antony protested. 'On behalf of a client –'

'Is it really?' Barrington didn't let him finish. 'I want to find out who's doing these things and put a stop to them. I assure you the situation is serious enough. If something isn't done –'

'In that case, why not call the police?'

Suddenly, unexpectedly, Barrington smiled. 'I can't believe you're making that suggestion seriously. So far the press are intrigued, quite willing to play up the angle of a dramatic performance that has been haunted by the man who first conceived the plot. But once the police come on the scene that's something quite different.'

'Yes, I can see it would be,' said Antony slowly, and indeed he did realise it only too well. He glanced at Meg and found her eyes fixed anxiously on his face. 'Do *you* think I can help?' he asked.

'Brian thinks you can and I agree with him, darling,' said Meg. 'That's why I called you.'

'If I felt . . . but it's not in my line at all.'

'You have a sort of sixth sense where people are concerned,' said Roger, 'and that's what seems to be needed here.' He had been so silent that his sudden incursion into the conversation startled them all, and Maitland turned to give him a reproachful look. But then he realised that his friend was worried, desperately worried. He wasn't sure where all this would end and he didn't want Meg to get hurt, but at the same time he wasn't going to ask her to give up something that obviously meant so much to her. 'Besides,' Roger added, 'there's still a few days to go before the Hilary term starts.'

'Yes, but I ought to put in an appearance in chambers a little before that. And as for understanding people . . . as much as the next man, no more.' He turned back to Barrington. 'When is the next rehearsal?'

'Tomorrow, of course, and we'll probably put in a bit of work on Saturday, too. We've lost so much time over these incidents this week I thought we'd better call an extra one, though normally we leave the weekends free so early in the game.'

'I see. Well, those I can certainly attend, but I hope to goodness you don't think I'm at all competent to be able to do

54

anything constructive. I can ask a few questions but I've no earthly right to do so and if anyone objects that's the end of it.'

'Let me worry about that,' said Barrington more buoyantly. 'Is there anything else *we* can tell you?'

'If you really mean all this,' said Antony, though it was quite obvious that three of his audience were quite serious in what they were asking of him, 'there are two points we must consider straight away. Motive, of course, and opportunity. But first, what about this magpie?'

'You're thinking it must have been caught and caged and brought up from the country. I'm afraid that doesn't help us much. Most of us have country cottages not too far away and only stay in town when we're working.'

'Would that apply to the two who are only starting their careers?'

'Mark and Roberta? She goes to her parents' home between whiles, and I understand Mark has been staying with Stella and Mary at weekends.'

'Jeremy could hardly keep a bird caged in his hotel room without the whole staff knowing about it,' Jenny pointed out.

'I'm too fond of Jeremy and Anne to consider him seriously, love,' Antony assured her, 'but if we have to talk about it at all we have to cover every possibility. A policeman with a suspicious mind, for instance – and which of them doesn't have such a thing? – would say that bribery of somebody familiar with country ways was open to anyone. And we still have to consider Cartwright.'

'He inherited his aunt's house in Haslemere, that's where he found the outline in the attic. I can't imagine him going into the street there and trying to entice a bird into captivity.'

'In that case we'd better go back to motive.'

'Well, before we do that let me get you another drink,' said Barrington. 'As I gather you think that anyone with an interest in the success of the play may have a motive in publicising it,' he went on, coming back with a tray in his hands, 'you'd better put me at the head of the list.'

'Somehow I'm not really ready to do that,' said Antony. As soon as he had spoken he was surprised at his own words, knowing well enough that for every villain there were a dozen people ready to say 'he wouldn't do a thing like that'.

'There's Jeremy, too,' said Jenny. 'I won't have you suspecting him.'

'All right, I won't. What about the members of the cast?'

'Their only financial interest is in their salaries,' said Barrington. 'But of course the longer the play runs the better it is from that point of view. There's also the question of reputation – you must never forget that. And that takes Meg off the list,' he added, dividing a smile between his leading lady and her husband. 'She's so well established nothing could affect her, either success or failure.'

'What about Stella Hartley?'

'Meg will be cross with me if I answer that honestly,' Barrington told him. 'She's an excellent actress, and more than competent in the part she's playing, but I think she's reluctant to give up the leading roles she's always played, and for all her good looks she doesn't look as young as . . . well, as Meg can do.'

For a moment Antony looked at Meg, realising as he did so that she was by now so familiar a friend that sometimes he hardly noticed her appearance. She was a small woman with dark hair which, except when a stage part called for another style, she wore in a plait that was twisted round her head. The years had given her an elegance that was by now almost unconscious, except when she was deliberately dramatising herself or a situation, but nothing would ever change her forthright nature. He knew from experience that she could play the *gamine* as well as the *grande dame* and though she had never had Stella Hartley's spectacular good looks she was perfectly capable of projecting any image she cared on an audience stunned by her acting ability. 'We'll leave her on the list, then,' he said. 'Stella, I mean. About the others . . . are any of them particularly hard up, for instance, perhaps because they've been resting for a while?'

'That would be most likely to apply to the two youngsters, Mark and Roberta. Mary Russell never wants for work, and I think she only took on the understudy because she wanted to be connected with the same performance as Stella. You may have gathered she's devoted to her.'

'And the others?'

'Matthew, I imagine, is quite comfortably off financially. As for Joseph and Edward, they've been working, but I daresay they haven't been particularly well paid. Besides, they're both very young still and can't expect to have made a reputation for themselves yet.'

This didn't seem to be getting them anywhere. 'Your financial backers perhaps,' Antony suggested, not very hopefully.

'Can you imagine old Tremlett creeping around with an aerosol can of paint?' asked Roger, obviously taking some pleasure in the thought. 'In any case, he could certainly well afford to write the whole thing off as a tax loss, and I'd be surprised if that didn't apply to the rest of them. He wouldn't go into anything if he wasn't sure all his colleagues were in excellent shape financially.'

'Yes, of course, you would know about that,' Antony agreed. 'And from what you said, Mr Barrington, I can't see any of them getting into the theatre and playing all these pranks without being detected.'

'It does seem unlikely.'

'Opportunity, then. We've already considered the magpie, but surely you must have been thinking about the other things.'

'Indeed I have, and I don't think it will be the slightest help to you. Nobody has seen anyone doing anything suspicious; it would be much easier to calm their fears if they had. And except when they are on stage anyone can go roaming around the theatre at will, into the greenroom or the dressing rooms or anywhere.'

'I believe I've heard that Mr Benbow is on stage most of the time.'

'Yes, so he is. So is Meg for that matter. But Matthew's presence is only during the first act. You may remember he's murdered after that.'

'It occurs to me though that you yourself must be in evidence during the whole time the rehearsal is going on.'

Barrington gave him a long look. 'I see you're taking this seriously,' he said.

'Don't you want me to? I thought that was the whole idea?'

'Yes, of course. And in the same vein I'll answer you. We do have breaks, you know.'

'I realise that, but take the substitution of flour for face powder in Miss Hartley's dressing room. If you were taking a break she'd be there, wouldn't she?'

'She might just as easily be in the greenroom making life hell for everyone,' said Barrington with one of his sudden fits of frankness. 'And the same goes for the writing on the wall. I could have done it during the break when the others had decided for once to go to their dressing rooms. There is a certain amount of clannishness, as Meg could tell you. They often prefer to be in several small circles – pulling the rest of the cast to pieces, I daresay – rather than form a single large group.'

'I see. I think we'll leave you out of this all the same. The same thing goes for Jeremy and Meg, doesn't it?'

'I certainly don't think you could involve Meg in all this,' said Barrington with his warm smile. 'Jeremy . . . well he doesn't know his way around the theatre as well as I do. Hugh Clinton does and could easily provide an excuse wherever he might be seen, but he doesn't come under the heading of motive. As to the rest of the cast I don't think any one of them can be excluded. I did ask some questions after each incident but nobody would admit to having seen anything suspicious. As I told you.'

'There are a few other people about the theatre I'm sure, in spite of what you said just now.'

'You're wasting your time if you concentrate on them. There's nobody else with a whiff of motive and not so many people about at this stage of the proceedings as you might imagine.' In spite of being asked to repeat himself he managed to keep the least trace of impatience out of his voice.

'Well – I suspect Meg knows this already – I think it's a publicity stunt and the person responsible is Chester Cartwright.'

'Poor Chester, aren't you being rather hard on him?'

'No, I don't think so. I'm basing my conclusion on the fact that he has more to lose – or should I say more to gain – than any of you. Neither you nor Mr Skelton needs publicity. And he's the one person without definite duties around the theatre who could most easily have found time to do everything that was done.'

Barrington still looked doubtful. Meg said, 'I do agree with you, Brian, it's horrible to think it might be someone we know. But all these things have happened, unless you really agree with the rest of them that it's Sir John Cartwright's ghost.'

'Do they *really* all think that?' asked Antony incredulously.

'I should say the remark was half true,' said Barrrington thoughtfully. 'That is, at least half the cast believe in the ghost implicitly and the rest say they don't but have some sneaking qualms. As for me, I daresay your explanation is by far the most likely one, but I have to admit to being a little uneasy.'

There didn't seem to be much to be said in face of that. They went out to dinner soon after but the subject kept recurring throughout all their attempts to talk of other things . . . and just as usefully, thought Antony rather sadly as he and Jenny made their way home later, as during their previous talk.

Friday, 9th January

I

Maitland wasn't due at the theatre until ten o'clock, so he and Jenny both went downstairs as soon as they had finished breakfast and regaled Sir Nicholas and Vera, who were still finishing theirs, with an up-to-date account of the happenings at the Cornmarket Theatre. 'This is something new for you, Antony,' said Sir Nicholas cordially when the rather disjointed account was finished. (Disjointed because Jenny had insisted on taking a hand.) 'Ghost hunting,' he added thoughtfully. 'Well, at least it's an innocent enough occupation. Have you thought of consulting –?'

'I don't for a moment believe it's a ghost,' said Antony, interrupting without ceremony. 'I don't know if you've thought about it yet, but there's a sort of logic about the progression of events that doesn't sound like the supernatural. What do you think, Vera?'

'Believe in ghosts when I see one,' said Vera gruffly. 'All the same, quite see for Meg's sake you ought to get to the bottom of it. Somebody's being spiteful and I don't wonder Roger's worried.'

'I suppose it'll be interesting, in a way, to attend a few rehearsals,' Antony admitted, 'particularly as we've met most – if not all – of the people concerned, but as I told Barrington I don't see that my presence will do the slightest good at all.'

'If they knew who's doing the things they couldn't still think it was Sir John,' said Jenny. 'You know that's what Mr Barrington wants you to find out.'

'Even that wouldn't be much use unless I could prove it, and the only way to do that would be to catch someone in the act. And if I'm prowling around, nothing will happen while I'm looking on,' Antony pointed out reasonably.

'You must do what you can,' said Sir Nicholas still with that suspicious amiability. 'Is Jenny going to accompany you?'

'No, we talked about it but decided she wouldn't. She saw the rehearsals for Jeremy's other play, because at that time Anne was shy about going alone, but I think on the whole she'd rather wait and see the whole thing on the first night.'

'Well, you may consider the affair as having my blessing,' his uncle told him. 'But don't forget that the new term starts on Monday.'

'I haven't forgotten. I was going to ask you, sir, if you'd see if there's anything I ought to look over before then and bring it home to me tonight.'

'With the greatest of pleasure. I should like to hear of your adventures in any case, and I'm sure your aunt would too. Have you any engagement, Jenny, or may we come up after dinner?'

'You may as well eat with us,' said Jenny inevitably. 'There's plenty of time to tell Mrs Stokes not to get anything ready so she won't get in a huff, and that way we'll have time to talk.' And so it was arranged.

Antony left Jenny planning her menu and set off on foot for the theatre. Since they had left Barrington the night before he had been asking himself at least once in every one of his waking hours how on earth he had managed to allow himself to be manoeuvred into such an invidious position. Making enquiries on behalf of a client was one thing, but this was quite another. He could form an opinion about who was responsible for the incidents, in fact he had already done so, though part of his mind kept pointing out that the theory had perhaps been reached on too little evidence. But how could he prove what he suspected, and if he did prove it to his own satisfaction what could he do about it?

He put this question to Meg when he encountered her on his arrival at the theatre but it obviously wasn't one that worried her. 'If you can convince Brian and Jeremy,' she said, 'they'll do something about it, don't worry.' There was nothing to do but leave the matter there, so he regaled her instead with a description of Uncle Nick's reaction to his ghost hunting activities.

'He even let me get away with interrupting him,' he told her, 'without calling down fire from heaven on my head.' But this obviously had the opposite effect to the one he had intended.

'There, you see!' said Meg triumphantly. 'If Uncle Nick approves that shows I'm right.' Which left Maitland with nothing to do but shrug his shoulders and attempt no further argument.

Going into the body of the theatre they found the entire cast, plus the three understudies, in a nervous huddle in the centre of the stage. Jeremy Skelton, with Chester Cartwright beside him, was sitting at ease in one of the front stalls, while Brian Barrington seemed to be giving the members of his company an exhortation of some kind. He broke off when he saw them coming, however. 'Oh, there you are, Meg. And Mr Maitland.' His gesture in Antony's direction seemed to say, It's up to you now.

'Clever Mr Maitland,' said Stella, coming forward with hands outstretched as though to take his, though considering the height of the stage above the auditorium this would have been a difficult manoeuvre to accomplish. He was to find that she called him by his Christian name or his surname indiscriminately, and decided without any proof at all that the use of the more formal address was intended to remind him of those of his past activities that had been commented upon unsympathetically by the press. 'B.B. has been telling us,' she went on, 'that you've come to solve all our troubles.'

'I'm not so sure about that,' said Antony, a little taken aback by this greeting.

'Oh, but I know you are!' He realised even before she went on that she was saying the exact opposite to what she meant. 'You're an expert in exorcism, or why should B.B. have asked you for your help in dealing with Sir John? Of course everything will be all right now you're here. How do you go about it?'

'Stop teasing, Stella,' said Matthew Benbow, as gruffly as Vera herself might have done. 'You know perfectly well B.B. doesn't believe we're being haunted; he thinks there's some trickery afoot and that Mr Maitland can get to the bottom of it.'

'Oh, I see, you do disappoint me.' She drooped a little, registering the emotion. 'We were quite sure – weren't we, Mary? – that that was what you were going to do.'

'I'm afraid not,' said Antony, doing his best to sound serious though the humour of the situation had suddenly struck him very forcibly, so that he was tempted to add, Even if I were in Holy Orders, I understand that would require a clearer conscience than mine. Instead he went on, 'I don't actually think there's anything I can do, even on the natural plain.'

'Because there is no natural explanation,' she said triumphantly. 'You agree with me, don't you, Mark?'

'Yes, of course,' said Kenilworth, but Maitland thought he sounded a little doubtful, though perhaps it was only that he didn't like making the admission. 'We ought to have known from the beginning . . . that message on Meg's mirror. Cartwright doesn't like us playing about with his brainchild.'

'Is that what you all think?' asked Antony, looking round at the assembled company.

There was a moment's complete silence. Then, 'I believe what Stella says absolutely,' said Mary Russell quickly.

'Oh, so do I,' said Edward Brome in his languid way. Matthew Benbow contented himself with looking extremely uncomfortable.

'It certainly seems,' said Joseph Weatherly soberly, 'to be an unlucky play.'

'*You* don't believe that, Mr Maitland.' Arthur Webb's tone was challenging and he had a protective arm around Amanda Chillingworth's shoulders.

'No, I don't,' Antony replied bluntly.

'What *do* you think, then?'

'I think –' he began, but Barrington interrupted him, perhaps afraid of what he might be going to say.

'Mr Maitland thinks it's a publicity stunt,' he said. 'And you must admit the things that have been happening have certainly got our names into the papers.'

Stella Hartley began to laugh. There was more than a touch of hysteria in it. 'That's all we needed!' she said. 'Really, B.B., how stupid can you get? We need someone from the Society for Psychical Research, and all you bring us is a lawyer with a reputation for getting his clients out of trouble whether they're innocent or not.'

'With a record of successes in the sort of investigation where a knowledge of what makes people tick is helpful,' said Barrington evenly. Matthew Benbow, in a completely unexpected gesture, turned to put a hand on each of Stella's shoulders and began to shake her.

'I know you're upset,' he said. 'Mr Maitland will forgive you. Perhaps the – the happenings will stop now he's here; perhaps he'll decide your suggestion is a good one, in which case I think B.B. may well take his advice. In the meantime there's nothing we can do but get on with our rehearsal and we can't do that if you let yourself get upset.'

Stella wriggled herself free. 'I know,' she said, 'the play must go on! Can't you think of anything a little less corny than that?'

'It seems a good idea at the moment, corny or not,' said Weatherly mildly. 'Though I must admit I'm curious. B.B. says you're going to investigate, Mr Maitland. How do you propose to go about it?'

'To begin with I'm going to sit down next to Jeremy and Mr Cartwright and watch you rehearse,' Antony told him. He thought he might prowl about the theatre later on when they got used to his presence, but at the moment the backstage area was almost a complete mystery to him and though Roger had escorted him sometimes to Meg's dressing room on a first night he didn't think he could have found his way even there by himself. But there was no point in telling them his intentions at the moment. It also occurred to him that if anything else happened it might prove educational. He had every intention of keeping an eye on Chester Cartwright, but that again was something that was better left unsaid.

'All right then, children.' Barrington was brisk again. 'We'll take it from the beginning and I hope everyone is word perfect by now. Tommy,' – he turned to a young man who had been hovering unobtrusively at the edge of the group – 'get into your place and if anyone needs help don't make it too obvious. That's our prompter,' he added, turning to Antony. 'As I told you, I don't think you need consider him. Everyone's been so jittery there's been a lot of drying up and his absence from his appointed place would certainly have been noticed.'

Antony nodded his agreement and slipped into his place beside Jeremy, who gave him a grin and said, 'I'm glad you're here. It's quite obvious something has got to be done, and I can't think of anyone more likely to get results. You may care to see the "cast in order of appearance",' he added, 'otherwise you'll get terribly mixed up.'

There was enough light from the stage for Maitland to read what was typed on the sheet Skelton handed him:

Sir Benjamin Oldfellow	Matthew Benbow
Becky, Lady Oldfellow	Margaret Hamilton
Bess Brownlees, her maid	Amanda Chillingworth

63

Richard Twells, manservant to Gilbert Bold	Arthur Webb
Lucy Simpering, Becky's friend	Stella Hartley
Jack Bashful	Edward Brome
Gilbert Bold	Joseph Weatherly
Understudy to Miss Hamilton	Mary Russell
Understudy to Miss Hartley and Miss Chillingworth	Roberta Rowan
Understudy to Mr Benbow, Mr Brome, Mr Weatherly and Mr Webb	Mark Kenilworth

The first act started with a scene between Sir Benjamin and his wife. Benbow moved about the stage with a limp. ('He's got gout,' said Jeremy in an undertone. 'In the play, I mean.') They might have been nervous but it was uncanny to see how these old campaigners transformed themselves, he into a much older man, Meg into a very young girl.

The point was made quite early on and very amusingly, that Becky was utterly bored with the quiet life he wanted to lead, and equally it seemed that Sir Benjamin was quite unconscious of any dissatisfaction on her part. Meg, speaking aside to the audience or grimacing behind his back, was in her element. 'La, Sir Benjamin, you'll be the death of me yet, the pace you want to live,' she said prettily to her elderly husband at last and tripped off the stage. Sir Benjamin stood looking after her and the droop of his shoulders conveyed to Maitland for the first time that he might realise well enough his wife's feelings and lack of affection for him. After a moment's pause he too made his exit at the opposite side. ('But I can quite see,' said Antony in a low voice to his neighbour, 'why you felt you had to change the method of murder. The old boy must have said "stap me vitals" at least half a dozen times already.')

There followed the sound of thunderous knocking off-stage and Bess Brownlees entered on the same side as her mistress had exited. A moment later she was joined by Richard Twells. They embraced fervently and then engaged in a spirited dialogue, during which it emerged that Twells had been sent with a message from his master for Lady Oldfellow's eyes alone. Bess told him roundly that she knew all her mistress's affairs and would see that the letter was safely delivered. Mr Bold, it seemed, would be following up his missive with a morning call, hoping to see some sign from Lady Oldfellow that she agreed to a clandestine meeting. Their scene together was entertaining and they needed Tommy's services only twice. Amanda was obviously nervous but playing up manfully to her more stolid husband. They separated and went off in different directions when the knocker sounded again, this time to herald the entrance of Lucy Simpering escorted by Jack Bashful. If these two were intended as comic relief, as the names seemed to imply, Antony thought this was an embarrassment of riches. All the talk so far had been quick and amusing. They were left alone for only a moment before Becky joined them with Sir Benjamin Oldfellow limping in a few minutes later. Becky made much of her friend and sat with her on the sofa centre stage exchanging gossip about their mutual acquaintance, while Sir Benjamin took his favourite chair and Jack Bashful one at the other side of the stage where he sat sucking the knob of his cane and eyeing the two ladies admiringly.

Lady Oldfellow and Miss Simpering did not get through their dialogue quite as smoothly as Becky had done with her husband earlier and Lucy at one stage lost the thread of what she was saying. The prompter was slow in reminding her and she turned on poor Tommy – invisible in the wings – quite viciously.

Barrington intervened in a moment. 'Steady on, Stella,' he said. And then, tactfully, 'You're both going on so smoothly I don't suppose Tommy expected you to dry up.'

'That's what he's there for, isn't it?' asked Stella crossly. 'Anyway, I remember now.' But she was still nervous and kept casting glances over her shoulder as though somebody might be creeping up behind her to do her an injury. Brian Barrington pulled her up over this several times until Jack Bashful who, having had very little to say as yet, might or might not have been nervous, told him roundly, 'No good blaming Stella. She's doing her best.'

'I suppose you all are,' said Barrington sarcastically. 'Good heavens, Stella, I've seen you act a dozen times with never anything to complain about. This is an important scene.'

Jack Bashful paused in his exercise of sucking the silver-headed cane. 'No ghosts then,' he said flatly. 'That makes a difference, you know.'

'All right then, get on with it.' Just for the moment Barrington was doing nothing to hide his exasperation. 'But do try, Stella, not to look as if you expect to be murdered at any moment. You're paying a morning call on your friend, you know there's some intrigue afoot and are longing to find out what it is, but there's nothing at all to worry you '

'All right, B.B., I'll try.' For once Stella seemed to have forgotten her usual abrasiveness, and this time her glance around obviously met with the director's approval. 'I think that dear Sir Benjamin has just fallen asleep,' she cooed.

Becky followed her look and a distinctly feline smile showed on her face. Jack Bashful had left his seat and was examining something at the side of the stage, where Maitland presumed there would eventually be a wall and perhaps a painting hanging on it. 'Alas,' said Lady Oldfellow, 'I fear Sir Benjamin grows old.' She produced a note that up to then had been concealed in her hand. 'Only see, dear Lucy, what Mr Bold has writ me.'

'Remember, Meg,' said Barrington, 'when you're in costume that note will be produced from your bosom.'

'I'll remember,' she promised.

Lucy Simpering had taken no notice of this exchange. 'I see you wear it next to your heart,' she said, and tittered.

The ensuing dialogue concerned the pros and cons of Lady Oldfellow's agreeing to a meeting. She seemed strangely reluctant. 'I have long thought, dear Becky,' said Lucy reproachfully, 'that you have formed a romantic attachment. Can it be that I was wrong?'

This time it was Lady Oldfellow who simpered. 'Not wrong at all, but perhaps wrong about the object of my affections,' she said. And that was a bit of clever acting if ever there was one, Antony thought. She succeeded in conveying perfectly well that she didn't trust her friend an inch and was only willing to confide in her up to a point.

Jack Bashful had come back to his chair and resumed his silent staring, but when Sir Benjamin woke with a start the talk became general and continued that way for some time. Then, just as Miss Simpering and her escort were about to take their leave, the knocker was applied again, voices were heard in what was presumably the hall off-stage, and Gilbert Bold entered. There was a little more general conversation before the other two visitors left, and then Sir Benjamin, who had heaved himself out of his chair to make his farewells, limped across the stage to his wife's side. 'Do you entertain Mr Bold,' he told her. 'I find myself weary.'

'To be sure, sir, I fear our guest will be disappointed. Will you not, Mr Bold?'

Gilbert Bold looked from one to the other of them whimsically. 'I looked to have the company of you both,' he said, 'and I am sorry for Sir Benjamin's weariness. But I should be churlish indeed not to welcome the chance of conversing with so charming a lady.' And he too succeeded in conveying to the audience, without a word said to disillusion the old man, his delight in this unexpected opportunity. Sir Benjamin nodded as though in approval of the sentiment and patted the younger man on the shoulder as he passed on his way off-stage. A moment or two later he came tiptoeing back, crossing the stage and coming to a halt in the opposite corner at the rear. 'When the stage is set there'll be a screen there,' hissed Jeremy in Antony's ear.

Even if he hadn't spoken Maitland would have had to assume as much: the two younger people at the front of the stage took no notice of the old man. Like Bess and Richard Twells before them they fell at once into an enthusiastic embrace and there were some murmured endearments. It was obvious that Becky had been intent on deceiving her friend as well as her husband. But after a moment they drew apart, though Gilbert's hand still rested on her shoulders as though he couldn't bear to let her go. 'Dear heart –' he began, but before he could complete the sentence there was a stunning crash, something hurtled down from the flies above the stage, and Stella in the wings – perhaps inevitably – started to scream.

II

Antony was already at home when Sir Nicholas and Vera came upstairs that evening. His uncle had been into chambers that day, as he knew, and handed over a couple of files before he followed Antony back into the living room. 'Nothing very urgent,' he said negligently. 'I don't think Mallory is very pleased with you though.' (Old Mr Mallory was Sir Nicholas's clerk, and a tyrant of the first water.)

'Dereliction of duty,' said Maitland sadly. 'Gibbs succeeded in conveying the same thing when I came home in the middle of the afternoon. I wish I had your knack, Vera, of dealing with Uncle Nick's old retainers.'

'I feel sure the fault is yours, my dear boy,' Sir Nicholas told him. 'As for Mallory, I don't think he would appreciate the description. His position is far too powerful for it to be really apt.'

'It's all very well for you, Uncle Nick, he eats out of your hand,' said Antony, knowing well enough that this form of speech would annoy his uncle. 'What horrors has he involved me in this term?'

'Nothing very immediate,' Sir Nicholas assured him, with unusual forbearance. 'Though if you will take the trouble to read the papers I brought home for you –'

'I'll read them all right.' Jenny was already busy pouring sherry and he reached past her to place the files on the writing table and went to his own accustomed place near the fire. Sir Nicholas had already taken possession of his favourite chair, with Vera at the end of the sofa nearest him. 'Of course, if you think I should get at those files immediately –' Maitland hazarded.

'By no means.' That was the second opportunity Sir Nicholas had missed of annihilating his nephew, which could only mean that his curiosity had been thoroughly aroused. 'Can't you see that your aunt is all agog to hear what you have to tell us?' he went on, confirming this. 'How did the ghost hunting go?'

'It's turned into a poltergeist,' said Antony baldly.

'Come now, you can't leave it there.'

'No, sir, of course not. You knew I was going to the theatre today and something else did indeed happen. But to take things in order, I had a few words with the actors first, they really are jittery, and I meant to take a stroll behind the scenes later on to see who was around and whether there would be any difficulty in finding an opportunity of doing all these things. Not to mention that I needed to get the hang of the set-up generally. But first I wanted to see something of the play, and if you tell me that in the circumstances that was inexcusable curiosity . . . well, I don't agree with you.'

Sir Nicholas ignored that. 'And before you could carry out this programme Sir John Cartwright decided to take a part in the proceedings himself, I suppose, and started throwing things,' he said.

'You might put it that way,' said Maitland, and allowed himself a moment's amusement, though he was immediately serious again. 'It wasn't funny at the time,' he said, 'but I'd better tell you about the rehearsal first, at least so far as I saw it. They went, Jeremy told me, nearly through the first act.' He outlined the action for them in a good many fewer words than Jeremy Skelton had taken. 'It took almost two and a half hours; which I gather isn't extraordinary in the circumstances. I thought they were pretty good myself, except for drying up occasionally, but Barrington said afterwards they were frightful. Except Meg, of course, who I think could act under any circumstances. Anyway, towards the end of the act, she and Joseph Weatherly were doing a scene together and Matthew Benbow was at the back of the stage, where I understand there's going to be a screen for him to hide behind when things are set up properly. And all of a sudden there was an almighty crash and a huge chunk of wood – eight by eight and about eighteen inches long – hurtled down from the flies on to the stage.'

'Nobody was hurt,' said Jenny in quick reassurance. She had already heard the story.

'No,' Antony agreed, 'but whoever rigged the thing up couldn't have known that for sure. It gave me a hell of a fright, I can tell you.'

'Rigged it up?' said Sir Nicholas with a question as well as some distaste in his voice.

'Yes. Stella Hartley was having hysterics, of course, she must have been standing in the wings watching what was going on on stage. Then one of the stage-hands appeared. I don't know what he'd been doing, I don't know enough about these things. He was practically in hysterics too. Apparently he'd just set foot on one of the catwalks and this chunk of wood, which had no business to be there, became unbalanced and fell.'

'Did Barrington tell you anything about him? Was he a man who might have had a grievance?'

'Barrington knew him, Uncle Nick. A very solid chap, he called him. And I honestly don't think he could have had anything to do either with what happened today or with any previous event. For the first happenings he wasn't even in the theatre, I gather, and if he was acting when he came down and rushed on to the stage today he was even more clever than any of the very capable cast that Barrington has assembled for this play.'

69

'What happened next?' Sir Nicholas maintained his look of indolence, but Vera's interest had obviously been caught and she didn't care who knew it.

'Matthew Benbow slapped Stella to shut her up, and Barrington and Clinton – he's the stage manager – between them soothed the stage-hand.'

'Who so far remains anonymous.'

'Come to think of it, I never did hear his name. But I really believe, Uncle Nick, he had nothing to do with what happened. Except as an innocent agent, of course. He never denied that he'd triggered the whole thing.'

'You were there and I wasn't,' said Sir Nicholas, dismissing an obviously unfruitful course of enquiry. 'If the rehearsal had gone on so long you must have been wanting your lunch by that time.'

Antony grinned at that, knowing well enough that events would have to be dire indeed to make his uncle forget such an important point. 'It was obviously no use going on anyway; the cast were completely demoralised. Barrington said they'd start again tomorrow because they'd been losing so much time, though I think he'd meant to call a Saturday rehearsal anyway. After that he took Jeremy and myself to lunch – Anne wasn't at the theatre today – but we waited until everybody else had left before we went.'

'Mr Chester Cartwright was not included in the invitation?'

'No. You see Mr Barrington wanted to ask me my opinion, and I'd already told him my previous theory.'

'Which I take it you've now changed?'

'Well, what happened today makes a difference . . . don't you think? The fact that no one was hurt doesn't alter the fact that somebody might have been, or even killed. That wasn't a publicity stunt. It was spite, and it was done by somebody who just didn't care what the result might be.'

'Meg was on stage, you say.'

'Yes, and Matthew Benbow and Joseph Weatherly. I didn't mention that Barrington had included her in the luncheon invitation, but she wanted to get home and Benbow said he'd take her.'

'Was she dreadfully upset?' asked Vera anxiously.

'I'm sure she was but she didn't show it. You know Meg, Vera, she'll play up like anything over something that isn't in the least important, but when something like this happens . . . *ye'll no fickle*

70

Tammas Yownie, as she'd probably say herself.'

'Good girl,' said Vera approvingly. 'Not that I've the faintest idea what you're talking about.'

'John Buchan,' said Maitland briefly. 'Anyway, the fact of who was actually on stage hasn't any real relevance. Nobody could have known the stage-hand was going to put his foot on the catwalk at that precise moment. The piece of wood must have been pretty delicately balanced, but that might have been done at any time, it might have even been there for several days. So I'm bound to think, and I'm sure you'll agree with me, that all these episodes were engineered by someone with a malicious motive.'

'With the intention of making the production impossible?' asked Sir Nicholas.

'That seems to be most likely, which is why I've written Chester Cartwright off completely as a suspect.'

'Have you indeed?'

'Yes. I was fairly sure it was him because I knew he was less aware of the effect all these things would have on the actors than anyone else. But what happened today was different; it couldn't be written off as publicity. So what I think, Uncle Nick, is that it must be someone with a grievance against Cartwright himself or against Barrington, or against Jeremy. That's the most obvious possibility, I think. But any of the actors might have been the intended victim. I shall have to find out a lot more about their relationships with each other.'

'You have the whole of tomorrow,' said Sir Nicholas cordially.

'Yes, sir,' said Antony meekly, and his uncle gave him a suspicious look.

'I imagine,' he said thoughtfully, 'that part of the attraction this affair has for you is that the police aren't involved, at least at this stage. Am I right?'

'I think perhaps you are,' Antony conceded reluctantly, 'though I wouldn't say it attracts me particularly as a way of occupying my time. I did take up the question of calling the police with Barrington again, but he's quite right – it *could* have been an accident, and that's what they would think. They wouldn't be interested in the practical jokes, which is how they'd write the rest of the things off. I don't think it was an accident, mind you, but it could have been, and as no one was hurt I think Barrington was quite right in his decision. I'm beginning to be afraid of what may happen though. Roger insists on coming to the theatre with

71

me tomorrow; he's even more scared than I am, I suppose.'

Sir Nicholas took his time to think that out. 'You're trying to tell me, I think, that somebody – the person who is responsible for all these tricks – may be working himself up to a climax of some sort.'

'Something like that. You must admit the possibilities are – are rather uncomfortable. I don't care about the play so much . . . well, I do, I suppose, because I like Barrington, and Jeremy and Anne are pretty special people. But Meg's involved. I have to hand it to Roger that he hasn't so far tried to persuade her to back out, because I know she wouldn't. But if she gets hurt –'

'I suppose all possible precautions will be taken, to prevent any further booby traps being set, for instance.'

'Certainly they will. That was the first thing Barrington thought of.'

'Very well, then.' Sir Nicholas took time to sip his sherry. 'What would you say was the first priority? After keeping Meg safe, I mean.'

'To reassure the cast, I suppose.'

'Exactly the point I was about to make. And to do that we have to persuade them that Sir John Cartwright is resting peacefully in his grave, not wandering around the theatre indulging in some rather undignified pranks. To begin with, he's supposed to have written an outline of the plot on which this play is based, isn't he? Why then should he object to its being put on?'

'I can tell you that,' said Antony. 'At least, I can tell you what the actors think. There was that first message on Meg's mirror, *This is no play of mine.* And Chester Cartwright's first impulse was to dislike the change in the murder method that Jeremy had made.'

'You said he'd come round to that later on.'

'Yes, I think he saw it's more effective this way, and in any case he's quite aware on which side his bread is buttered. That's one thing. The other is that the play has been modernised to the extent of containing the action in two acts. To a restoration dramatist that might not be a popular move. In addition, he may just not like Jeremy's treatment of what, after all, was his idea. I think it's pretty good myself, but perhaps I'm prejudiced.'

'Meg thinks so too,' said Jenny, 'and she knows more about the stage than either of us.'

'Do you know,' asked Vera, 'how the play goes on?'

'You mean from the point where the block of wood fell on the stage and today's rehearsals stopped? Jeremy told me over lunch. You remember that Matthew Benbow, or perhaps I should stick to the stage names and call him Sir Benjamin, was at the back of the stage, supposed to be concealed behind the screen. There's quite a long scene between Lady Oldfellow and Gilbert Bold, rather outspoken in the manner of the day –'

'Which will offend nobody of this generation,' Sir Nicholas put in rather dryly.

'– and they finish up by making an assignation for that evening. Then Gilbert leaves. Lady Oldfellow and Bess, her maid, have a brief scene together. I gathered from watching the earlier part of the play that Becky doesn't altogether trust her friend Miss Simpering, but it turns out she does trust Bess. Then Bess goes off and the audience is expecting Sir Benjamin to come out from behind the screen and confront his wife with the evidence that he has been cuckolded. Instead of that there's a sudden dreadful cry – I'm putting this more or less in Jeremy's words – and a moment later the old boy staggers out to centre stage and dies in a suitably dramatic manner, having been run through by a rapier.'

'I take it the audience never sees the assassin.'

'No, that's right. Jeremy said one end of the screen is right up against the wings. Where would the mystery be otherwise?'

'And the second act?'

'Well Gilbert Bold is suspected, naturally, even by Becky, and of course the idea is cleverly conveyed that if he is guilty she may find consolation elsewhere. When Bold left the stage the audience could hear the front door shut but nobody is able to say they actually saw him leave. That applies to the other visitors too. Apparently Miss Simpering and Jack Bashful didn't leave the house together as everybody thought. She went upstairs to fetch her mantle, and when she came down again Bashful was nowhere to be seen. The only member of the cast who couldn't have done it, besides Becky who is in full view on stage all the time, is Gilbert's manservant Richard Twells, and he turns out to be a detective *manqué* and solves the mystery in a series of really brilliantly funny interviews. It seems to me rather a pity ... you can't help liking Sir Benjamin but none of the people in the play seem to be at all sorry he's dead and Jeremy says the audience will soon forget all about that side of things. At least, Becky pays a little lip service to his memory, but only to maintain her as a sympathetic character in the audience's eyes. The murderer, of course, is Jack Bashful who has been in love with Becky all the time. When he heard what she said to Lucy Simpering about having formed a romantic attachment but not caring for Gilbert Bold he thought she must have been referring to him and that he had a very good chance of winning her if the old man was out of the way.'

'All this sounds fascinating,' said Sir Nicholas in a tone that meant exactly the opposite, 'but it isn't getting us anywhere. What is known about Sir John Cartwright?'

'I don't see how that can help us,' said Antony, 'but if you really want an answer I can give you one because I looked him up in the encyclopaedia. He was born in 1620 and as a young man fought in the Civil War.'

'In view of his later career I must presume that he fought for the king and not for the parliament,' said Sir Nicholas.

'Yes, of course. He was in the cavalry, under Prince Rupert, and went into exile with the prince. If you remember that was before the king finally surrendered himself to the parliament.'

'To the Scots,' said Vera, who liked to get these things straight. '*They* handed him over to Cromwell.'

'So they did. But to get back to Sir John, nothing much is known about the next years though as he was devoted to Rupert he may have stayed on under his command when the prince became Admiral of the Fleet, such as it was.'

'And as Charles II and Rupert were good friends, in spite of being uncle and nephew –' Sir Nicholas prompted him.

'Yes, in spite of that,' said Antony, smiling. 'You're quite right, Sir John came back to England when the monarchy was restored, his estates were returned to him, and he occupied what leisure he had left playing the gentleman farmer. You all know how successful he was as a playwright, though it didn't last very long. He died in 1675.'

'That's all very well but I'm more interested in his character,' said Sir Nicholas. 'Which should have been your question, my dear,' he added, smiling at Jenny.

'The encyclopaedia didn't say anything about that, nor did the *Companion to English Literature.*'

'Well, what can we deduce from the plays?'

'He was very much a man of his time, Uncle Nick,' said Antony, 'as far as I can judge from the little I saw of the

74

rehearsal. Even if we grant the authenticity of the outline Cartwright found –'

'Do you really think Jeremy could be wrong about a thing like that?' asked Jenny. 'Anyway, I thought you'd stopped suspecting Chester Cartwright.'

'So I have. That doesn't mean I've accepted the outline as authentic though, I still have my doubts about that. He might have spent years preparing it, learning to copy Sir John's writing, and from what I've been told about his attainments in the scholastic world the outline itself shouldn't have been beyond him. But even if it *is* genuine it only means that Sir John had a certain ingenuity in thinking up what was then a completely new idea; I don't think it tells us much about him as a person.'

'I wonder,' said Sir Nicholas slowly. 'Your encyclopaedia must have told you this, Antony. Was he ever engaged in an affair of honour?'

'Yes, I see what you mean. As a matter of fact, he was.'

'In his youth or in his later years?'

'During the last period in England. I should imagine that the war kept him busy enough when he was young, and anything may have happened during what they call not very originally the lost years. But he fought three duels during the fifteen years which he spent in England before he died.'

'Was he the challenger?'

'It only said he was the challenger in one case, Uncle Nick. In the others the cause of the dispute was unknown.'

'Was he married?' Vera put in.

'No, he seems to have copied Prince Rupert in that, too. But come to think of it that's rather odd. Chester Cartwright said he was descended from a junior branch of the family, but if Sir John had no offspring surely Chester's ancestors must have inherited the title.'

'Not thinking straight, Antony,' Vera told him. 'Doesn't follow, you know, because Sir John might have had any number of younger brothers.'

'And there's a further question,' said Sir Nicholas rather dryly, 'whether Sir John was a knight or a baronet.'

'I don't know the answer to that, sir, and in any case it doesn't really make any odds. If you're looking for something about Sir John that would make it unlikely that he'd be spiteful enough to persecute the actors in his play I don't think we've got very far, do you?'

'It would hardly reassure Meg's colleagues to be told he was evidently a man of somewhat choleric disposition,' Sir Nicholas agreed. 'Perhaps we can get at it another way, then. The second lot of writing on the wall was a quotation from Shakespeare – would he have been likely to have been familiar with it?'

'That's something else I looked up and it won't help either,' said Antony rather sadly. 'There was a folio edition – twelve hundred copies, I believe – of Shakespeare's work published in 1623, and a second impression in 1664. Sir John might have been brought up on the first, or got hold of a second when he came back to England with the king.'

'In any case,' said Vera, 'he used a Shakespeare quotation for his title.'

'There's some dispute about that,' said Antony. '*The Passionate Pilgrim*, which the encyclopaedia describes as an unauthorised anthology of poems, was published in 1599 and attributed to Shakespeare. But the general feeling seems to be that most of it was by other people.'

'I suppose,' said Sir Nicholas, 'that I should congratulate you on your erudition, my dear boy.'

'More appropriately on being able to read. I told you, I looked it all up quite recently.'

'In any event, I can't see that it is the slightest help. Nothing you can tell the cast of Jeremy's play will convince them that it couldn't have been Sir John Cartwright doing all these things.'

'No, I'm afraid you're right about that, sir.'

'Meg wants this play to succeed very much, doesn't she?' asked Vera.

'Naturally she does. And we all do for Jeremy's sake and Anne's. Also I've come to like the director, Brian Barrington, very much indeed, as I think I told you, and what I saw today made me think the play deserves to succeed.'

'You say, however, that they will be rehearsing again tomorrow.'

'As far as I can make out it's a question of their superstition battling with the old saying, the show must go on. And Barrington says they've lost enough time already.'

'But you're wondering what may happen next?'

'Yes, Uncle Nick, I am. But I do see Barrington's point about not calling the police. So far, the press can pass off everything that has happened as a joke, though they played up the ghost angle for all they were worth, tongue in cheek. And he phoned them himself today about the block of timber that fell to make sure they reported it as an accident. If the police were involved –'

'If the police were involved I should not be so happy about the part you are playing,' said Sir Nicholas. 'As it is it seems a harmless enough occupation and you'll probably be able to join the Society for Psychical Research on the strength of it. Otherwise, it seems to me a complete waste of time,' he added dismissively.

'I don't agree with you at all,' said Jenny, firing up as she very occasionally did when criticism of her husband seemed to be implied. 'Even if Antony can't stop anything else happening you know yourself he's good at finding things out. Don't you agree with me, Vera?'

'On that score, yes,' Vera said. 'But Nicholas is right too, you know, it's different when a client is involved. In this case Antony has no shadow of an excuse for asking people pertinent or impertinent questions.'

'Brian Barrington has asked him to and he told Antony the others would do what he wants,' said Jenny.

'That seems reasonable,' said Sir Nicholas judiciously. 'All the same, Antony, I should very much like to know exactly what you intend to do. I should be very surprised to know that you haven't already thought out a course of action.'

'Well –' Maitland sounded a little deprecating. 'Chester Cartwright, Brian Barrington and Jeremy stand to gain most by the play succeeding. Therefore, I think I should try to find out if anyone feels spiteful towards any one of them. It would also be interesting to know a little more about the relationships of the actors to each other. That couldn't possibly do any harm,' he concluded, rather tentatively.

'There, you see!' Jenny sounded triumphant, but he knew well enough that her pleasure was on Meg's behalf not on her own. 'You'll know who's responsible in no time at all and everything will be clear sailing right up to opening night.'

Maitland let that pass without comment, but it cannot be said that he was altogether easy in his mind, or that he felt an equal confidence in his own abilities. He was tired, and the old injury to his shoulder was always more painful than usual when that was the case.

Saturday, 10th January

I

Roger, taking Meg to the theatre, picked Antony up in Kempenfeldt Square the next morning. He dropped his two passengers off at the entrance to the theatre and drove on to find a parking place.

They found the auditorium empty, except for Jeremy Skelton, who pounced on them eagerly. 'Have you thought of anything that will help us?' he demanded, after the briefest of greetings.

'I talked to Uncle Nick and Vera last night,' Maitland told him. 'The most urgent thing seems to be to reassure the cast, as Uncle Nick very properly pointed out, so we went through Sir John Cartwright's background as far as I could find out anything about it from the encyclopaedia.'

'Sensible,' said Jeremy approvingly. 'But was it helpful?'

'Not so as you'd notice it. As he fought three duels in the last fifteen years of his life it seems likely that he was a pretty violent sort of fellow, who'd be quite likely to come back and throw things if he felt one of his ideas wasn't being treated with proper reverence.'

'But you don't accept that?' asked Jeremy.

'I told you I didn't. It's just that there's nothing that makes it seem unlikely from a believer's point of view.'

'Anyway,' said Jeremy, ignoring this, 'we're giving him full credit. The playbill reads "by John Cartwright and Jeremy Skelton". What more does he want?'

'He might think,' Antony ventured, 'that you took liberties with his plot. I'm only saying what Miss Hartley, for instance, may have in mind,' he added hurriedly.

'I took the greatest care,' said Jeremy thoughtfully, obviously

79

taking the suggestion more seriously than Maitland felt it deserved, 'and I'll swear the only change I made was in the manner of killing and that was really irresistible. And I did make the thing two acts, because that's how most plays are put on today. But who could object to that?'

'We're talking,' said Antony solemnly – he really couldn't resist entering into the spirit of this exchange – 'about a possibly testy ghost.'

'Well, I still maintain stabbing Sir Benjamin is more dramatic,' said Skelton. 'In the outline he dies quietly off-stage of poison, and though Bess Brownlees would have come in at the end of one of the acts and made a dramatic announcement to that effect if I'd followed the outline, the way we're doing it is much better. You remember, Meg, Chester felt at first it wasn't a good idea to change a single thing, but when he'd read the whole play again and thought about it he came round to my way of thinking.'

'Yes, he's certainly enthusiastic now. But we're not talking about Chester's opinion,' Meg pointed out. Roger rejoined them at that point, and she laid a hand on his arm but didn't break off what she was saying. 'We're talking about what Sir John Cartwright may think about what you've done to his brainchild.'

'Oh, pooh!' said Jeremy. 'You're pulling my leg, both of you.'

'Not altogether,' Antony told him. 'Just trying to see it from the actors' point of view and whether there's any way to reassure them. We did think perhaps that Sir John Cartwright might not have been too familiar with Shakespearean quotations, and so be an unlikely source of the painting on the greenroom wall. But the research I did, such as it was, didn't confirm that idea.'

'Well, I'm grateful to you for taking so much interest,' said Jeremy. 'Ah, there's Barrington,' – the director came up as he spoke – 'isn't anybody here, Brian?'

'They're all backstage and you can cut the atmosphere with a knife,' said Barrington gloomily. 'So you decided to come back again, Mr Maitland, I'm glad of that. And glad to see you too, Roger.'

'Antony says there's no chance of persuading your players that Sir John Cartwright is an unlikely ghost to have done all these things,' said Jeremy, almost equally morosely. 'But I gather that's his idea of a joke.'

'Not altogether,' Maitland protested. 'All I said was –'

'Yes, I know. From their point of view there's nothing that makes it unlikely. Are you going to sit with us and watch the rehearsal, or have you some ploy of your own to carry out?'

'Are you going to start from the beginning again?' Antony asked.

'Yes, I mean to. Are you bored already?' asked Barrington with a thread of amusement in his tone.

'No, not at all. I was thinking that while Sir Benjamin and Becky are doing their opening scene I might talk to Bess Brownlees and Richard Twells. Amanda Chillingworth and Arthur Webb, I mean,' he added. 'I don't know how you manage to keep the two sets of names separated all the time.'

'When you remember that Amanda is also Mrs Webb you've a real puzzle,' said Barrington sympathetically. 'I'll send them to you right away. Why not use the greenroom to talk?'

Meg said, 'See you later,' and then added looking back over her shoulder, 'Are you going to watch, Roger, or go with Antony?'

'If you're quite sure, Mr Barrington, that nothing's likely to fall on the stage again –'

'Quite sure,' said Barrington firmly, and carefully refrained from pointing out that even if such a mischance were to recur there was nothing to be done about it from a seat in the stalls.

'Then I'll go with Antony. If I shan't be in the way.'

'No, that will suit me very well. Where is this greenroom of yours?'

'Come with me,' said Barrington. 'I'll show you.'

It was about five minutes later when the sprightly Amanda and her rather nondescript-looking husband, Arthur Webb, joined them in the greenroom. Antony had been interested enough in the meantime in taking stock of his surroundings. To begin with the room wasn't green at all but a rather pleasant eggshell blue. One of the walls, in fact, had been recently painted, but the message beneath could still be made out. For the rest there were photographs of people well known now and in the past, generally in costume. The Cornmarket was an old theatre, so there were

81

plenty of these. While he was looking round Roger had arranged a group of decidedly comfortable chairs around a glass-topped table that he thought would be suitable for their purpose, and it was he who guided the two newcomers to it when they arrived.

'B.B. tells me you're trying to sort out this mystery of ours,' said Arthur Webb in his quiet way. 'Do you think that there's anything you can do?'

'Don't be silly, darling, you know perfectly well he's done this sort of thing before,' said Amanda, which left Antony in no doubt that she knew all there was to know about him, and that probably the rest of the cast did, too. Meg's dislike of gossip was almost pathological, so the man from the *Courier* at the party – what was his name? Richard Trevor? – must be the cause of that. As usual the reminder angered him, but he did his best to keep his voice light.

'I think perhaps Mr Webb would make a better detective,' he admitted. 'I understand that's your part in the play.'

'Yes, it is. You've only seen part of the first act, haven't you? Well, Richard Twells blossoms out quite a bit after the murder. I hope you really can do something,' he added seriously. 'We've a good crowd here . . . well, most of them. Besides, I think the play has great potential.'

'And for some of us it would be a tragedy if it failed,' said Amanda. 'It's all very well for you, Arthur, you're established already. And when that hellcat tries to upstage you, you know how to deal with it.'

'Mr Maitland isn't interested in our inter-company squabbling,' Arthur Webb assured her. 'What he wants to know . . . well, what do you want to know?' he demanded.

'To begin with, I'd like an explanation of what your wife just said,' Antony told him. 'If she doesn't mind telling me, that is.'

'I don't mind at all. This is my first big acting chance, and I daresay I wouldn't have got it if it hadn't been for Arthur being so perfect for the part he's playing.'

'Amanda –' Arthur Webb started.

'Don't be modest, you know it's true.'

'As a matter of fact that wasn't what I meant.'

'No, I can see you think I'm being indiscreet. I'm only telling

Mr Maitland and Mr Farrell what any of the others could tell them . . . Stella's doing her very best to see my chance doesn't come to anything. When we're on stage together, which happens quite a lot in the last act, she feeds me my lines so that I can only answer in a certain way, and sometimes with my back to the audience, which is what upstaging really means. In any case, so that I can't make the most of them. And it's a wonderful part and wonderful playing opposite Arthur. But –'

'That's enough, Amanda!' Webb was suddenly incisive. 'None of this has anything to do with what has been happening.'

'But at the moment we're completely in the dark,' said Roger, seeing his friend wasn't ready with an immediate question. 'Mr Maitland needs information about anything and everything. Was that what you meant, Mr Webb, when you said they were a good crowd, or most of them were? That Miss Hartley isn't the most comfortable of colleagues?'

'If you must have it, that's exactly what I meant. But I haven't been playing tricks, and neither has Amanda. After all, they haven't been specifically aimed at Stella.'

'I know that.'

'And if it is Sir John Cartwright –' Amanda began.

'Do you really think it is?' Antony asked.

'Why should he have said, *This is no play of mine*, if it wasn't?'

'Anybody might have written that to convey a certain impression.'

Amanda shook her head, obviously unconvinced. 'What about you, Mr Webb?' asked Roger, joining the conversation again. 'What's your opinion?'

'None of the actors wrote that quotation from the Scottish play,' said Arthur, jerking his head towards the newly painted wall. 'You can be quite sure of that, if of nothing else. And I know that isn't a complete answer, but it's the best you're going to get.'

'If someone is playing tricks,' said Antony, thinking that perhaps this rather ambiguous statement might be the most tactful way of putting it, 'it must be somebody who knows his or her way about the theatre. I thought at first it was all a publicity stunt –'

'And suspected Chester,' said Arthur Webb, nodding wisely.

'Yes, as a matter of fact I did at that stage,' Maitland admitted, rather startled and wondering how he'd given himself away. 'I see now that I was wrong. After what happened yesterday, it was obvious there was more than that involved, some genuine spite against somebody, the desire, perhaps, to close down the whole production.'

'That certainly lets Chester out, he's mad keen to make a go of it.'

'That's my impression, too. So there's just a chance that the motive might arise out of some malicious feelings among the cast, but it's far more likely that someone has a grudge against one of the three people who have the most to lose.'

'The author, the director, and the discoverer, if I may put it that way,' said Arthur Webb. 'I see what you mean but I can't help you. None of us knew Chester before, why should we grudge him any honours that may be coming to him as the finder of a previously unknown idea of his illustrious kinsman? The same applies to Jeremy Skelton . . . we'd heard of him before because of his other play, but we didn't know him personally. And everyone likes B.B.'

'Do you agree with that, Mrs Webb?'

'It would be much easier if you'd both call me Amanda,' she complained.

'Yes, I suppose it would. As far as I'm concerned, Meg always tells me that lawyers are a stuffy lot.'

Amanda smiled at him with sudden brilliance. 'No, I don't think that at all,' she said. 'And it couldn't possibly apply to Meg's husband either. But I do agree with Arthur whole-heartedly. Except that perhaps –'

'Perhaps what, Amanda?' asked Maitland when she hesitated.

'B.B. doesn't like Stella –'

'Who does?' enquired her husband of the world at large.

' – and that might mean she doesn't like him either.'

'Have you seen any signs of that?'

'Not exactly.' She sounded doubtful. 'I told you I don't like her, so you may not believe what I say. But she does make catty remarks whenever she possibly can about just about everybody.'

'Everybody?' asked Roger.

'If you mean, does that include Meg, Stella's pretty careful but she tries to get a dig in occasionally. And of course I didn't mean Mark, she's besotted about him.'

'And he with her?' Antony prompted.

'How could he be? He's years and years younger. And I think,' said Amanda consideringly, 'that sometimes Mary Russell gets a bit fed up with watching Stella making such a play for him. But Stella doesn't really try to annoy her deliberately.'

'And that, my pet,' said Arthur Webb, getting up with sudden decision, 'is just about enough indiscretion for one day.'

'It doesn't really matter,' Amanda assured him, following his example and getting to her feet, 'because whatever anybody says, I don't think any person – any living person – is doing all these things.'

'All the more reason for not airing our squabbles. I'd be happier about it,' Webb added, looking from Antony to Roger, 'if I thought what we told you could help you. But honestly I don't see how it can.'

'I don't either,' Maitland assured him, and only later wondered whether this could be construed as a belief in an outraged ghost. 'I'm grateful to you all the same,' he went on. 'Do you think I shall find your colleagues as helpful?'

'Give any of us a chance to talk about ourselves and watch us make the most of it,' said Webb humorously. 'I don't think you need worry about that, Mr Maitland. And I'm sorry if I seemed to imply that you're being no better than a busybody, I'm sure you mean well. Do you want us to send any of the others to you here?'

'No, I'll come out with you and nobble Miss Hartley and Mr Benbow as they come off-stage. And if you're afraid that anything Mrs – that Amanda told us will get back to the wrong quarters, you needn't worry. An indiscreet lawyer wouldn't last very long, and the same applies to a stockbroker.'

'I'm pleased to hear it,' said Arthur, and held the door for his wife to precede them into the corridor. 'If you want to get into the auditorium I'd better show you the way,' he went on, 'or do you know it, Mr Farrell?'

'Not really, things always look so different when you're going in the opposite direction.' They followed their guides with some difficulty, there was a good deal of work going on backstage today, but eventually they found themselves back in the darkened auditorium and with the aid of the light that fell from the stage made their way to Jeremy's side.

'Where has Mr Barrington got to?' Maitland asked quietly.

'He went up to the balcony to see if he could hear from there. He said Stella was mumbling her lines. They sounded clear enough to me, but she's terribly nervous, worse than any of the others.'

'I wouldn't say the same of Mr Benbow,' said Roger, who was watching the stage.

'Or of Meg. They're marvellous together, aren't they? I don't think anything could fluster either of them.'

They fell silent, watching the scene run its preordained course, but Maitland was more occupied with the talk they had just had with Amanda and Arthur Webb. Somewhere he felt something useful had been said, but he couldn't quite put his finger on it. He heard the voices from the stage without registering their meaning, and then suddenly there was a louder sound reverberating through the theatre and bringing him up straight in his seat.

'*No longer mourn for me when I am dead,*' proclaimed the voice in tones of thunder, '*than you shall hear the surly sullen bell give warning to the world that I am fled from this vile world, with vilest worms to dwell.*'

'What in hell's name was that?' asked Roger as the echoes died away. Antony followed his glance towards the stage where the actors had fallen silent, and then Roger had left his seat and was standing looking up at them. 'Are you all right, Meg?' he asked. 'There's nothing to be frightened of.'

'I know that, darling,' she told him, but Antony thought it was something of an effort for her to keep her voice steady. 'And I can answer your other question, Roger. I think that was Sir John Cartwright's ghost again.'

II

So it happened that Meg and Roger and Antony arrived back at Kempenfeldt Square in a body just before luncheon. That was a meal that the Maitlands usually took downstairs on a Saturday, so it was Maitland's intention to kidnap Jenny and take her back to their own quarters. Vera, however, had other ideas and more courage than any of them where Mrs Stokes, Sir Nicholas's housekeeper, was concerned. 'You'll find there's plenty for everybody,' she said firmly, 'and if there isn't we'll just have to manage with some extra rolls and butter.'

To everyone's relief Gibbs showed his displeasure at the change of plans by absenting himself from the luncheon table, which he certainly wouldn't have done if he had realised how anxious they all were to talk. So Antony, between mouthfuls, was able to give an immediate account of the morning, finishing up with a description of the booming voice that had so startled them all. 'It *was* uncanny,' he admitted, 'but perhaps the queerest thing of all was that, of all the people in the theatre, Sir Benjamin and Lady Oldfellow on the stage were the only two of whose whereabouts we could be absolutely sure. And Jeremy and Roger and myself, of course. I'd meant to look for Stella Hartley, but I got interested in watching the play all over again.'

'You said there were some carpenters backstage.'

'Yes, but they weren't around when the earlier episodes took place. Anyway, this time they could all vouch for each other. And then they downed tools and went home in a body; Mr Barrington was in an awful state about that.'

'Matthew Benbow said they'll be back,' Roger put in. 'I daresay he's right.'

'It will be more helpful, I imagine,' said Sir Nicholas, 'to consider the people more nearly concerned. Not from the point of view of their likelihood at the moment, but whether they could have played this particular trick or not.'

'You haven't explained how the booming effect was produced, Antony,' Meg reminded him.

'Someone used a loud hailer. We found the thing at the back of the dress circle, it was pretty dark up there. But at first when we heard the voice we were looking all ways at once, it was absolutely impossible to know where it was coming from. You'd agree with that, wouldn't you, Roger?'

'I certainly would.'

'And Mr Barrington had left the auditorium, Jeremy told you, with the express intention of going up to the dress circle,' said Sir Nicholas pensively.

'To the balcony, actually, but I see what you mean. He spent a little time there but was on his way downstairs when the voice started up. And that's quite likely, I mean that he might not have met whoever did it. There are a dozen different ways into the circle.'

'I suppose so. What about the others?'

'For once Chester Cartwright wasn't in the theatre today,

though Jeremy said he'd announced his intention of coming during the afternoon. Matthew Benbow was on stage with Meg, as I told you, so he couldn't have done it.'

'Could a woman have produced such an effect?'

'Yes, I think so. We did some experiments afterwards. It could have been a woman pitching her voice low, or a man. Amanda Chillingworth and Arthur Webb had just left us, as you know, but they were due to enter from opposite sides of the stage and had separated. Mary Russell admitted in a rather embarrassed way that she'd been to the ladies' room, Stella Hartley says she was in her dressing room, and Edward Brome and Joseph Weatherly tell exactly the same story. As for the two understudies, Mark Kenilworth said he was in the wings watching, the opposite side from the prompter who of course is someone else whose position we can vouch for. Nobody saw him . . . Kenilworth, I mean. And Roberta Rowan was at the other side of the stage, standing behind the prompter. She could give him an alibi if he needed one but he can't say she was there, he was too concentrated on what was happening on the stage. I think it's quite likely she's telling the truth though. She says she wanted to study Meg's performance, and that seems very reasonable to me.'

'And where was the stage manager all this time?'

'Hugh Clinton? He was directing the carpenters' activities, so he's accounted for. I haven't been considering him very seriously as a matter of fact.'

'As you've allowed yourself to be involved at all you should consider every possibility,' Sir Nicholas reproved him. 'What happened after this rather odd announcement?'

'It had been heard even in the dressing rooms. The three who said they'd been there appeared in a body and Stella Hartley had hysterics again,' said Antony and smiled at the recollection.

'No laughing matter,' said Vera. 'No wonder the poor woman was upset, I don't blame her at all.'

'Nor I,' Sir Nicholas agreed. 'But the interesting thing to me is what construction they all put on the words that were used.'

'I can tell you what Miss Hartley said as soon as she could speak again, and Mary Russell agreed with her. They took the words *When I am dead* as indicating that this was certainly a message from the deceased playwright. And as with the *Macbeth* quotation – sorry Meg, the one from the Scottish play – everyone thought there was a vaguely threatening aspect to it, particularly the talk about going out of this world "with vilest worms to dwell". It isn't a pretty thought, whichever way you look at it.'

'It's perfectly horrible,' said Meg, shuddering. She was beginning to recover from the shock, and at the same time to rediscover her tendency to dramatise any given situation.

'Forget about it,' Sir Nicholas told her rather severely. Having adopted Meg and Roger as members of the family long since he considered himself at liberty to treat them as such – sometimes a mixed blessing. 'What did they do after that? Go on with the rehearsal?'

'The odd thing is they did. That was largely due to Hugh Clinton and Brian Barrington, who between them succeeded in persuading everyone that it was the only thing to do. But there was no asking any more questions, they were far too upset to make any sense, and when I decided to leave Barrington said Meg and Roger might as well come along with me. She's about the only one besides Matthew Benbow who's word perfect, and he thought it would do Mary Russell good to have a chance to take on Becky's part. They'd all have time to calm down a little tomorrow, and if they do I'll have another crack at them on Monday.'

Sir Nicholas closed his eyes for a moment as if in extreme pain, but opened them quickly to eye his nephew with disfavour. 'May I remind you, Antony – ?'

'Yes, I know, Uncle Nick, but I looked at those files you left late last night, and there's absolutely nothing that I need go into chambers for immediately.'

'Don't be horrid, Uncle Nick,' Meg put in. 'Of course he must come to the theatre again, we need him. I thought you understood that.'

'I suppose it has been considered that the police could perhaps discover who had purchased this loud hailer,' said Sir Nicholas reflectively. 'After all, it isn't the sort of thing anyone has on hand, although I believe one would be fairly easily obtainable.'

'Yes, of course. I pointed that out to Barrington and Jeremy when we were talking together before we left. They still insist it isn't a matter for the police, and after all what could they do? It isn't a crime, however annoying it may be, to interrupt a rehearsal in that way.'

'Well, as you've obviously made up your mind, I can't stop you,' said Sir Nicholas, and Jenny and Vera exchanged an

89

amused glance, knowing pretty well how his mind was working. 'The magpie is more intriguing,' he went on, 'but I expect you'll find there's quite an easy answer to that too if only you could think of it.'

'I agree, sir, I suffer from a certain lack of facilities in conducting an enquiry of this sort,' Antony conceded. 'I don't know why I let myself get talked into all this, Meg, I don't think I'm doing any good at all.'

'It did me some good today,' she told him firmly, 'having you and Roger there. I was scared stiff when that terrible noise started reverberating all through the theatre. You must admit it wasn't like a human voice at all.'

'If anything else happens Stella Hartley will have you believing in her nonsense,' said Antony almost crossly, but he couldn't help remembering her first reaction to the disturbance. 'And as a matter of fact I think it's very likely that was the last manifestation. Unless someone really wants to wreck the production there's no need for them to go on.'

'Famous last words,' said Meg lightly. But none of them contradicted him, and afterwards they were all to wonder at themselves for being so innocent as to believe for a moment that he might be right.

Hilary Term, 1976

Monday, 12th January

I

Sunday had passed quietly except for an argument in the evening between Roger and Meg as to whether she should go back to the theatre the next morning, or – if she did so – whether it should just be to tell Brian Barrington that she was giving up her part.

'I can't possibly do that, darling,' Meg expostulated. 'In any case there's no need. Antony said himself that it was possible nothing else might happen.'

'Possible, not certain.' Roger pounced on the admission.

'Well I'm not going to anyway,' said Meg stubbornly.

'If you tell me the show must go on,' said Roger bitterly, 'I won't be answerable for the consequences.'

'Well, darling, it must. And they can't rehearse anything at all without me, I felt bad enough coming away on Saturday.'

Roger, most uncharacteristically, was obviously on the verge of an explosion, and Antony hastened to intervene. 'Will it set your mind at rest if I remind you that I'm going to the rehearsal tomorrow?' he asked.

'Of course it would if I thought you could put your finger on the joker. But you said yourself last night that this was a different sort of thing from working for a client.'

'I think working for a friend is more important,' said Antony smiling. 'There are a few more questions that may profitably be asked so there's no need to despair just yet, and I'm in Mallory's bad books already so a few more days playing truant won't do any harm.'

Meg looked at him uncertainly. 'But darling –'

'I've nothing coming up that won't wait,' he told her firmly. 'Nothing at all that will take me to court, for instance, and not even a conference till Friday.'

Jenny, seeing Roger's relieved look, forbore to point out that his absence from chambers would involve a good deal of burning

93

the midnight oil at home, and added her persuasions to his. 'Well, all right,' said Roger at last, reluctantly. 'If Antony has any hope of clearing this up of course I waive my objection. Except that I think it's a bit of an imposition on you,' he added apologetically to his friend.

And there matters rested until Monday morning, when Roger dropped both Antony and Meg at the Cornmarket. Maitland left Meg in the wings and made his way to the front of the theatre where Jeremy Skelton had already taken his usual place in the stalls, while Chester Cartwright was standing a little aloof in one of the side aisles. Too good a chance to miss, Antony thought, and made his way promptly in that direction. 'Would it trouble you if we had a few words together?' he asked. 'If we sit right at the back I'm sure we shouldn't disturb the rehearsal.'

Brian Barrington was on stage, haranguing Bess Brownlees and Richard Twells, though it seemed with great good humour. Maitland guessed that he had picked up where they left off at the previous rehearsal, in the middle of the second act. Chester said, 'Of course we must talk,' and began to walk towards the back of the theatre. 'How do you think our friends the actors seem?' he asked, seating himself.

'Surprisingly well, all things considered.'

'I must admit I was worried when I heard what had happened on Saturday morning, thinking we may never reach the first night even. Though Brian tells me there's no chance of that – the show must go on.'

That phrase again. 'I never realised before how seriously they take it,' said Maitland.

'Neither did I.' Chester Cartwright tittered suddenly. 'My illustrious namesake is going to have to think of something better,' he said.

'You're not telling me, Mr Cartwright, that *you* believe in Sir John's ghost?'

'No, of course I don't. But I did think, as I told you, there was a good chance they'd be so upset that the production wouldn't go forward. And that wouldn't suit me at all.'

'That's why I want to talk to you particularly. Did you know any of these people before?'

'I'd seen Margaret Hamilton a dozen times I suppose on stage, and most of the others, too. That's quite different from knowing them personally.'

'And Mr Skelton?'

'No, I didn't know him either until I went to see him with Uncle Jack's outline.'

'What made you pick on him?' Maitland, to all appearances, was in one of his vague moods this morning, and the question seemed to imply no more than the most desultory interest.

'He seemed the best person for the job. He's very well known as a mystery novelist, as you of all people must be aware, and after the success of his first play . . . well it seemed a good idea.'

'There are a number of even more experienced playwrights who might equally have jumped at the chance.'

'There were several people I considered, of course,' said Chester, 'but I admit I was a bit afraid of a snub. Someone with a row of successes behind him . . . I'm sure you know what I mean.'

'But you had a first-rate idea.'

'Not my own, though,' Chester corrected him. 'However, that's beside the point. There was also the question of the dialogue. I didn't know how a purely modern playwright might like going back to the seventeenth century, whereas Jeremy had done one or two books set in that period and managed the conversation pretty well.'

'So that was the first time you made his acquaintance. How did you come to pick on Brian Barrington to direct?'

'It wasn't so much a question of our picking him as of his picking us,' said Chester. 'It isn't the easiest thing in the world to get backing for a play, even with Jeremy's previous success in that line behind him, but we were well enough satisfied when Brian agreed to take it on and you see what a good job he's doing of it. So far as he's allowed, of course.'

'Yes, that was my impression too, though I've only seen a very little of the rehearsals compared to what you must have observed I suppose you might say,' Maitland added thoughtfully, 'that Mr Barrington has a bigger stake than any of you in the success of the play.'

'His reputation is already made,' Cartwright pointed out.

'Yes, but he'll want to retain the goodwill of his backers, won't he?'

'That's right. You're looking for motive,' said Chester as though the idea had only just occurred to him, though Antony was pretty sure he'd been aware of the fact for several minutes. 'Jeremy has his own reputation secure in his own field; but as far as plays go, after having one success it's terribly important to him that the second attempt will live up to the first. As for me – I'm being frank with you, Mr Maitland – I quite simply need the money. Also, Sir John being so well known, my finding the outline in his own hand has caused something of a stir in academic circles. That may well be of help to me . . . professionally, you might say.'

'Wouldn't the publicity there's been already ensure that latter point, without the play's actually getting as far as opening night?'

Cartwright took his time to think that over. 'To an extent you're right,' he said at last. 'Perhaps you don't realise what a good job Jeremy has done on this. When the play is put on I'll swear there's not a soul will be able to tell it from the real thing.'

'But you're not saying –'

'Oh, no, no,' said Chester rather impatiently. 'We've been perfectly honest about it, but I think there's no doubt at all that the work Jeremy has done on the basis of the outline I gave him will enhance my claims to its genuineness.'

Maitland too thought for a moment before he spoke again. 'You quite obviously see the trend of my questions, Mr Cartwright,' he said after a while. 'Can you think of anybody, anybody at all, who may have a grudge against you?'

'I've been wondering about that, of course, but quite frankly, Mr Maitland, I find it difficult to take it seriously. One doesn't go through life making enemies . . . at least I don't.'

'No, I'm sure of that, but there's no end to the things people get it into their heads to take offence at, for no reason at all,' said Antony.

'There has occasionally been some correspondence in the papers about my books, quite acrimonious at times,' Cartwright told him, as though the thought pleased him. 'But that's no good to you, is it? It would have to be somebody with access to the theatre.'

'In view of the number of things that have been happening . . . yes, I think it would,' Maitland agreed.

'Well, I met the actors for the first time at the party which you and your charming wife attended,' said Chester. 'Now they might dislike Brian Barrington, he always seems to be picking on them, but I suppose that's his job. As for me, I'm a quiet sort of fellow, and I can't imagine any of them could have taken offence at anything I've said or done in the brief time we've known each other.'

'Have you commented to them on the production at all?'

'Only in a congratulatory way. And I don't think they could have come to dislike Jeremy either. For so brilliant a man he's been remarkably self-effacing, confining himself to making any alterations Brian might ask for.'

'Without argument?' asked Antony, smiling at the thought, because what he knew of Jeremy Skelton made him wonder if that could possibly be true.

'I know it sounds unlikely, but that's the way it's been. Stella complained once or twice that she couldn't speak the lines he'd written for her, and he made changes there too quite meekly. I think,' said Chester, smiling in his turn, 'that he's an added proof that he's keen on making the thing a success.'

'You've had some chance during the past week to observe the members of the cast and the three understudies,' said Maitland. 'Can you tell me anything about the relationships between them? Is there any evidence of envy, hatred and all uncharitableness, for instance? As an outsider I should think you're in a good position to know.'

'Stella Hartley has a tongue and knows how to use it, but I don't think any of the others take very much notice. Most of them are probably used to her.'

'You agree then that whoever is trying to wreck this production is doing so because he has a grudge against one of the three men who stands to gain most from it?'

'Yes, I do. And of the three I can only see it's being Brian Barrington. He knew most of the actors before, if not all of them. It could be a grudge that has been slowly corroding for years, or some of his more recent remarks may have cut too near the bone.'

'You didn't hear the voice yesterday morning?'

'I didn't, but I gather it was pretty impressive. I also,' said Chester regretfully, 'read a full account of it in this morning's paper, complete with the quotation used from Sonnet seventy-one, accurate in every detail.'

'Yes, I saw that too. Somebody had spread the tale, but I can't believe any longer – not since that block of timber fell – that it's merely a matter of getting publicity. What did you make of the quotation?'

'It had a fine sinister air,' said Cartwright critically. 'More than enough to make an impression in the present climate in this theatre. I think I could have found something more appropriate though.'

'The question is, appropriate to what?' said Maitland in a thoughtful tone. 'Last night I wondered if we were all getting rattled for nothing, and probably nothing else would happen.'

'If I'm right about what's happening, our friend X – is that what Jeremy would call him? – won't be content until the cast is completely demoralised and the whole project abandoned,' said Chester. 'Which God forbid,' he added piously.

After a few minutes Antony left him, apparently quite content with the seat he had taken in the back row. Brian Barrington was standing in the middle of the centre aisle, not far from where Jeremy Skelton was sitting, and as Antony approached he flung up his hands in an exaggeratedly despairing gesture and said to the world at large, 'All right, children, we'll take a break. And for heaven's sake, Edward, use the opportunity to learn your lines a little better.' He turned to Maitland. 'Ah, there you are, you haven't deserted us yet. Have you had any more bright ideas on the subject of our joker?'

'Not exactly, but there's something I'd like to discuss with you.' Antony looked around vaguely and Barrington seized his arm.

'Come with me,' he said. 'We'll find an empty office.' Maitland allowed himself to be conducted once again to the door that led backstage.

There was still some activity going on. 'Is it the same gang of men, or did you have to hire new ones?' Antony asked.

Barrington turned his head briefly to smile at him. 'They came back,' he said. 'It's a tradition, you know.'

'I know,' said Antony hastily, before the trite phrase could be repeated. 'How are you finding your cast this morning?'

'Pretty dreadful,' Brian admitted. He opened a door and stood aside for Antony to precede him into a small, rather bare room. 'I won't say make yourself comfortable,' he remarked, 'because that's obviously impossible. But we can have our talk in here in complete privacy.'

'That's good. Do you think you'll be ready by . . . the thirteenth of next month, isn't it?'

'If I have anything to do with it,' said Barrington firmly, 'we'll be ready by then if we have to rehearse day and night in the meantime. But I admit it will make matters more difficult if our ghost continues to haunt us.'

'I've been wondering,' said Maitland, seating himself, 'how you feel about that now? You told me yourself you're superstitious –'

'That isn't the same thing as believing in ghosts,' Barrington told him. 'I think the idea that Sir John Cartwright is haunting us because he doesn't like what Jeremy has written is absolutely ludicrous.'

'Then the things that have happened don't worry you at all?'

'I didn't say that.'

'How then?'

'Not from my point of view,' Barrington explained. 'I did tell you, Mr Maitland, that my superstitions go by reverse, so the black cat dying in Stella's arms was, if anything, a good omen. I felt the same thing about the magpie, though I must admit that the quotation from the Scottish play made me a little uneasy. The other things were just annoying.'

'Would you say the timber falling from the flies was just annoying?'

'The way it turned out, yes. Nobody was hurt.'

'But somebody could have been,' Antony insisted.

'Well, if you want to know what I really think, that one happening most likely was an accident,' said Barrington. 'I told you that was the reason I wouldn't take your advice and go to the police. They wouldn't be interested in our joker obviously and we'd never have persuaded them that the one thing that might have been dangerous was done deliberately.'

'No, I suppose you're right about that. All the same it puts the whole affair on a different plane, a more serious plane. If it was done deliberately, as I'm sure you're about to point out, but if it really was accidental it was the devil of a coincidence. So I'm sticking to the idea that it was deliberate. Somebody might have been badly hurt, and whoever rigged the thing up just didn't care.'

'No, I remember what you said. You don't believe any longer that all these things are publicity stunts. Well, I can't say I blame you about that.'

'I've been talking to Mr Cartwright,' said Antony.

'He doesn't know much about the actors,' Barrington pointed out.

'No, nor about any of you really. He agreed with me though

that there are three people in and around the theatre every day who have the most to lose if the production is cancelled ... himself, you, Mr Barrington, and Jeremy Skelton. Neither he nor Jeremy knew any of the people concerned before – except, of course, that Jeremy knew Meg pretty well after her appearance in his first play – so I'm wondering whether you can think of anybody who might be harbouring revengeful thoughts about you.'

'Was that Chester's suggestion too? No, don't bother to answer, Mr Maitland, I imagine it was. Of the people who are actually in the play I've known every one before, some better than others. Mary Russell, too. As for the two understudies, I've seen them in small parts, but had no personal contact until I engaged them.' He smiled suddenly. 'Does Chester think I'm very unkind to them?' he asked.

'I don't suppose he understands much about directing and producing a play,' said Antony. 'Any more than I do,' he added honestly, 'except what I've picked up from time to time in conversation with Meg.'

'Well, I assure you – and I'm sure Meg would too – there's been nothing more going on than the general give and take between actors and director. Except perhaps thât what's been happening has put us all a little on edge. That would provide more reason for me to interfere than might normally be the case with such an experienced cast, and I might speak more sharply. I haven't been conscious of it, but I might. But to say any of them would resent it to the point of trying to wreck the whole thing ... well, that's just ridiculous.'

'Well, can you think of any reason why any of them should dislike Jeremy or Mr Cartwright?'

'No reason in the world. If anything they should be grateful to them both for providing a job.'

'That's what I thought. The only thing that remains then, Mr Barrington ... is there anything in their relationships with each other that would account for what's been happening?'

Barrington hesitated. 'You've had experience yourself of Stella's habit of making things uncomfortable for other people,' he said slowly at last.

'And you rescued me,' said Maitland, smiling at the recollection.

'Yes, but not, unless I'm very much mistaken, before she

100

succeeded in annoying you considerably. Did you feel so angry that you'd try to spoil things for her if you could?'

'No, of course not,' said Antony, rather startled.

'It's all right. I'm not suggesting anything. I'm only saying that her shafts quite often go home, but they wouldn't be enough to make anyone feel he had to get back at her. In any case, you know, there'd be no harm to her reputation if the play was cancelled. That's established already, even though she's playing second fiddle to Meg in this instance. Well, I have to admit she isn't in Meg's class, but she's very much in demand. She wouldn't be resting for long.'

'No, I see that. But it's a funny thing . . . it's always Miss Hartley's name that comes up when I ask a question like that.'

'Because we're a very peaceful bunch on the whole,' Barrington assured him. 'Stella's the exception, but don't take any notice of that. Put it down to artistic temperament or something of the sort.'

'So you can't really give me any help at all.'

'No, I'm sorry. I do realise, Mr Maitland, that between us we've wished an impossible task on you, but I do assure you your efforts are appreciated.'

'I only wish I thought I could do any good,' Antony told him. 'You see, it's quite different from a case where one of my clients is concerned. For instance, I've no right to be here except by your goodwill, and there's nothing really to get hold of. Usually when I come on the scene the police have already made a charge or been prepared to do so. I do see your point, Mr Barrington –'

'For heaven's sake stick to Brian if you can't manage B.B.'

'– about not calling them in,' Antony persisted. 'But they've all the facilities for making an investigation. If a crime had been committed and somebody accused, that's where I might be useful in mounting a defence. There'd be something for me to get my teeth into then.'

'Yes, I understand. I don't think you're quite fair to yourself though, Mr Maitland.'

'If we're to get on Christian name terms, you'd better stick to Antony. And whether I'm fair to myself or not, that's how it seems to me. I ought to be back in chambers tomorrow, but I'll do what I can for the rest of the day. After that, unless something comes up that gives me an idea, I think we may as well call it a day.'

'Then perhaps we can have dinner again, if it isn't too short notice for Mrs Maitland, and ask Jeremy and Anne too, of course. We can at least talk things over.'

'I should like that, of course, and I'm sure Jenny would. But please don't expect too much, Brian. I'm really quite out of my depth.'

'We'll talk about that tonight,' said Barrington. 'Meanwhile, I'd better get back to my rehearsal. It isn't going to be as bad as you think, you know,' he added, as they went back into the behind-the-scenes confusion. 'All things considered, it's really shaping very well.'

'That's what I thought earlier but you didn't seem to agree with me,' Antony told him. 'Perhaps if nothing else happens –'

Barrington stopped dead and turned to look at him.

'Do you really believe the – the manifestations might stop now?' he enquired.

'On Saturday I did, but that might have been wishful thinking,' Antony admitted. 'The trouble is, you see, I'd like to believe it.'

'Well, don't relax your vigilance,' Barrington advised him. 'Where do you want to go now?'

'I think I'll have a word with Jeremy. I gather from what Mr Cartwright said you don't need him too much now.'

'No, I think all the bugs he can take care of are ironed out,' Barrington assured him, mixing his metaphors freely. 'Go straight along here and don't fall over anything as you go and you'll find the door we came through.'

II

Maitland obeyed. There was nobody about but Jeremy when he got back to the auditorium, and when he suggested they should talk at the back of the stalls this was agreed to readily enough. Cartwright had disappeared by the time they reached their objective, which Antony couldn't help thinking was a good thing. He was beginning to feel self-conscious about this fruitless questioning and considered that the more privacy they could achieve the better.

'Well now, Antony, what's all this about?' asked Skelton as

they seated themselves. 'First Chester, then Brian, and now me. Are we your main suspects?'

'I think you know perfectly well that isn't true,' Maitland retorted, though he had a strong suspicion that in spite of his experience in the past the role was one that Jeremy would probably enjoy playing. 'In a way I wish it were. At least, I wish I had a suspect. But as you know, that falling timber, with the chance that it might maim or even kill somebody, changed all my ideas about that. If somebody's playing these tricks out of malice, as now seems must be the case, it also seems most likely that one of the three of you is the intended victim, not necessarily of violence to you personally, but –'

'That's obvious, of course.' He might have known that Jeremy would have seen all the possibilities already. 'So you want to know, I suppose, which of us has an enemy sufficiently bitter to try to wreck this project.'

'That's exactly what I want to know, though it seems to be a forlorn hope,' Antony said regretfully.

'I'm not saying,' Jeremy was thoughtful now, 'that I've never offended anyone in my life. In fact I'm damned sure I have. For instance,' he went on, and there was no doubt about the complacency in his tone, 'there's my secretary. I'm quite sure I often infuriate her, but apart from not having access to the theatre she isn't even in London but safely at home answering fan letters and things like that. And, of course, there's Anne; I've often wondered how she bears with me. But you're not suggesting that she's been playing these tricks, I suppose.'

'Far from it.'

'As a matter of fact,' said Jeremy inconsequently, 'I've told her not to come to any more rehearsals.'

'I thought that must be why I hadn't seen her around. Roger's worried, too, but of course it's different for Meg, she has a job to do.'

'You don't think –?' asked Jeremy in sudden alarm.

'No, I don't,' Maitland told him, not waiting for him to finish the question. 'There's about as much chance of Meg giving up a part she's enthusiastic about as there is – as there is of Sir John Cartwright coming and joining our discussion.'

'I've been wondering about that,' said Skelton, who had all the novelist's curiosity about what motivated his fellow men. 'What do you really think about the ghost theory? I shouldn't have been surprised, you being an imaginative sort of chap –'

'Who, me?' asked Antony, who had genuinely no idea that the description could fairly be applied to him. Then, seeing that his companion was really interested in his reply, he went on, thinking it out as he spoke, 'I've never seen one, but I wouldn't altogether rule out the possibility that they exist, though hardly in the numbers some people would have us believe. But I can't envision one quite so well organised as Sir John, or who would go into action for such a motive.'

'That's funny,' said Jeremy, 'that's the bit I could understand, only I don't happen to believe in ghosts.'

'Then you won't mind going back to my questions. I can see that I don't need to point out to you that the possibilities are strictly limited. I'm speaking of opportunity now, not of motive.'

'Limited to the people who have access to the theatre and some knowledge of its geography,' Jeremy agreed. 'Then let's take things in order. I first met Chester when he came to see me with that outline of Sir John's. As I agreed to do what he wanted, I don't suppose he can hold any grievance against me, particularly as he stands to gain financially from the production as well as in prestige. Or so I gather.'

'No, I don't see either how he could dislike you.'

'Oh, he might easily do that,' said Jeremy, and again he sounded rather pleased than otherwise by the thought. 'I've never set out in my life to win a popularity contest, but that isn't exactly what you're after, is it? As for Brian, I didn't meet him until after he'd read the play and signified that he'd like to meet me. He'd no need to be associated with it unless he wanted to, so I think that rules him out too. Besides, we've always got on pretty well together over all the preliminaries and now the rehearsals. Of course, he used to be an actor so he may just be pretending to feel friendly towards me, but I don't really think so.'

'I like Mr Barrington,' said Antony slowly, 'which if Uncle Nick were here he'd tell me is quite beside the point. Do you think any of the actors could hold a really bitter grudge against him?'

'No, I don't,' said Jeremy bluntly. 'If you're thinking he's come down a bit hard on them in the course of rehearsals I can only tell you I'd have said twice as much. In any case it's nothing out of the way, I've enough experience to realise that. Of course, any of the understudies – and i suppose one might say here Mary Russell in particular – might resent not being cast for an actual part in the play, but I really don't think that would be a serious enough reason for all this, do you?'

'I don't think so either. The trouble is someone has shown a high degree of perseverance, and also a singular disregard for the sanctity of human life; that is, supposing the block of wood was fixed deliberately so it would fall on the stage at some time or another, and anything else would be too much of a coincidence.'

'That's rather how I feel about it.'

'I've just been trying to explain to Brian Barrington that I don't see my way at all,' Antony told him.

'You take things too hard,' said Jeremy roundly. 'Brian is absolutely determined to carry on, ghost or no ghost.'

'He also says he doesn't believe in them.'

'That may be true, or he may believe it's true. But I'll tell you this, Antony, there's not a single person intimately connected with the play who is altogether unaffected by these rumours that have been going around. That sepulchral voice we heard on Saturday just about put the finishing touch to things.'

'Didn't finding the loud hailer reassure them at all? After all, Sir John Cartwright wouldn't have needed one.'

'They're past thinking of anything so reasonable,' said Jeremy. 'You heard it, Antony, didn't it give you the shivers?'

'Yes, I suppose it did for a moment. Well, for more than a moment really because when I thought about the quotation I didn't like it at all. But after what you've just said don't tell me you class yourself among the ghost hunters.'

'I don't,' said Skelton. 'But even if I believed in such things I'll tell you what would convince me that nothing from the spirit world is involved in this case. I made a damned good play out of Sir John Cartwright's outline. If he knew anything about the matter at all he'd be grateful to me.'

Antony had to smile at that, but he didn't pursue the subject. 'You must have observed this and that about the actors during rehearsal,' he added. 'What can you tell me about them?'

'Quite a lot.' Jeremy settled back into his stall, only too ready for a good gossip. 'Have you anybody in particular in mind?'

'All of them,' said Maitland firmly.

'Then I'll start with Matthew Benbow, who's one of the nicest chaps imaginable and a good actor as well. I'm only sorry he has to be eliminated at the end of the first act. Have you seen that bit by the way? I think it's really effective.'

105

'No, I only know what I've been told about it,' Antony replied, 'but it sounds good and Meg's enthusiastic. There isn't anyone's word I'd rather take about anything concerned with drama. You don't think then that Mr Benbow is the sort of person to have enemies, or to bear grudges against anybody else?'

'No, I don't, and perhaps he's the only one I could say that about for sure. Except Meg, of course, and I don't need to tell you anything about her. Stella Hartley, however, is a bitch of the first water.'

'There was some talk of her upstaging people,' said Antony, purposefully vague. 'I don't quite know what that means.'

'As far as I'm concerned it means she'll do as much scene stealing as she can,' said Skelton. 'She doesn't have much chance with Meg or Benbow – they're both far too old hands to let her play games with them – but with the other members of the cast she's pretty successful.'

'And the understudies? If Miss Hartley gave up her part Roberta Rowan would get her chance.'

'She'll get her chance all in good time anyway. Brian tells me she's a good actress, and she's quite young enough to wait.'

'What about Mary Russell? Is she on good terms with Miss Hartley?'

'On the face of it, yes. Unless Mary's called on to stand in for Meg nothing will arise out of the play anyway. You know perhaps that Mary moved in with Stella after Stella's most recent divorce.'

'On the face of it . . . does that mean anything?'

'Yes, it does. I was about to add that she's wildly jealous of Mark Kenilworth, who – as you may have gathered – is making up to Stella.'

'Yes, I had heard something of the sort,' said Maitland cautiously. 'There seems to be some argument about it . . . whether he's really taken with her, or whether it's his ambition that leads him to pretend to be.'

'I can put you right about that,' said Jeremy confidently. 'I don't think he cares a scrap for her, but he does think she might be of some help to him in the future. She, on the other hand, is genuinely intrigued, unless I'm very much mistaken. She isn't the sort of woman to live without a man, and it's a year or more since her latest divorce.'

'And Miss Russell resents whatever there is between them?'

asked Antony, declining to be diverted by this attractive byway.

'That's what I said. Arthur Webb and Amanda Chillingworth, however, – you did know they're married – seem to be a thoroughly devoted couple and so far he's managed to persuade her to keep a rein on her tongue.'

'How do you mean?'

'Not to answer back when she resents Stella's antics. Then there's our other pair of lovebirds, you must have noticed them. Joseph Weatherly and Roberta Rowan.'

'Yes, it did occur to me that there was something between them.'

'I think it's just what used to be called an understanding,' said Jeremy. Maitland was left to wonder whether this meant they were living together or not. 'Weatherly's a good actor, and Brian says that Roberta has the makings, so it may not work out too badly.'

'I suppose not,' said Maitland, and fell silent. He was thinking of Meg and Roger and wondering, as he sometimes did, whether it would be easier or harder for them if they both followed the same profession. Being married to an actress had its disadvantages, but on the whole Roger had taken it very well, and even succeeded to an extent in hiding his disappointment every time a new part came up that Meg simply couldn't refuse.

All this time the rehearsal had been continuing on its course and must, Antony considered, from what he'd been told of the plot, have proceeded to the second act. Whether he was right about this or not, at the moment Gilbert Bold and Lucy Simpering held the stage together. Gilbert was registering a rather exaggerated bewilderment, and Lucy an equally exaggerated nervousness. Barrington was back in what seemed to be his favourite position standing in the centre aisle of the auditorium and looking up at them.

'Children, children!' he said a little wearily. 'A little more emotion about it, if you please. Remember, Stella, you're beginning to have a very good suspicion that the man you're talking to is a murderer.'

Stella moved towards the front of the stage with something that Antony could only think of as a flounce, though he couldn't recollect ever having seen anyone perform such a manoeuvre before. 'There's no pleasing you, B.B.,' she said. 'If you'd given me somebody to act with who isn't a block of wood –'

'If you want to know what I think, Stella, it was you who was holding the scene up, not Joseph.'

'Yes, and we all know what your opinion is worth,' said Stella, looking down at him angrily. 'There's an old saying, isn't there: those that can, do; those that can't, teach. Well you're certainly good at criticising other people,' she added spitefully.

Jeremy had come to his feet. 'I think we'd better intervene,' he said quietly to Antony and began to walk quickly down the centre aisle. But before he could reach Barrington's side the director had turned away.

'We'll break for lunch,' he said. And then, less abruptly, 'I told you all to bring sandwiches today; you'll find Roberta has made coffee in the greenroom.' Jeremy and Antony came up with him then and Maitland noted with surprise that he was as white as a sheet. 'We can eat in my office,' said Barrington, with only a fair assumption of casualness. 'We'll collect Meg on our way, I think, to bring a breath of normality to the proceedings, and has either of you seen Chester around?'

III

They didn't succeed in finding Chester Cartwright but his goings and comings were unpredictable, Barrington said. Looking into the greenroom to detach Meg from the others, Maitland noticed that for a group that had previously been reported congenial, the actors were now strangely ill at ease with each other and for the most part munched their sandwiches in silence. On the whole, Barrington's office, though less comfortable, seemed a better bet.

Brian, who disliked coffee, produced instead Perrier water and said once, looking rather gloomily at his glass, 'I only wish it were something stronger.' Jeremy seemed contented enough with his own thoughts, but Antony was glad when they had finished eating and could separate again, a feeling he felt pretty sure Meg shared with him.

'What do you want to do next, Antony?' asked Barrington as they all got up.

'Avoid interrupting your rehearsal any more than I can help,' Antony replied. 'Are you starting again where you left off?'

Something in Brian Barrington's expression told him that the remark had been a tactless one; however, he replied evenly enough, 'I think we'll skip to Meg's entrance, you certainly won't be wanting her. As for the others, there's rather a lot of going and coming in the second act but Matthew, you remember, is dead already so he at least will be completely free if you'd like to see him first.'

'That would suit me very well, but may I use your phone to ring Jenny?'

'Yes, of course. You'll find Matthew's dressing room three doors down the corridor on the right. If you get there before he does, I'm sure he wouldn't mind your waiting for him. Afterwards I suggest you knock on the next door but one, with any luck you'll find Edward Brome there. He appears briefly at the beginning of the act, and not again until he has an abortive love scene with Becky. After that come and find me and we'll arrange something.'

'Thank you.' When he had completed his call and reached the room indicated Antony again found less glamour than he had expected. There were some framed photographs, however, some of them rather faded. He was fairly sure he recognised most of them, though they were of young men and women who when he saw them had already been approaching middle age. He was still puzzling over them, wondering whether he was right in his identification or not, when Matthew Benbow joined him.

'I hope you don't mind my bothering you like this,' said Antony, feeling suddenly and for no reason at all completely out of his element.

'Not at all, I find it very interesting,' said Benbow briefly. 'I'm not likely to be needed again this afternoon, you know, so otherwise I'd have nothing to do but go home and study my lines. Between you and me I know them already, as well as those of most of the rest of the cast.'

'I've often wondered how you all manage that, going from one part to another and never getting muddled,' said Antony. 'Meg says it's quite easy, but I shouldn't have thought it would be for everybody.'

'It's just a knack when you know how to do it,' said Benbow, 'but you're quite right, everyone doesn't have it to the same degree, otherwise why should we need a prompter? I was going to say though that I think it's very good of you to interest yourself in our affairs.'

109

'As far as that goes,' said Maitland, and smiled at him, 'I think I was more or less shanghai'd into the operation.'

'Did Meg persuade you? Now there's a girl who's an ornament to our profession, but I don't need to tell you that. You've known her for a long time, haven't you?'

'Ever since she first came to London. Did you see her Lady Macbeth? It was enough to make your blood run cold.'

'Yes, I saw a matinee. It happened that the play I was in at the time played on Thursday afternoons instead of Wednesdays. Was it she who persuaded you?' he asked again.

'She certainly influenced my decision, but I really meant Brian Barrington.'

'And you think we ought to have called the police?' said Benbow shrewdly.

'No, I can see his point about that. At least I did when he explained it to me. They wouldn't be interested in practical jokes, and the one thing that was really dangerous and might possibly have been construed as a breach of the peace or something like that could well have been an accident. My trouble is,' he added confidentially, 'I feel so helpless.'

'For once in your life,' Matthew Benbow suggested.

'There's nothing really I can do,' said Maitland, and whether this was an answer to the implied question it would be difficult to say. 'Short of flooding the theatre with guards I don't see how we can prevent another outbreak.'

'Do you think there will be one, then?'

'Funnily enough I had an hour or two of optimism the other night, thinking everything might be over. I don't really know why, unless it was because that booming voice was so very dramatic . . . a fitting climax, I suppose. But I don't feel that way now – I feel definitely uneasy. Only of course, as I explained to Barrington, I've no right at all to expect anyone to answer my questions.'

'Well I for one have no objection, but this isn't my kind of thing at all,' said Benbow, seating himself and waving Antony to the only other chair in the room. 'Have you come to any conclusions?'

So Maitland spelled out his thoughts on the subject yet again. At the best of times he hated explanations, but he did his best to keep both boredom and irritation out of his voice. 'You know what I think,' said Matthew, when he had finished. 'I think you're placing altogether too much emphasis on that block of wood falling. After all, you said yourself it might have been an accident.'

'It might have been, but I don't like coincidences. Too much has been going on around here for a thing like that to happen purely at random.'

'And you've come to the conclusion that the target of all these things must be one of the three men who stand to lose most by the production's being scrapped,' said Benbow. 'If you're right about that, and from what you've told me your conclusions are based on, I daresay you are – granting also your premise that the events aren't supernatural in origin – it would seem B.B. must be the one, because Jeremy and Chester are strangers to the rest of us, or were until recently.'

'Mr Cartwright pointed that out to me, and I do see the force of the argument,' Maitland agreed. 'Brian himself says he knows of nobody who feels that kind of hatred for him, but sometimes the outsider sees most of the game. Can you help me, I wonder?'

'I'm afraid not. He was acting himself until a few years ago, you know, and he had the kind of success,' said Benbow, obviously without envy, 'that I could never aspire to. Now the theatrical world is a small one, at least among those of us who are more or less successful, and you know yourself that in any group of people like that some dislikes, some jealousies, must arise. But I don't know of anything in this particular group that could account for what's been going on.'

'Stella Hartley spoke rather unkindly to him today,' said Antony. As he spoke he made a mental note to see what Meg would have to say about that.

'So she did, but she speaks unkindly to everybody. She wasn't too nice to Joseph for that matter.'

'I don't know that but hearing her made me wonder . . . why did Barrington change course in mid-career as it were and go into directing instead of acting?'

'That's always been a puzzle to me. I've known him quite well for years and I'd have said he loved the stage – as a performer, I mean – as much as I do. There have been a number of unkind stories circulating. Somebody suggested that he couldn't bear growing too old to play juvenile leads any more. But that's all nonsense, he'd been playing much more mature parts for years, and to tell you the truth I think that's something most of us look

111

forward to . . . having the opportunity to diversify a little. In this play, now, I know the dialogue's witty, really very clever indeed, but if there's one part that's less interesting than the others, it's Gilbert Bold's, for all that I suppose he might be designated as the hero. No, Mr Maitland, I'm very content with Sir Benjamin, and I'm surprised B.B. didn't feel the same way about not being as young as he used to be.'

'You spoke of practical jokes,' said Antony, 'though you did qualify your agreement with my conclusions. Does that mean that you, at least, don't believe in Sir John Cartwright's ghost?'

He'd expected a resounding Yes to that question and was surprised when Benbow took his time about answering. 'He was a man of the theatre himself,' he said, then slowly, 'and would have known perfectly well how each one of these events would affect us. I don't think I've ever thought seriously about ghosts and spirit manifestations before, but what with one thing and another I don't think I could say categorically now that I disbelieve in them.'

'He wouldn't have needed a loud hailer,' said Maitland bluntly.

'No, of course he wouldn't but we've got a theory about that. At least it was Stella's idea originally, but most of the others seem to have adopted it and I must say I'm not quite sure.'

'What theory is that?'

'That B.B. planted the thing there himself to try to reassure us.'

'I see,' said Maitland, rather taken aback by the idea. 'It isn't the sort of thing you'd have about you. Where would he have got it from?'

'If he didn't own one himself – and I daresay you're right and that's unlikely – there are places where these things can be bought. If you remember, everything was confused for quite a while after the voice was heard, and the loud hailer wasn't produced immediately by any means.'

'No, that's true. I don't believe it though,' he added firmly.

'And you're wondering why I gave it even a moment's thought,' said Matthew Benbow acutely. 'Well, Mr Maitland, you have a legal mind and that means that you're at the same time probably brighter and more stupid than the rest of us. Am I being very rude?' he added anxiously, seeing Antony's bewildered look.

'You are rather, but I don't mind,' Antony told him.

'Stupid was the wrong word, anyway,' said Benbow. 'What I really meant was less imaginative. And considering the career you chose it's probably just as well.'

'It isn't my reputation,' said Maitland sadly, thinking as he spoke of his earlier conversation with Jeremy, and of his uncle's only-too-frequent comments about the dangers of indulging in guesswork. 'I only wish it were.'

'Does it trouble you?'

'I only said that because I wish to goodness that Brian Barrington hadn't asked me to help.'

'You should be flattered,' said Benbow briskly. 'No, you said you felt helpless, didn't you? I'd help you if I could, Mr Maitland, but honestly I don't know anything to the point.'

'Even if Sir John Cartwright isn't responsible himself,' said Antony, and smiled as he spoke. But for some reason he was reluctant to leave his companion. Matthew Benbow was willing enough to be steered into a series of anecdotes about his long career, and it was more than half an hour later when Maitland glanced at his watch. 'Brian Barrington said I could very likely catch Edward Brome before he was needed,' he remarked. 'Do you think I may have left it too long and missed him?'

'It all depends how quickly they got on with the scene, but in any case, there's no harm in our going to see if he's in his dressing room,' suggested Matthew, and got up purposefully.

As soon as they got into the corridor they smelled it very strongly. 'Gas!' said Benbow, sniffing. 'Where do you think it's coming from?'

'I don't know. We'd better try each room in turn,' said Maitland, wasting no time in following his own advice. 'Be careful,' he added, seeing Benbow crossing the corridor to follow his example, 'It's pretty strong.'

He was coughing by the time he pushed open the door to Edward Brome's dressing room. He had his handkerchief over his mouth by now and his voice sounded thick as he turned his head to call 'Here!' He wondered for a moment whether he could face the fumes, but it was obvious that something must be done. A gas fire, similar to the one he had seen while he was talking to Benbow, was expelling its deadly fumes at the far side of the room; at least he couldn't see very well, but that was the only possible place . . .

113

Crossing towards it he tripped over someone but did not stop to make a further examination until he had got the gas tap firmly in the off position. Then, still coughing and half blinded by the fact that his eyes were watering freely, he started to return, and encountered Matthew Benbow, masked now like himself, trying to drag the apparently lifeless body of Edward Brome towards the door. He lent what aid he could with his left hand, and together they succeeded in reaching the corridor. 'We ought to get him somewhere where the air is clearer,' he said urgently.

'Did you open the window?' the older man demanded.

'I didn't even notice there was one,' Antony admitted.

'It opens on to a sort of air shaft. I'll wet my handkerchief and see to it,' said Benbow to Maitland's relief. The actor had obviously noticed that his right arm was of very little use to him, but at least he hadn't had to spell it out that unless it was a casement window or ran exceptionally freely he wouldn't have been able to manage this simple task.

'That should help matters a little, and now we can close the door,' said Benbow, when he came back from fulfilling his mission. Antony, his left hand clasped firmly round Brome's right ankle, had succeeded in dragging the unconscious man a little way. But the opening of the door of the dressing room had obviously spread the smell of gas at least into the backstage area and quite a crowd was gathering. Some of the actors were there, and as might have been expected contrary directions as to what should be done began to be heard from every side. To Antony's relief Hugh Clinton pushed his way through the throng – he still looked as cheerful as ever, perhaps he had no other expression – and took command of the situation.

'You'd better call a doctor,' he said over his shoulder, and fell on his knees beside Edward Brome.

Arthur Webb went off to comply with this direction and came back presently with Brian Barrington and Jeremy Skelton. 'Is he dead?' Barrington demanded. Even allowing for the circumstances he looked oddly white and shaken.

Clinton ignored the question, being already occupied with mouth-to-mouth resuscitation. But Antony had already stooped to pick up Brome's flaccid hand. 'There's a faint pulse,' he announced.

'Thank heaven for that, at least. Who found him?' Barrington demanded.

114

'Mr Benbow and I. We'd been chatting, and I wasn't sure if I'd left it too long and he'd be back on stage. Well, it's just as well we didn't leave it any longer,' he added, dropping Brome's hand and straightening his back again. He looked down for a moment at the unconscious man and the stage manager who was still working over him and obviously approved of what he saw. 'That should take care of things until the ambulance gets here,' he said. 'But now, Brian, I think you'll have to face the fact that you've got no alternative but to call the police.'

'Surely –'

'Another accident?' said Maitland. 'I've told you already I don't like coincidences, although I know they happen, but this one would be altogether too much of a good thing. And if you're going to tell me Brome is suicidal –'

'No, I don't think that.'

'Then somebody turned on the gas tap. Turned it on full,' said Antony, though Barrington's face should have told him that the emphasis was not needed. 'Apparently no attempt had been made to light the fire.'

'Where did you find Edward?'

'Halfway across the room. As if he had gone in, smelled the gas, and meant to turn it off. Could he have been overcome so quickly?'

'That, I imagine, would depend on the concentration of noxious fumes,' said Jeremy promptly, so that Antony thought immediately, he once wrote a book about something like this. 'As it seems to have happened –'

'Edward had no sense of smell,' said Barrington suddenly. 'I think most of us knew that.'

'In that case, there's no telling how long he'd been in the room. If it was coal gas,' said Jeremy, unconsciously confirming Maitland's thought, 'I could tell you about it because I once researched it for a book. I know this new stuff is mainly methane, but apart from that . . . well, what about it, Brian?' He turned to Barrington, and it was evident that he hadn't lost sight of the point. 'Antony's quite right; even if Edward was taking what some people call the easy way out – though I don't believe that for a moment – the police would still have to be called.'

'Yes, yes, I see. I'll do it myself,' said Barrington, and turned away just as the crowd of spectators parted to let the ambulance men through.

115

IV

In view of all that had happened, the council of war that evening with Brian Barrington and Jeremy Skelton had been called off. Maitland took the first opportunity to telephone Jenny again, and because there was a good deal going on at the theatre asked her to ring Roger for him. When the time came he took Meg home to Kempenfeldt Square so that the four of them could have a chance to talk things over. Sooner or later Sir Nicholas and Vera would want to know what had happened, but they were out that evening, and as it turned out that was just as well.

The recounting of what had happened fell, of course, to Antony. Jenny listened in her usual silence, but when he reached the point where Edward Brome's unconscious form was dragged from his dressing room Roger was moved to violent protest. 'I suppose you're going to tell me,' he said turning to Meg, 'that you still think it's safe to go on with this accursed play.'

'Darling, of course it is!' That was Meg in her role of wide-eyed innocence. 'If you'd give Antony a chance to go on with his story he'll tell you that Edward wasn't dead.'

'That doesn't make the slightest difference to my position,' Roger retorted. 'He might have been . . . mightn't he?' He swung round so that Maitland got the full force of his question.

'If Benbow and I hadn't found him when we did I think it's very likely he would have died,' Antony admitted reluctantly, because he could see that squalls were coming. He had already expostulated with Meg as they came home from the theatre, without any perceptible result, and he was afraid Roger would have no better fortune. 'As it was,' he added, 'in the interests of delaying the evil day, the ambulance men had brought oxygen with them and Brome soon showed signs of coming round.'

'That doesn't alter my position in the slightest,' Roger insisted. 'Someone wants to stop the production, and how better could they do it than by harming the leading lady?'

'They haven't tried so far, darling,' Meg pointed out.

'That first message was written on your mirror, wasn't it?'

'Yes, but that was probably just pure chance, because my room happened to be unoccupied. And if you're going to say someone might turn on the gas in my dressing room, I'd smell it in an instant.'

'I daresay you would, but that's not the only thing that might happen. Don't you see, Meg, I won't have a moment's peace while you're in the theatre and I know there's some murderous lunatic at large there.'

'I knew you'd say that,' said Meg. 'Are you asking me to throw up the part?'

'Yes, I am!' He paused a moment, only too obviously with the intention of continuing in some less vehement tone. 'You know I wouldn't do it for any other reason, Meg,' he went on almost pleadingly, 'but when it comes to your safety –'

'I don't agree with you about that. If somebody's doing all these things –'

'Don't tell me we're back to Sir John Cartwright's ghost again,' said Roger bitterly.

'– no one has any cause to harm me.'

'Except to stop the production.'

'There are a thousand different ways that could be done, but I don't think they'll succeed because B.B. is very determined.'

'And if it is Sir John Cartwright,' Antony put in, 'Meg's the last person he'd want to hurt, because of all of them she gets into the spirit of the thing by far the best.'

'I'm perfectly serious,' Roger snapped. 'Meg, you must be sensible for once.'

'I don't know what you mean by "for once", darling, but I am being sensible,' said Meg frostily. 'I have my pride, after all, and as long as the others are willing to continue how can I back out?'

'I can understand how you feel, but –'

'She's right, you know, Roger,' said Jenny. Her intervention took them all by surprise, so that there was a long moment of silence while they turned and looked at her. 'When Antony asks you to help him with something that may not be quite safe,' she said carefully, 'Meg's never made any objection. I don't know if you realise it but it's not very nice just sitting and waiting –'

'Of course I realise it!'

'– so I think you should give her the same – the same latitude now. I don't like what's happening any more than you do, but it's Meg's right to decide what she should do about it.'

Roger stared at her for a long moment, rather as though he

117

couldn't believe his ears. After a while he turned to Maitland. 'I suppose you agree with her, Antony,' he said.

'I'd like Meg to retire gracefully as much as you would, but I don't think we've either of us any right to –'

'To play the heavy husband,' Meg supplied, seeing him for a moment at a loss for words. 'In any case, Brian's promised that precautions will be taken. I don't see how anything else can happen.'

That was almost the end of the matter. After a while Roger gave in, though reserving to himself the right to arrange for Meg's dresser to start her duties immediately, and stay in the dressing room as an insurance against the laying of any booby traps. 'Though if it had come from anyone but you, Jenny –'

'Your sense of fairness would have convinced you Meg's right sooner or later,' Jenny assured him. She was as anxious as either of the two men, but trying valiantly not to show it. 'You told us what happened today as far as the arrival of the ambulance men,' she went on, and Meg gave her a grateful look.

'Yes, did I mention that Brome showed signs of coming round after they'd given him oxygen? Still, they insisted on taking him back to hospital with them, so the body had been cleared away by the time the police arrived. And if you think I'm speaking rather callously,' he added, 'it's because Jeremy has such a very prosaic way of talking about these things.'

'After all, they are his bread and butter,' said Jenny.

'I know. Apparently he wrote a book once in which a murder was committed by coal gas poisoning, only in that case the murderer crept into the victim's bedroom at night and turned on the fire. But he isn't up on methane. However, it turned out that Edward Brome has little or no sense of smell. Brian Barrington told us that, and Mary Russell and Matthew Benbow were able to confirm it. None of us knows when the gas was turned on. He hadn't been to his dressing room since morning, so he might have been wandering around for quite a while before he was finally overcome.'

'So we reach the arrival of the police,' said Roger.

'Yes, they turned up quite quickly – two local chaps. They'd read about the so-called hauntings in the newspapers, of course, and come to the same conclusion as I did at first, that it was a publicity stunt. They were quite thorough though; they questioned everybody about Brome's state of mind, and I daresay they looked for a suicide note in his room, too, but if they found one they didn't say so. What they did tell Brian Barrington, and he passed it on to us, was that there were no fingerprints at all on the gas tap . . . except my thumbprint when I turned it off. Which to my mind rules out all possibility that Brome did it himself.'

'Yes, I should say so, too. Didn't that make them at all suspicious?' Roger asked. He was trying very hard to treat the matter as though it were of no direct concern to him.

'They were fiddling around for the rest of the day and they called in their usual experts and despatched their doctor to the hospital to talk to Brome. I could see their heart wasn't in it, but they went through the motions of asking about motive and opportunity and so on. Alibis were hopeless – nobody knew when the gas was turned on. Even if Benbow hadn't opened the window I don't think anyone could have been sure about that.'

'Besides,' said Meg, who seemed to have recovered her spirits, 'I'm quite sure they consider theatre people to be an odd lot of whom anything at all might be expected.'

'And if you'll believe me,' said Antony, 'while all this was going on Barrington was continuing as well as he could with his rehearsals. It isn't as callous as it sounds, he was quite aware by then that Brome was going to get better. Mark Kenilworth was playing Jack Bashful, and I must say he did it pretty well. I think in any case Barrington would have wanted to go on with the production, and now his blood is up and I'm beginning to think nothing will stop him. But seeing how well young Kenilworth did was certainly an encouragement. So you'll get your chance of attending the first night, Jenny love,' he added.

'If nothing more drastic happens,' said Roger, but his annoyance seemed to have passed and he sounded more resigned than anything else. 'But with everyone in the state of nerves you described I don't see how it's possible for them to act at all.'

'Am I in a state of nerves?' Meg demanded.

'I'm not so sure you oughtn't to be,' Roger told her.

'Well, even if I were . . . don't you understand, darling, there's no reason for Lady Oldfellow to feel nervous, so when I get on the stage –'

'You become a different person,' said Antony. 'A small, nightly miracle,' he added, looking at Roger, who this time smiled back at him without reserve, so that Maitland was emboldened to add, 'Brian Barrington phoned the hospital while we were at the

119

theatre. Brome is doing well and he was able to speak to him, but he found that rather upsetting because Brome declined to have anything further to do with the production. What's getting to him, as far as I can gather, is that he might have been blown sky high if he'd lit a match. Not that I blame him, but I can see that it puts Barrington in rather a spot.'

'You said this other man – this understudy – was doing the part very well,' Jenny reminded him.

'Yes, love, but it leaves him without an understudy for the other men. I think Brian is still hoping that he can persuade Brome to change his mind; we'll just have to wait and see.'

'Did you manage to talk to the rest of the cast?' Roger asked.

'Not really, there was rather a tendency for them to huddle together, and you know as well as I do that it's no good talking to people *en masse*. But that's another reason, Roger, that I don't think you need worry too much about Meg. As long as she sticks around with the rest of them, and I think she has sense enough to do that –'

'You made it quite clear to me, darling, that I'd better,' said Meg rather fiercely. But she softened suddenly. 'I really do see that he's right, Roger darling,' she said, 'and I will be sensible.'

Roger might have become resigned but he was not altogether ready to give up his grievance. 'If you are it'll probably be for the first time in your life,' he said rather sourly. 'Will you be going to the theatre tomorrow, Antony?'

'No, I've got a conference that came up suddenly, and a whole pile of papers waiting for me, but in any case I'm not doing any good. I might just as well be back in chambers. It's in the hands of the police now.'

'I suppose you've no idea –?'

'No idea in the world,' said Maitland promptly. 'The whole thing's a mystery to me.'

'You always have ideas, Antony,' Jenny protested.

'Well this time I haven't.' Maitland sounded positive. 'There's one thing I did want to ask you though, Meg. What has Stella Hartley got against Brian Barrington?'

'Darling, she's like that with everybody,' said Meg. 'What makes you think there's a special cause of grievance there?'

'I'm not blind, *darling*, or deaf, either,' Maitland told her, with a rather savage emphasis on the endearment.

'Well, I can't tell you anything about it.'

120

'Can't . . . or won't?'

'I've known them both for ever,' said Meg, 'but not intimately.'

Knowing her hatred of gossip, Antony left it there. He could probably force her to be a little more frank with him if it became necessary, but as things were at present it didn't seem worth the trouble. Roger still had a question to ask.

'What do you make of this latest – what's a good word for it – mischief-making?' he asked. 'Though that seems rather a mild word to use under the circumstances,' he added consideringly.

'I can tell you what Stella makes of it,' Meg put in. 'As soon as she heard there were no fingerprints she said, "That proves it was Sir John." Antony did try to point out to her that it was very unlikely the room had been so thoroughly cleaned that there were no old ones on the tap, but she wasn't having any of that.'

'You're not so sure she isn't right,' said Roger, eyeing her rather closely.

'Well, you must admit it's a little bit odd, darling. That ought to make you feel better about it,' she added, suddenly inspired. 'I mean, I do rather feel as though I don't particularly want to be alone at the theatre.'

'That's good.' It was hard to tell whether he found the argument convincing or not. 'But I asked you what you thought, Antony.'

'So you did, and I'd tell you if I knew. Someone's out to make an effect, and I'd say he's getting a bit desperate about it.'

'Unless the whole series of events were designed to confuse the issue,' said Jenny. 'Mr Brome is alive, but he might equally be dead. Have you any idea of anyone who might have a motive for killing him?'

'You mean, love, that if his death was the motive there's no cause for Roger to worry,' said Antony, rubbing in the point she was obviously trying to make. 'I have to say, though, I've no idea at all. He seems on the face of it a particularly inoffensive sort of chap. Unless Mark Kenilworth wanted a chance to play the part of Jack Bashful. I've been told he's ambitious, but that seems to be taking ambition rather far.'

'Not a motive that would drive a normal person to murder, but are murderers normal?' asked Roger rhetorically. 'If three of the actors knew he had no sense of smell it's a hundred to one the rest of them knew it too. Except, perhaps, the two understudies, and that seems to militate against the only theory you've come up with yet, Antony.'

'Not the only theory,' Maitland objected, 'I'm still inclined to believe that someone has a grudge against one of the three people most concerned with the play's success. I'm talking about alibis –'

'We weren't,' Meg pointed out.

'No, but there's just one thing I was able to deduce. Brian Barrington knew I was going to look in on Brome after I'd talked to Matthew Benbow. He wouldn't have encouraged me to do that if he'd turned the gas on himself, because if Benbow and I hadn't got talking about other things I'd probably have walked in on Brome long before he was overcome by the fumes.'

'That might work either way,' said Roger. 'If murder wasn't intended, but only some dislocation of the rehearsals –'

'I see what you mean, of course, but I still think Barrington would be the last person to want that. Anyway it's no business of mine now, so let's forget it while we can. Not that I think the last word on the subject's been said between Meg and Roger,' he added to Jenny, much later when they were alone together.

'Meg's quite determined, and I do see her point.'

'Yes, love, I know that. You did your best to smooth matters over and I daresay Roger agrees with you in his mind, as I do, but his heart's a different matter.'

'Poor Roger,' said Jenny, sighing. 'Only he can't expect Meg to – just to run away from the situation.'

Antony looked at her with amused affection. 'My dearest love,' he said, 'you're worried about her yourself.'

'Of course I am,' said Jenny rather crossly. 'Only *I'm* not so silly as to expect the impossible of her.'

Tuesday, 13th January to Thursday, 15th January

The next day was a busy one for Maitland, and Sir Nicholas was in court, so it wasn't until Antony got home in the evening to find that the Hardings had already arrived for their dinner engagement that he was able to tell them of the most recent development in what Sir Nicholas had begun to call satirically the Ghost Story. They both looked serious when they heard of the mishap to the unfortunate Edward Brome, but it was Sir Nicholas who commented upon the matter first. 'I hope you succeeded in persuading Meg to give up what seems to be rapidly becoming a forlorn hope,' he said.

'I tried to, but without any success at all,' said Antony. 'So did Roger, in fact they came as near to "having words" as I've ever heard them. Jenny stopped that by appealing to Roger's sense of fairness, and on consideration we both agreed she was right.'

'Are you going back to the theatre again?'

'If I thought any good would come of it I'd go like a shot. But my enquiries aren't doing any good, and there's nothing I can do to protect Meg as far as I can see.'

'There I am bound to agree with you,' said Sir Nicholas thoughtfully. 'You were there yesterday, and if somebody had turned on the gas tap in Meg's dressing room would you have known anything about it?'

'No, of course I wouldn't, but she'd have smelled it all right. I don't think there's anything to worry about on that score and Roger has arranged with her dresser to come back to work, though of course she isn't needed yet, so there'll be no chance of anyone rigging up a booby trap or anything of that sort. And Meg has promised not to wander about alone, so I really don't think –'

'All the same you're worried about her . . . you and Jenny,' said Sir Nicholas accusingly. 'I thought better of your powers of persuasion, Antony, even if Roger is too much in love with her to

123

insist on her retiring from this particular play.'

'The trouble is as I told you, I can see her point of view, at least since Jenny pointed it out,' said Antony meekly. 'And quite honestly, Uncle Nick, short of tying her up, or locking her in the boxroom, I don't see what's to be done.'

'See your difficulty,' said Vera, and for the moment the matter was allowed to drop.

The Farrells came in after dinner, with no further mishaps to report. Sir Nicholas, however, who regarded them both as family and accorded them the attendant privileges – which mainly consisted of having him speak his mind freely to them whenever he felt so inclined – had a good deal to say, both on the subject of Meg's stubbornness and Roger's weak-minded attitude in allowing her to go her own way. Roger retorted by inviting Sir Nicholas to have a go himself at persuading her, but Meg argued her point quite fiercely and it wasn't until Vera said, 'Agree with Jenny on the whole,' that peace was restored after a fashion.

Again the next evening there was nothing to report, but on Thursday, when the Farrells arrived at Jenny's invitation in time for dinner, Meg answered the inevitable query by shaking her head sadly and saying, 'Poor Miss Miggs.'

Maitland cast his mind quickly through the list of characters in the play. 'I don't remember anyone called Miggs,' he said. 'Who the devil is she?'

'The wardrobe mistress, and of course that isn't really her name.'

'Why call her by it then?' Antony sounded rather impatient. Roger seemed calm, but Meg's evident safety might account for that, and he couldn't quite conceal his anxiety that some further mishap might have occurred.

'We used to have a dressmaker's dummy in the attic at home,' Meg explained, 'and for some reason it was always called Miss Miggs. It just seemed a natural thing to call her.'

'It may have seemed as natural as anything,' said Maitland, no longer making the faintest attempt to conceal his impatience. 'What happened to her? Don't tell me she's had an accident too.'

'Nothing like that, but she was getting on marvellously with the costumes and then this morning she went to the theatre and found that everything had been ripped up.'

'You mean the seams are all to do again?'

'No, there'll have to be new material bought. Somebody

124

slashed them with a knife, not at the seams at all but right down the bodice and the back and the sleeves and everything. Luckily she hadn't started on the men's costumes yet.'

'I was beginning to hope –'

'Yes, so was I,' said Roger with feeling.

'He's started worrying again,' Meg confided. ('I'd never stopped,' said Roger.) 'But it's a pity about what happened because I think B.B. had got Edward almost talked round into coming back to his part again. But this has wrecked that idea, of course.'

'How is Brome? Have you heard?'

'Oh, yes, he's fine now. The funny thing is he's haunting the theatre ... no, I shouldn't have used that word, should I? It sounds too much like what poor Sir John Cartwright is supposed to be doing and I don't want to get into an argument about that again because it makes Roger so cross. But I thought he'd be too frightened to come anywhere near us.'

'I was talking to him while I was waiting for Meg tonight,' said Roger. 'I think he's made up his mind that it's only actual members of the cast who are at risk. Which is an idea I don't find at all comforting considering that Meg is by far the most important of them. I've a good mind to attend the rehearsals in future.'

'You could look at it in another way, Roger,' Jenny suggested. 'Perhaps whoever is doing these things got a bit frightened when he nearly killed Mr Brome. If that's so he may have decided to confine himself to comparatively harmless things like slashing the costumes.'

'Harmless, darling?' Meg was horrified. 'It's a terrible setback.'

'Never mind that. Jenny may well be right, Roger, and I think you should take comfort from that.' He turned back to Meg who was still simmering gently. 'What do the police make of this latest episode?'

'Oh, it just confirmed what I'm sure they thought already, that there's a practical joker at work; after all, even turning on the gas wouldn't have been so serious if Edward could have smelled it as soon as he went into the room.'

'I suppose that's reasonable enough from their point of view.' He met Meg's indignant look blandly, and made haste to turn her thoughts to some less controversial subject. 'How is Mark

Kenilworth coming along?'

'I think he's marvellous, darling. In fact I'm not at all sure he isn't better than Edward was, but perhaps I'm being unfair about that.'

'I should have thought the handsome hero was more in his line,' said Antony thoughtfully.

'Yes, I daresay you would, but that's where acting comes in. A real actor can take any character at all and make something of it, and that's the sort of ability Mark seems to be showing. And Jack Bashful in the play is a complicated character, you must admit that.'

'I do, as far as I've been able to see and from what I've been told. The question is, what's going to happen next?'

'That's obvious, darling. Miss Miggs will start work again on the costumes,' said Meg precisely, 'and the rest of us have the whole weekend for rest and reflection. B.B. thought that was a good idea, so we're not starting rehearsals again until Monday.'

'Well, give some thought to what Jenny suggested about the joker, Roger,' Antony advised.

'I thought we might as well give him what comfort we could, love,' he told Jenny when they were alone again. 'But it's like – like terrorist activity. You can't guard against it because you don't know where they'll strike next.'

'Do you really think Meg may be in danger?' asked Jenny anxiously.

'Only because we're both so fond of her, love, and like Roger that makes me worried. My head tells me that as leading lady she'd have been the first target if any real harm had been intended to the members of the cast. All the same,' he added reflectively, 'it might not hurt to have a word with Sykes over the weekend. He's sure to have heard what the local chaps made of the Edward Brome affair.'

Saturday, 17th January

A phone call on Saturday morning revealed the fact that Detective Superintendent Sykes was not on duty that weekend, and, after a little skirmishing, Maitland's invitation was reversed and it was arranged that he and Jenny should take tea with the Sykeses that afternoon. 'For I know well enough, Mr Maitland,' said the superintendent, the amusement in his tone very evident, 'this way there'll be no awkward questions from Sir Nicholas, if it should so chance that you want to keep the fact that we've had a talk from him.'

'My life is an open book,' said Antony virtuously, though he couldn't have denied that there had been many occasions in the past when the suggestion would have been a welcome one. Sir Nicholas both liked and respected the detective, but it was an undoubted fact that he looked askance at most of his nephew's dealings with the police.

So that afternoon Jenny drove them both down to Streatham and offered tactfully, but quite unnecessarily (even though Mrs Sykes, a good Yorkshirewoman, favoured a hearty tea), to help with the arrangements while the men had their talk.

Superintendent Sykes was a square-built man with a placid disposition and a cheerful expression, without which – as Maitland had often thought – he would have looked far more like a farmer than a detective. 'Well now, Mr Maitland,' he said, having seen his visitor comfortably settled, 'what can I do for you? The last time we got together, if I remember rightly, it was at my instigation.' This was said, as Antony realised well enough, to put him at his ease if he had a favour to ask. They had become close friends over the years, and each of them felt himself to some degree indebted to the other; though as both were conscientious men each of them exaggerated the benefit he had received from the other's help.

'I wanted to know,' said Antony, coming to the point without delay because he knew that when the ladies joined them the talk must become general, 'whether any gossip had reached you about the goings on at the Cornmarket Theatre.'

'The haunted theatre?' said Sykes, amused again. 'I read about it in the papers, of course, but that isn't what you mean, I take it.'

'No, I meant about the chap who nearly got snuffed out by gas. It wasn't murder, though it might have been, and it wasn't even Scotland Yard's business, but I'd be very surprised if you hadn't heard about it.'

'I have, of course. The chaps who dealt with it reckoned nowt to it as a matter of fact. Publicity, they thought, and the accident to this actor fellow a part of the same thing that had gone a bit too far on account of his having no sense of smell; that, or a genuine accident. Which it could have been.'

'I don't like coincidences,' said Maitland flatly.

'I knew you were going to say that,' said Sykes in a pleased tone. 'Well, låd, no more do I. But I have my share of curiosity, you know, and it's been a puzzle to me what you were doing there when it happened.'

'I allowed myself to be talked into trying to find out who the joker was,' said Antony. 'To my great sorrow, I might add. I suppose it was partly Meg's influence, though it was Brian Barrington who finally persuaded me. I agreed with your chaps at first, about it all being a publicity stunt, I mean, but then I began to think someone didn't want the play to open and must have a grievance against one of the people who stood to gain most by it. It had to be someone with access to the theatre, and who knew his way about. It didn't seem possible that anyone had a grudge against the backers and that brought it down pretty well to three men, the director, the author, and the man who owns the outline that Sir John Cartwright wrote. The trouble is I can't find the smell of a motive for anyone disliking them to such an extent.'

'Nor could my colleagues for anyone wanting to murder Edward Brome, or for his committing suicide,' said Sykes. 'Was that what you were interested in?'

'I have considered, of course, whether everything else might have been a cover-up for that one incident, but on the whole I don't think so. I mean, why terrorise the cast? And even Meg, though she hasn't exactly admitted it, is beginning to wonder, unless I'm very much mistaken, whether Sir John's ghost isn't behind everything.'

'I've always understood that theatre people have their superstitions,' said Sykes indulgently.

'Besides,' said Antony, ignoring this, 'there's been a further incident. On Wednesday night someone ripped up all the work that Miss Miggs, the wardrobe mistress, had done so far. A waste of money and time because they have had to buy more material, but that's the extent of the damage . . . except that, of course, the cast think it's Sir John again trying to prevent their going forward with what he seems to think is a travesty of his original idea. Also, Meg tells me, poor Miss Miggs is extremely upset. But there's a fact that none of them seem ready to recognise and that is that someone has kept the press posted about all this. You may not have noticed, but there was a mention of this last incident this morning.'

'That would seem to be an argument in favour of your original notion . . . publicity,' Sykes pointed out.

'I think that's the idea, which makes me all the more certain that I was right in abandoning it after the first near accident. And if I'm right about that, closing the production down must be the main motive.'

'Yes, it would seem so. You're worried about this business, aren't you, Mr Maitland?'

'I'm worried for Meg, and for the people I've met and liked at the theatre. And I can't help wondering what's going to happen next.'

'I'm not surprised,' said Sykes. 'I only wish I could help you, but nothing I've heard would be of any assistance at all. There is just one thing, though, and it's why I suggested you might not want to tell Sir Nicholas about our talk.'

'Not that man Godalming again?' asked Antony sharply.

'The Assistant Commissioner, yes. You won't have supposed, Mr Maitland, that you endeared yourself to him by getting the charge against Mayhew and Harris dismissed last year.'

'No, of course I didn't. I've been meaning to ask you how Mayhew was getting on, though I hoped everything would be all right – well, as all right as possible in the circumstances – for him now. Harris, as you know, has been taken under my uncle's wing; he's now working as a clerk in Joseph Whitehead's chambers and reading law in his spare time.'

'You know it was decided not to proceed against Mrs Mayhew.

The only evidence against her was what she said herself in court, which would have been difficult to introduce, and I think the Director of Public Prosecutions felt some sympathy for Mayhew, even if Sir Alfred Godalming didn't. They've separated, of course – the Mayhews – but it's not quite so bad for him this way.'

'Not so bad,' said Maitland reflectively, 'but I don't think either of us is under any illusion as to how he really feels. But what I was really wondering about was, how are things going for him at work? If Sir Alfred's trying to take his frustration out on him that would be the last straw.'

'I won't say there's no resentment there, Mr Maitland,' said Sykes slowly, 'because I know enough about the AC to realise there must be. When we discussed it at the time I think we both decided he wouldn't dare to – to take it out on Mayhew, not after what had happened.'

'Which is a good thing, if true,' said Antony when he paused.

'Yes, in its way. But I won't deny to you, Mr Maitland, that the whole affair seems to have left Sir Alfred feeling even more bitter towards you. Which isn't reasonable, of course, when all you did was prevent a particularly unpleasant injustice being done, but there it is.'

'That's no more than I expected,' said Antony. 'But I don't know what you're getting at, Superintendent. I wanted to pick your brains in case they contained anything useful to me in this rather unusual problem, but at the moment my conscience is reasonably clear. I mean, I can't see that any of my recent activities can possibly be of interest to your revered superior officer.'

'You wouldn't think so,' Skyes admitted, 'and that just goes to show how deep this – this phobia he's got goes. He heard somehow you'd been at the theatre when this Mr Brome was gassed. Well, you've got to admit it was a queer place for you to crop up, and that roused his interest immediately and he started asking questions.'

'Questions about w-what, for heaven's sake?'

'About your previous association with any of the people concerned.'

'I've known Meg forever.'

'Yes, I know that, but if Mr Farrell was more intimately concerned in this business that would have roused Sir Alfred's greater interest. As it is he's concentrating on the fact that you once defended Mr Jeremy Skelton on a murder charge, and that he was the author of the play Leonard Buckley was appearing in when *he* was arrested for murder, and you took over the defence.'

'Damn it all, Sykes, it's m-my job. The world's l-littered with people I've had p-professional dealings with at one t-time or another.'

'So it is, but given Sir Alfred's view of your –'

'Of my unscrupulousness.' Maitland provided him with the word when he hesitated. 'Th-that doesn't explain what interest the p-present events can have for him.'

'I think he's persuaded himself that your friend Jeremy Skelton is responsible for everything that's happened, in the interests of publicity, but whether he believes you're directly involved at this juncture, I'm not quite sure. But if anything of a more serious nature should happen –'

Maitland, who had been on the verge of losing his temper, suddenly began to laugh. 'Jeremy has a sense of humour,' he said, 'which some people regard as distorted, but I'm as sure as I can be of anything that he's nothing to do with all this.'

'It's not a thing to be taken too lightly, Mr Maitland,' Sykes warned him.

'I don't think I altogether agree with you. In one way it's annoying, of course, but looking at it from a different point of view, why should I grudge Sir Alfred his fun? And leaving that aspect of things to one side I've probably got the wind up unnecessarily. The joker may have shot his bolt and we'll hear no more from him.'

The superintendent still looked doubtful, but as the ladies rejoined them at that moment bearing sustenance he was unable to say anything more. Mrs Sykes was not so well known to the Maitlands as her husband was, but she was an agreeable, down-to-earth person and the next hour passed pleasantly.

Antony, who had learned after a good deal of trial and error that anything was preferable to Jenny to having bad news kept from her (though it is not to be denied that he suffered an occasional relapse), told her about the private part of his conversation with the superintendent as they drove back to town. She listened in silence, and when he had finished resisted the temptation to turn her head to look at him. 'Are you going to tell Uncle Nick?' she demanded.

'As a matter of fact, love, I am. I mentioned at lunchtime

where we were going this afternoon –'

'I know you did, Antony, and you also told him why. But I expect he'd be quite satisfied if you just said you'd asked Inspector Sykes –'

'Superintendent,' he corrected her automatically.

'Yes, of course, I don't suppose I shall ever remember,' said Jenny remorsefully. 'But I was going to say if you told Uncle Nick he couldn't help you I don't suppose he'd be at all surprised.'

'It wouldn't be exactly untrue,' said Antony, 'but it would convey a falsehood, none the less. Is that your recommendation?'

'No, it isn't,' said Jenny emphatically. 'Even if you could convince him you were telling him the whole truth – and he knows you awfully well – I wouldn't recommend it. But I thought I'd have to persuade you to tell him, so what I'd like to know is why I didn't have to do so.'

'Jenny love, I never thought I'd see you resort to low cunning,' her husband told her affectionately. 'I'm going to tell Uncle Nick, and Vera too, of course, because – as you've told me something like a thousand times – they'd be hurt if I didn't. And if you're going to point out that in this case they might never find out I may as well end this fishing expedition straightaway and tell you I'm not at all easy in my mind that nothing else will happen.'

'I thought that was it,' said Jenny. She concentrated on her driving for a moment and then added, rather tentatively, 'Something horrid?'

'The answer to that is that I just don't know. I've never felt more helpless nor more bewildered. I agree with Roger in that I'd be happier if Meg had agreed to resign her part, but I also agree with your and her points of view as well that it's really too much to ask of her. But there are other people concerned that I've come to have a regard for, even leaving Jeremy and Anne out of the picture, and I wish for all their sakes that the whole thing could be cleared up.'

'Besides, there's this idea of Roger's about going to the rehearsals,' said Jenny. 'He can't neglect his business for a whole month.'

'If it was necessary . . . but I've been thinking, Jenny. If there's going to be more trouble, his presence there might encourage the person concerned to make a dead set at Meg, just to show what could be done . . . what Sir John's ghost is capable of, if you like. Meg's promised to behave herself, and I think if we can persuade

132

her it's for Roger's peace of mind she might be able to make him realise she meant it. And if you have a word with him –'

'He'd be far more likely to listen to you,' said Jenny.

'No, I don't think so. He has a great regard for your judgement. Didn't you realise that? If I thought he'd be doing any good by hanging around the theatre . . . but I don't. No good, and possibly some harm.'

'Well, if you really think I should try I will,' Jenny promised.

'But I still think it would have come better from you.'

Sir Nicholas and Vera were at home when they got back to Kempenfeldt Square, so they both went into the study and Antony gave a full account of his talk with Sykes. After which, Jenny, seeing that Uncle Nick was in one of his more carping moods, remembered that she had done nothing yet about dinner and succeeded in extracting her husband and whisking him upstairs before the older man could really get into his stride. 'It's only delaying matters,' Antony protested. But on the whole he was relieved at the way things had worked out.

Before the evening was over they were also able to report to one another some success in their plan to talk sense to the Farrells. Jenny inveigled Roger into the kitchen on the excuse that there were trays that needed carrying, and was able to tell Antony later that Roger had agreed that if nothing else happened he'd stay away from the theatre. Similarly Meg, after a short lecture on the subject of her wifely duty, which Maitland said would have done Uncle Nick credit, had promised Antony she'd do her best to persuade Roger of her own good intentions. 'And knowing her, Jenny love,' said Maitland later, 'I'm pretty sure that's the end of that bit of nonsense.'

Saturday, 7th February

After that there was a period of comparative peace. Maitland was busy and preoccupied, and though he and Jenny still listened eagerly to Meg's anecdotes about the course of rehearsals they didn't include any further disasters. Until the Saturday before the opening, when she and Roger were due to dine at the Maitlands' and arrived a little later than they were expected. They let themselves in, as was customary, but Antony heard the creak of the front door and went into the hall to greet them.

'You'll never believe what's happened!' said Meg with all the dramatic fervour at her disposal.

'Something else?' asked Maitland sharply. 'Roger, is she all right?'

'Of course I am,' Meg answered for herself. 'You're not still worrying about me, darling, are you? Even Roger realises I'm being as careful as I possibly can be.'

'I couldn't have helped you in this instance,' said Roger rather grimly. 'Hello, Jenny,' he added, as Jenny came out of the kitchen.

She ignored the greeting, looking from one of the new arrivals to the other. 'I heard your voices,' she said. 'Something's happened.'

'Another *accident*,' said Roger.

'Are you all right, Meg?'

'Perfectly, darling, but it is rather dreadful all the same and the last person I'd have wanted to get hurt.'

'Who?' asked Maitland, rather too loudly.

'Matthew Benbow.'

'What's happened to him? He isn't dead, is he?'

That brought Meg up sharply for a moment. 'That's what you've been afraid of all along, isn't it? No, he isn't dead – one of the trap-doors on the stage collapsed when he was standing on it and he's broken his leg.'

'And is that supposed to have been an accident, or ghostly intervention?' Antony asked sarcastically.

'Well, if it was done on purpose,' said Meg, with the air of one trying to bring reason into an unreasonable conversation, · 'it couldn't have been aimed at any particular person. I don't think it would have collapsed unless someone stood on it. But –'

'How did it happen?'

'Hugh Clinton said immediately that the bolt must have slipped, so he went down to look and found it had been sawed almost through. And Matthew is such a dear!' she added tragically.

'I quite agree, I like him too. I suppose he's in hospital.'

'Yes, of course.'

'Well, it's no good our standing round discussing it in the hall. You'd better come in, both of you, and I'll get you a drink.' There was a pause while this programme was carried out and then he asked, 'I imagine even Brian saw that you must call the police in again.'

'Yes, and I phoned Roger, and he arrived just as they were taking Matthew away. You know, Antony, you said a police enquiry might bring something to light, but there's nothing to go on, nothing to get hold of at all. Nobody knows when it was done, and the trap-door might have been walked across a hundred times before it actually gave way, so there's no question of producing alibis. And though the police seem to have taken it a bit more seriously, they kept coming back to the theory that it was a deliberate attempt to hurt Matthew, nothing to do with the other things. And everybody knows how nice he is – nobody could have a grudge against him.'

'No, I'm inclined to agree with that too. Perhaps if he's well enough I could come with you to see him tomorrow,' Antony suggested. 'In the meantime, what on earth is happening to the play? Your one male understudy is already taking part, and there's so little time now.'

'Well, after the police had gone we had a sort of council of war about that,' said Meg. 'It was Amanda who came up with the answer and asked Brian why he didn't do the part of Sir Benjamin himself.'

'Did he agree?'

'He didn't answer immediately. The first thing was that Stella

136

was down at the front of the stage positively cooing at him. "Darling B.B., it will be so wonderful playing with you again," ' Meg mimicked.

'I can't stand that woman,' said Roger.

'It sounds like a pretty innocuous remark all the same,' said Antony.

'Well, I suppose it does on the face of it, but it was the way it was said,' Roger told him. 'And she added, "Just think of it, B.B., the part is absolutely made for you," ' (Roger, of course, didn't attempt to take off Stella's voice) 'which was pretty unfair considering he'd have to make up nearly twenty years older to do it.'

'So then Amanda and Roberta set themselves to persuade him,' Meg took up the story, 'and Mark Kenilworth, with a good deal of tact, I thought, distracted Stella's attention by holding her in conversation until they'd got a rather unwilling yes out of Brian.'

'Well, I suppose that's all right if nothing else goes wrong,' said Antony rather doubtfully, but if he'd been about to add anything he was interrupted by Roger who said angrily,

'If you think it's all right, I don't! It might have been Meg standing on that trap-door when it collapsed.'

'I don't think so, you know. She's very much lighter than Matthew Benbow,' Maitland pointed out. He paused and looked at his friend more closely. 'What's on your mind, Roger?' he asked.

'I'm not going to start another row about whether Meg should give up the part or not,' said Roger. 'I do realise now that's rather too much to expect of her. The thing that's worrying me is whether there's anything I can do to keep her safe. If you meant it when you said my presence at the theatre might antagonise the person who's doing all this it seems I'll just have to stand on the sidelines and hope for the best.'

'I did mean it,' Antony told him, 'but it's only an idea and I may be wrong. The trouble is, you know, there's nothing whatever you could do if you were there, so on the whole I think it best not to risk it. Meg's taking her own food and thermos flask with her, and her dresser will see that no noxious substance is added to them, or any booby trap set up in her dressing room. As for the rest, as long as she doesn't wander about alone I don't see what can happen.'

137

'Benbow wasn't alone,' Roger objected. 'He was on the stage in full view of everybody.'

'Yes, darling,' Meg interposed, 'but that kind of thing won't happen again. Brian has set up a corps of watchmen, consisting of some of the stage-hands he's known for years. There'll be no more interference of that kind, and it's less than a week till we open,' she reminded him.

'I suppose you're right, all of you,' said Roger reluctantly. 'If you want to go to see Matthew Benbow with Meg tomorrow afternoon, Antony, I'll come here and keep Jenny company. Do you really think Brian Barrington can be ready by next Friday?' he asked, turning to Meg in an obvious attempt to put his fears behind him.

'He knows the part backwards, of course, and exactly how he wants it done. In fact,' said Meg, 'I think he knows everybody's part by heart. We've four whole days to get it right before the dress rehearsal on Thursday night; that should take care of it.'

'It sounds a bit tricky to me,' said Roger doubtfully.

'I've the utmost confidence in him,' said Meg. 'And do you know what Mary Russell said to me after it was all arranged? She said, "I'm glad B.B. is getting back into his proper place again. I always thought it was the greatest shame he gave up acting, even though he's a really good director."'

'I wonder what persuaded him to make the change,' said Antony, not for the first time. But that was a fruitless field of speculation, because if Meg knew anything she wasn't saying, so by mutual consent they abandoned the topic and it wasn't until they'd finished dinner and were gathered round the fire again that it forced itself once more on their attention.

Since Vera's arrival, Gibbs – who enjoyed playing the martyr – had abandoned his annoying habit of toiling upstairs with any messages for the Maitland household in favour of using the house phone which had been installed for his convenience when the house was first divided. Nothing, however, would alter the censoriousness of his tone when he announced that there was a young lady to see Mr Maitland. Antony had long since got used to the implication that invariably accompanied such an announcement that something improper was going on, and asked only, 'Didn't she give you her name, Gibbs?'

'A Miss Hartley, Mr Maitland.'

'Thank you, I'll come down and fetch her. Another of my illicit

138

relationships has reared its ugly head,' he told Jenny. 'Stella Hartley this time, and though the adjective young was hardly appropriate I expect she looks that way to Gibbs.'

'She's an extremely attractive woman,' said Meg rather reprovingly, but spoiled the effect a moment later by adding curiously, 'I wonder what on earth she wants.'

'We'll soon know.' Maitland was already on his way to the door. And indeed, when he got down to the hall and found the actress waiting for him, he had to admit that her red hair and glowing complexion made a very attractive picture. Anything more to do with affairs at the Cornmarket Theatre was the last thing he wanted just then, but there was nothing for it but to greet her politely and invite her to precede him up the stairs.

Stella was looking about her in a rather disparaging way as she went. 'What on earth do you live up here for?' she asked when they reached the second floor landing and Maitland went past her to open his own front door. 'Such a bore, all those stairs, though I daresay it's good for the figure. It's a good address, of course.'

'Convenient, which is more to the point,' said Antony equably. 'And we find it comfortable. I don't think I need make any introductions,' he added as they reached the living room, 'though you only met Jenny once, so perhaps –'

'I remember Mrs Maitland very well,' said Stella graciously. 'And it's so nice to find Meg and her husband here. You don't mind if I call you Roger, do you, because Meg and I are such good friends?'

Roger's rather incoherent reply fortunately drowned Meg's muttered, 'You could have fooled me.' Jenny judged it time to take matters into her own hands, and piloted the visitor to one of the wing chairs by the fire.

'It's very nice to meet you again, Miss Hartley,' she said.

'And I should be apologising for dropping in on you without warning,' said Stella, not to be outdone. 'But, my dear, I'm a creature of impulse. And I was shattered by what had happened to Matthew, absolutely shattered. So then I thought there was only one thing for it and that was to come and see your husband. If anybody would listen to me, he would.'

By this time Roger had seated himself again and Antony had taken up his favourite stance a little to the side of the fireplace. He exchanged rather a doubtful glance with his wife, now sitting rather more primly than usual beside Meg on the sofa. 'I don't know what it is you want to talk to me about,' he said, 'and whatever the problem is – I presume from your mentioning Mr Benbow that it's something to do with what's been happening at the theatre – I don't see how I can help you.'

'B.B. has every confidence in your good sense,' Stella told him.

'That's only because he succeeded in persuading me into a course of action very much against my will. And I'm afraid it didn't do him much good anyway. But does this mean, Miss Hartley, that you've decided after all there isn't a ghost involved in all these happenings?'

'Oh, no. Why do you think that?'

'Because whatever else I am, I'm certainly not an exorcist.'

She laughed gaily, as though he had made an excellent joke. 'You told me that once before,' she said. 'But surely it's obvious that Sir John would like to put a stop to the production. You agree with me, don't you, Meg?'

'Nothing at all about this business is obvious to me,' said Meg uncompromisingly.

'I must say,' said Maitland, 'this last accident – if you like to call it that – rather makes nonsense of the idea of ghostly intervention. I can't imagine the spirit of Sir John Cartwright under the stage with a saw.'

'They – the spirits of the departed – have to work with whatever comes to hand,' said Stella solemnly. 'I don't see any difficulty there, and even if Meg doesn't agree with me – and I suspect she does really and just doesn't want to admit it for fear of being laughed at – I'm quite sure the rest of the cast do.'

'What is it you want to tell me, then?' Antony asked.

'You know what's going to happen next, don't you?' She looked from one to the other of her companions as she spoke but Antony was the only one who attempted to answer.

'Perhaps nothing,' he said. He didn't believe anything of the kind, but it didn't seem to be exactly the time to spread alarm and despondency.

'You know B.B. has taken over Matthew's part?'

'Yes, Meg told me.'

'I've warned him,' said Stella, 'but he's quite determined. In fact he's really being so stupid I almost let matters take their course, but then I thought perhaps it was my duty to try to stop it.'

140

'Yes, but what is it you want to stop?'

'All these things that have been happening – there's only one possible ending to them dramatically,' said Stella. 'And you must remember that Sir John Cartwright was a dramatist.'

'I know he was, but I still don't believe –'

'He wants to stop the play . . . he wants to stop it at any cost. So what's going to happen?' She paused there, either for effect or to make sure that she had the attention of her entire audience. 'When B.B. staggers from behind the screen fatally wounded,' she went on, 'it really will be a fatal wound. He'll die right there on the stage!'

That held Antony speechless for a moment, and it seemed to have had the same effect on the others, too. 'Do you really think so?' he asked at last rather feebly.

'Why else do you think I'm here? It's the only thing possible dramatically,' she reiterated, 'and if you think I'm making it up, just ask Meg if she doesn't agree with me.'

'I hadn't thought about it that way,' said Meg hesitantly, 'but I'm beginning to think I see what you mean.'

Stella gave Maitland a triumphant look. 'And there's another thing,' she said. 'If Sir John has taken exception to the play, as he obviously has, it's because the method of murder was changed. Also perhaps because it's a two-act play now so that the emphasis may fall in a way he didn't intend. So to have Sir Benjamin succumb to the new method of killing would be an irony, wouldn't it? One that Sir John would have appreciated.'

Antony stared at her. 'I believe you're really serious about all this,' he said incredulously.

'Of course I'm serious. Do you think I'd be here if I weren't?'

'I suppose not.' He turned his head a little. 'Meg,' he said, and the word was at once a question and an appeal.

'I'm not sure about Sir John's ghost,' said Meg, 'at least when I'm away from the theatre I don't believe in him. But Stella's quite right – it is the obvious thing dramatically, and whether it's really Sir John or just somebody trying to make us believe it is, he may well have thought it out on the same lines as Stella has done.'

Maitland looked at her for a long moment. She sounded nervous, altogether unlike herself. Then he turned back to Stella. 'What do you think I can do about it?' he asked.

'You can talk to B.B., he may listen, I told you he has

141

confidence in you. You will try, won't you?'

'I don't see how I can convince him of something I don't believe myself.'

'Oh, you're hopeless!' She was suddenly really angry. 'Haven't you any sense of drama at all?'

'I'm a barrister, you know, not an actor or a playwright,' Antony pointed out to her. 'I don't think my clients would altogether appreciate it if I imported drama into our proceedings.'

'Then you'll just watch a man die and do nothing to stop it,' said Stella. 'I admit I'd rather it was B.B. than Matthew, I hate having to act with the man. But I thought you regarded him as your friend.'

'So I do. Assuming you're right, Miss Hartley, when do you think all this is going to happen?'

'I'd say at the dress rehearsal,' said Stella, still dogmatically. 'That's the first time we shall be in costume and all the props will be at hand. And I say the dress rehearsal rather than opening night because I don't think Sir John wants the play to come on at all before the public.'

Roger roused himself to take part in a discussion that seemed to have had as stupefying an effect on him as it had on Jenny. 'If you really think Sir John Cartwright wants to stop the performance, Miss Hartley, why don't you retire from it . . . give up your part?'

'That wouldn't stop it, it would just mean that silly child Roberta would take it over. I'll do nothing of the kind.'

Comparing notes afterwards, neither Antony nor Roger felt this to be altogether reasonable, but they let it pass. 'I haven't been to the theatre lately,' said Antony. 'Is the scenery in place yet?'

'Yes, it is.'

'Then how is the screen positioned, the one that Sir Benjamin hides behind?'

'As you're looking at the stage,' said Meg, who knew perfectly well that she'd confuse him if she started to talk about prompt and off-prompt sides, 'it's to the left at the back. You remember Sir Benjamin tiptoes across to it from the other side, almost the full width of the stage.'

'Yes, but does the screen join the wings? When he's stationed there could somebody get at him unseen?'

'I'm afraid they could,' said Meg reluctantly. 'It has to be that way or there'd be no mystery. The audience can't see who kills – who's supposed to have killed him.'

'All this is beside the point anyway,' said Stella. 'A spirit can materialise anywhere.'

'All the same, if you'll forgive me, Miss Hartley, I'm more inclined to take your idea seriously now I know it's possible for it to be carried out without supernatural intervention.'

'That must be as you please,' she told him coldly. 'At least will you talk to B.B.?'

'Short of cancelling the play, what can he do about it?'

'We've seen already that Sir John uses material things to carry out his ends,' said Stella earnestly. 'He can tell Hugh Clinton to make sure it really is a stage rapier that's left behind the screen and has to be dropped at a certain point in the action. And perhaps B.B. could just change his position from the one he usually stands in.'

'In case the ghost is short-sighted,' Antony couldn't resist saying. And then, before she could express her offence all over again, 'Do you mind telling me, Miss Hartley, why you dislike Mr Barrington so much?'

'Do I dislike him?' She seemed to be asking herself the question quite seriously. 'There was a time, but that was long ago.' She turned suddenly, confidingly, to Jenny, perhaps thinking her the person most likely to sympathise with her point of view. 'In fact I've been married and divorced twice since then.'

Knowing that the question was on the tip of her husband's tongue Jenny put it for him. 'Since when, Miss Hartley?' she asked.

'Since Brian and I . . . he thought it would be a good idea to get married but I wasn't so sure. And then at last I was quite sure and everything broke off between us. But I'd say that gave him cause to dislike me rather than the other way round, wouldn't you?'

'It sounds that way certainly,' said Jenny cautiously, and glanced at her husband who obligingly drew Stella's fire again.

'I had the impression during the rehearsals I've attended, Miss Hartley, that you weren't altogether happy with his direction.'

'He isn't infallible, you know,' she assured him spitefully. 'And I don't think failing as an actor qualifies him to tell other people what to do.'

143

'But he didn't fail,' said Meg indignantly. 'He chose to change the direction his career took, that's all.'

'He enjoyed a certain reputation,' said Stella grudgingly. 'But I've appeared opposite him, which I daresay you haven't, and I assure you he wasn't up to the standard of most of my leading men. In fact, the last time we acted together was the last time he appeared on stage. It was a modern drama and he really wasn't up to it.'

'And you told him so?' asked Jenny. The gentleness of her tone must have disguised from Stella that this was what all her friends would have considered a most un-Jennylike remark.

'Yes, naturally I did. And I shall continue to remind him,' said Stella, 'whenever he tries to interfere with my reading of the role of Lucy Simpering.'

'As you did the other day,' said Maitland thoughtfully. He succeeded in making the remark sound more like a compliment than anything else. 'Was the talk you had during the last play he appeared in anything to do with his leaving the stage, do you think?'

'If it made him realise his own inadequacy . . . no, I don't think that at all. I think he was just getting cast for more mature parts and he couldn't bear the idea of not being young any more.'

'He's still very handsome,' said Jenny.

'Do you really think so?'

'Yes, I do,' said Jenny firmly.

'Well, my dear, you're entitled to your own opinion. But we're wasting time. Will you talk to B.B., Mr Maitland?'

'I'll tell him you think some further trick may be played and that it may be aimed against him,' said Antony slowly. 'And if you dislike him so much I don't quite see –'

'I've just been explaining to you that it is he who dislikes me, not the other way round.' Stella Hartley paused and then laughed rather self-consciously. 'I'm making a fool of myself, aren't I? Of course I dislike Brian, but I don't want anything to happen to hurt the play any further.'

She went away soon after that, leaving the rest of the party eyeing each other a little wildly. 'She's really serious about this ghost business,' said Antony after a moment. 'Do you really think she believes a spirit could harm Brian Barrington?'

'I'm rather afraid she does, and I'm not at all sure Meg doesn't agree with her,' Roger replied. 'Unless, of course –'

144

'Unless she's thinking of killing Brian herself, *not* at the dress rehearsal, and this is an elaborate attempt to distract suspicion from herself before the fact.'

'That would be too subtle, darling,' Meg assured him.

'Well . . . perhaps.'

'Did you mean it, Antony, when you said you'd talk to Barrington?' Roger said.

'Yes, because I do realise that Meg and Stella have a better sense of drama than I have. Perhaps it *is* the next logical move for the joker to make.'

'I see what you mean. You still think I should stay away from rehearsals?'

'What I said stands. You can't do any good, and it's just possible that your being there might put ideas into someone's head. I think it might be a good idea for us both to attend the dress rehearsal though. Will you come with me?'

'Of course I will.' He didn't need to add, Just try to keep me away: his tone did it for him.

'And meantime, Meg, will you tell Barrington I'd like to see him. I suppose he'll think I've run mad too,' he added gloomily.

'You forget, darling, he's an actor,' said Meg. 'There's one thing I think I should say, though you know I hate gossip. Stella may be . . . well let's say she may be putting a wrong construction on what happened between her and Brian years ago.'

Antony asked her what she meant, of course, but farther than that, she refused to be drawn.

Sunday, 8th February

The next afternoon Roger arrived in Kempenfeldt Square in good time to take Meg and Antony to the hospital for the afternoon visiting hours. He then went back as promised to keep Jenny company.

Matthew Benbow, they found, had a private room. His leg was in traction, and though he was obviously making an effort to take his misfortune calmly it was equally obvious that he was extremely upset by it. 'Do you still think the joker may be Sir John Cartwright's ghost?' asked Antony, after greetings had been exchanged and the proper sympathy expressed, partly to distract the older man and partly because he was genuinely interested in the reply.

'It could be,' said Matthew cautiously.

'A ghost with a metal saw?' said Antony in a rallying tone.

'Who knows how they get their effects? I've had no personal experience myself before this,' Benbow told him, with every appearance of seriousness.

'But Sir John Cartwright could have nothing against you,' Meg protested. Either this was one of her non-believing times or she just wanted to help the conversation along.

'I'm playing one of the leading roles in what he must consider as his play,' said Benbow. 'If he dislikes what's being done with it . . . I think it's quite reasonable that he should want me out of the way.'

'What do you think the next move will be, in that case?' asked Maitland.

'I'd say there'll be an attack on either Jeremy Skelton or Chester Cartwright,' said Benbow promptly. 'I've had plenty of time to think about it, lying here.'

'Miss Hartley has a different theory,' Antony told him.

'What does she think?'

147

Antony outlined what Stella had said the evening before. 'You know,' said Matthew slowly when he had finished, 'I think she may have something there. Everything points to some more dramatic move, and there could be drama and irony too if Sir Benjamin were to die on the stage, and by the very weapon that had been introduced in defiance of what Sir John had written.'

'Not you too, Mr Benbow,' said Antony reproachfully, but Matthew, it appeared, was still perfectly serious.

Meg turned for the first time from the flowers she had been arranging in a vase on the table by the bed. 'If you think it's likely that Brian will be injured, or even worse,' she asked, 'what do you think will happen after that?'

'Just what I've outlined, that is if the production continued at all, which seems doubtful. But I do see that Stella may be right and that would be the first move.'

'But it's so – so drastic,' said Meg.

'Wasn't this drastic?' asked Benbow, gesturing towards his bandaged leg. 'But you don't – either of you – believe in Sir John Cartwright's ghost,' he added, looking from one of them to the other. Antony glanced at Meg, but she had for the moment no comment to make. 'Well, all I can say, Mr Maitland,' Matthew went on, 'if you're right in not believing in ghosts I wish you'd find out who the joker is who did this to me.'

This was in its own way so reasonable that there didn't seem to be much to say in reply. 'I only wish I could,' said Maitland, and sounded so depressed that Meg promptly changed the subject by telling Benbow that Brian Barrington was taking over his part for the time being.

'You see,' she continued – and Antony couldn't decide whether it was tact that prompted the words or whether they were the strict truth – 'he says he's going to take exactly the same line with the character that you did, Matthew. They say imitation is the sincerest form of flattery, don't they?'

'Well, I have to admit,' said Benbow, who obviously had his fair share of proper pride, 'that I gave a great deal of thought to the character and B.B. never saw fit to make any changes in my interpretation. But he's a fine actor, whether or no, and I'm sure everything will go well as far as Sir Benjamin is concerned. I only wish I could be there for the opening.'

'Never mind,' said Meg. 'If there's a run you'll be back in the part before you know it.'

'I think you're being too optimistic,' said Benbow sadly. 'Something else will happen, even if we're none of us right about exactly what it will be. This play isn't destined to be a box office success.'

There was no turning him from his opinion, so Maitland asked instead whether the police had been to see him again. It turned out they had been that morning, but had obviously found no neutral ground at all. Between Matthew Benbow's certainty that nobody could have wanted to harm him and that no human agency had been concerned, and the police's polite insistence that somebody must have had a motive, Maitland took away with him a very fair, and extremely amusing, idea of how their conversation must have gone.

They got back to Kempenfeldt Square to find that Sir Nicholas and Vera had already joined the others upstairs for tea, and Sir Nicholas, as might have been expected, had made a corner in the buttered toast. 'How is the invalid?' asked Vera when greetings had been exchanged.

'Bearing up, and quite convinced that Sir John Cartwright is to blame for his mishap,' Antony told her. 'Has Roger been telling you everything that's been happening since we saw you at lunchtime yesterday?'

'Roger and Jenny between them,' said Sir Nicholas in rather a hollow tone. But he relented then and smiled at his niece, whose efforts at explanation were notoriously difficult to follow. 'You must have made a great impression on this Miss Hartley, Antony,' he went on, with gentle malice, 'for her to think of turning to you in her predicament.'

'Very likely,' said Antony, knowing well enough no compliment was intended. 'What I don't understand is why she didn't just let matters rip seeing that she hates Barrington . . . or if that's too strong a word, seems to dislike him intensely.'

Sir Nicholas had closed his eyes briefly to signify his dislike for the colloquialism his nephew had used. 'But in any case you intend to warn him?' he asked in a failing voice.

'Yes, because . . . not that I think there's the slightest danger really, now that everyone's on their guard. But I couldn't square it with my conscience not to,' Antony admitted.

'Do you think the play will ever open?' Sir Nicholas enquired.

'Vera has kept Friday evening open, but –'

'Of course it will, Uncle Nick,' said Meg, ignoring his known dislike for being interrupted. 'Unless of course,' she added doubtfully, 'any more of the men get injured. It's a little bit tricky being completely without an understudy for them.'

Thursday, 12th February

I

Nothing happened for the next few days except that Meg, coming in with Roger on Monday evening, reported that the part of Sir Benjamin Oldfellow fitted Brian Barrington like a glove. 'Of course it will look better when he gets his make-up on,' she added. 'He looks far too young for the part. Even Matthew did, and he must be at least fifteen years older than Brian.'

'You don't agree with Stella Hartley about him, then?'

'No, I don't.' Meg seemed to be about to add something to that but then thought better of it. 'I gave him your message anyway and he'd like to have lunch with you on Thursday. We'll be rehearsing in the morning, but then have the afternoon off to rest before the dress rehearsal. Is that all right with you?'

'Quite all right. In fact, from my point of view, it's probably the best day he could have chosen,' Antony assured her, and as Roger seemed in a comparatively peaceful mood that evening nothing further was said on the matter.

Brian Barrington had chosen a well-known and extremely expensive restaurant for their meeting, and the table they were shown to – whether by prearrangement or not – was well out of earshot of the other customers. 'I don't know what you wanted to see me about, Antony,' said Barrington abruptly as soon as the waiter had departed to fetch their drinks, 'but it will have to wait. I've something to tell you first.'

'Not another . . . not somebody else hurt?' asked Maitland anxiously.

'No, and I suppose I should be thanking the Lord for that. But another – another manifestation,' said Barrington, obviously having a little difficulty in finding the right word. 'And from the point of view of morale just about as bad as it can be.'

'You'd better tell me.' Barrington had a distracted air, quite different from his usual composure, and the sooner he got what

151

was troubling him off his chest the better, Antony considered.

'There's been another message.'

'Somebody resorting to the loud hailer again?'

'No, a written one. Shakespeare again, and from the Scottish play.'

'Come now, I know how you people feel about that but it might be worse,' said Maitland encouragingly. 'How was it delivered?'

'It was on stage, a single sheet of paper lying on the chair that Lucy Simpering uses in the first act, which was what we were doing this morning. Stella found it, of course, and after that there was no hope of hushing it up. And the words were bad enough but that wasn't the real trouble. Chester swears it's in Sir John Cartwright's handwriting!'

'Does he though?' said Antony, taken aback.

'Yes, and I have to agree ... there's a copy of Chester's biography of Sir John in my office, and one of the illustrations is a page in his handwriting. Like the original outline, which both Jeremy and I have seen, to my eye there's no doubt it's the same as this new message.'

'A distinctive hand?'

'Yes, very. If you're thinking anybody could have got the book and imitated it –'

'Have you noticed whether the book has been missing from your office at any time? This note you're talking about might have been the result of a good deal of painstaking practice, not just dashed off in a moment.'

'I know that. I couldn't be sure about the book because I haven't had occasion to refer to it, but it's in print and anybody could have got hold of a copy. I'm trying to keep my head, Antony. I said all this to the people at the theatre this morning, but I can't deny it's given me a queerish sort of feeling. And today of all days!'

'Well timed,' Maitland agreed. 'You'd better tell me what it said.'

'Part of a very well-known speech,' said Barrington, 'but with a great chunk left out in the middle. *Is this a dagger*,' he started, then broke off and smiled for the first time that morning. 'We're pretty private here,' he said, 'but I'd better moderate my stage voice a little or everyone in the room will hear me.'

'Tell me quietly, then,' said Maitland, unconsciously lowering his own voice in sympathy.

152

'*Is this a dagger which I see before me, the handle toward my hand?* There are several lines missing there,' said Barrington, 'and it goes on, *Thou marshall'st me the way that I was going; and such an instrument I was to use.* What do you think of that?'

'In the circumstances I agree with you – about as unpleasant as our joker could have chosen. Tell me, Brian, what are you going to do?'

'Why, nothing of course.'

'You implied you were beginning to have some qualms as to whether Sir John's ghost was really haunting you.'

'Well, I admit that for a moment at the theatre this morning . . . but it's all nonsense of course. The person who's been clever enough to create all these incidents wouldn't be put off by a spot of forgery,' said Barrington, and Antony was relieved to see that he looked now much more like himself. The trite phrase, 'A trouble shared is a trouble halved,' passed fleetingly through his mind.

'Well it makes me wonder too, but not about supernatural intervention,' he said. 'It ties in rather neatly with what I wanted to talk to you about. Did Meg happen to tell you that Miss Hartley had been to see us on Sunday night?'

'Not a word. What on earth did Stella want to see you for?'

'She thinks that dramatically the joker's next move is bound to be a real attack on Sir Benjamin Oldfellow, probably when he's hiding behind the screen, so that when he staggers on to the stage he'll die in good earnest. I know you were shaken for a moment this morning, Brian, but now you've had time to think about it you don't believe in Sir John's ghost any more than I do. All the same, Mr Benbow also saw the dramatic possibilities of Stella's idea, and who knows who else she may have talked to about it. I do think at the very least you ought to take care.'

Oddly enough, what might have been taken as a threat seemed to restore Brian Barrington to his usual frame of mind. 'When is this tragic event supposed to take place?' he asked.

'At the dress rehearsal perhaps, or even on the first night,' said Maitland. 'Mr Benbow thought Chester Cartwright and Jeremy Skelton were more likely to be the victims if some deadly sort of violence is resorted to, but he quite saw that the attack on you might come first.'

'Yes, but I think he's a fan of Sir John's ghost too,' said Barrington, half amused. 'And now he's nothing else to think of.

. . . you'd something else in mind when you mentioned this to me, didn't you, Antony?'

'Yes, I had,' Antony admitted. 'I asked Miss Hartley why she dislikes you so much. First she said it was the other way round, you disliked her. But afterwards she admitted that it was mutual.'

'Are you implying that she herself might attack me?'

'She wouldn't be on stage while you were behind the screen, but if it occurred to her to do so and she wanted to create an alibi she has at least two members of the cast who are devoted to her.'

Barrington laughed then, sounding genuinely amused. 'If you can see poor Mary Russell rushing around with a rapier,' he said, 'I think you're letting your imagination run away with you just as much as the ghost hunters.'

'I know it sounds ridiculous, but Mary *is* jealous, you must admit that, and she might be only too willing to do almost anything to reinstate herself in Stella's good graces. Anyway, I was really thinking more of Mark Kenilworth. I've been told he's ambitious and just acting the part of the lovesick swain, but the fact remains that as far as appearances go, he's quite under Stella's spell and might be willing to accept any suggestion from her, however wild.'

'Oh, no, no. You're misreading these people altogether. Nobody's going to hurt me,' said Barrington confidently.

'Mr Benbow has a broken leg, and Mr Brome was nearly gassed –'

'Or might have been blown up,' said Brian, smiling.

'It isn't really amusing,' said Antony, too intent on his list of horrors to feel relieved that his companion seemed to be himself again. 'And it's only a matter of luck that nobody was hurt when that block of wood fell from the flies. I think you should take the possibility seriously, Brian, I really do.'

'Very well then, I'll keep a sharp look out. Meanwhile,' – he turned to signal to the waiter – 'let's have another drink before we order. Meg did tell me you and her husband want to attend the dress rehearsal. Is what you've been telling me the reason? Do you mean to stand guard over me backstage?'

'I don't think that would do the slightest good. If anyone has any lethal intentions they'd just take another opportunity. Meg says the rehearsals with you as Sir Benjamin are going marvellously, but when we visited Matthew Benbow she was careful to tell him you didn't mean to make any changes in his interpretation.'

'I couldn't better his playing of the part,' said Barrington generously. 'I only hope I can do as well.'

'Meg also said – but that wasn't while we were at the hospital – that it'll be better when you're in make-up,' said Antony, 'because you can't make the point that Sir John Cartwright intended, looking as young as you do.'

Brian grinned at him. 'What's all this leading up to?' he asked.

'I wasn't inventing any of that,' Maitland protested. 'But I do wish you'd tell me, Brian, aren't you happy to be back . . . is "on the boards" the right expression?'

'It'll do as well as another,' said Barrington. 'It's an odd thing but I'm very happy about it, though I wish it had happened any other way. Matthew is the best of good fellows, you know. I could also wish that Stella wasn't on stage for so much of the first act, but that can't be helped.'

'You chose her for the part of Lucy Simpering,' Antony pointed out.

'So I did, at the instigation of one of our backers, and in one way I've regretted it ever since, and in another I've been congratulating myself because she's ideal for the part. However, I die gracefully at the end of the first act – and I think I can promise you that this will be a piece of consummate acting, as they say, and not the real thing – and after that I'll be out of everybody's way.'

'Are all the costumes in order again now?'

'Miss Miggs – as Meg will insist on calling the poor woman – has been working night and day, and luckily the wigs hadn't been delivered when that particular episode took place. I got hold of some members of the Corps of Commissionaires to supplement the night watchman's activities, so everything should be all right on that score. I'd meant to recruit some of the stage-hands, but this seemed a better idea.'

'Yet that note found its way on to the stage, since yesterday presumably.'

'No difficulty about that. We were all milling about for a while before we got down to rehearsing, and the note wasn't found until Lucy Simpering came to call on her friend Becky and was just about to sit down.'

'I see. So the costumes are ready and all the scenery presumably in place.'

'Yes, that was clever of Jeremy, giving us all the action in Lady Oldfellow's drawing room. You wouldn't believe the saving in costs. You'll be there on opening night, won't you, as well as this evening?'

'Certainly I shall, and Jenny and my aunt and uncle, too. We never miss one of Meg's first nights if we can possibly help it, and of course Jeremy is an old friend.'

'The police think he's the joker,' said Barrington unexpectedly. 'At least, they came back a second time after Matthew's accident and asked some rather searching questions about him. Not that I believe it myself; he has a sense of humour or he couldn't write the sort of dialogue he does, but he's far too nice a chap for that sort of thing.'

'Yes, I agree with you, and if it weren't too long a story I'd explain to you who set them on to that,' said Antony. 'I'm afraid it's because he was once a client of mine, and there are certain members of the police force who look rather askance at my activities.'

'That explains it then,' said Barrington, realising immediately that it was lack of inclination rather than lack of time that left the story untold. 'I expect Meg told you that the curtain will go up, all being well, at seven o'clock this evening.'

'Yes, she did. Will the police be in attendance?'

'I shouldn't think so, they seemed to be taking it for granted that we'd finished until the opening, and I didn't bother to disillusion them. Frankly, they're in the way.'

'I suppose they are. Why are dress rehearsals always held in the evening?'

'The atmosphere doesn't seem to be right for it at any other time. Not that it will tell us anything really. We always start out with the idea of timing the performance, and then it drags on until the early hours of the next morning.'

'How do you feel about them yourself, Brian? If you don't mind my asking you,' Antony said.

'I think you mean do I subscribe to the superstitions concerning them,' said Barrington. 'Usually everything goes badly and everyone says "it'll be all right on the night". And generally it is.'

'So I suppose what *you* really like is for everything to be perfect,' said Maitland, thinking it out as he went. 'Is that right?'

'More or less. Though I think I'm a little inconsistent about that,' Barrington admitted. 'You see things never do go right, so it's no good hoping they will. I've just given up thinking about it.'

'Well, I hope this time you'll give it at least some thought,' Antony advised him. But Brian seemed to have had enough of the subject for the moment, and opened one of the menus and thrust it in front of his guest in what could only be called a marked manner.

II

Brian Barrington's mind might or might not be at ease concerning the dress rehearsal, but if indeed it was, Antony thought he must be the only one of the cast to whom this could possibly apply. He put in an hour or two in chambers after lunch, but went back to Kempenfeldt Square early, as Jenny had promised to provide a snack before he left with Roger and Meg for the theatre. Meg certainly was a prey to the jitters, and whether this was because of stage-fright, in which case he knew from experience she would forget all about it as soon as she made her first entrance, or some deeper worry, he couldn't tell. But Roger seemed if anything reassured by the nature of that day's communication and joined his host in doing justice to the repast. Between mouthfuls Maitland told them about his talk with Brian Barrington, as far as it concerned Stella Hartley's warning. 'He's probably right and there's nothing in it,' he assured Meg, 'but at least he'll be on his guard.'

There was nobody in sight when they reached the theatre, except for Chester Cartwright who was prowling up and down the centre aisle. But even if you disregarded his restlessness, which was probably akin to first-night nerves, Maitland was immediately convinced that his premonition had been right . . . everybody else connected with the play was on edge. He knew he was sensitive to atmosphere, but even someone who wasn't couldn't have mistaken this . . . you could have cut it with a knife.

The curtain went up on time, but that was probably the only thing that went according to plan. Hugh Clinton was very much in evidence: it seemed that the furniture had not been arranged to his liking. Barrington too was frequently consulted, so that the action didn't start till nearly seven-thirty, and though the scene between Sir Benjamin and Lady Oldfellow went smoothly it was immediately obvious when Lucy Simpering and her escort arrived that something was radically wrong. 'I thought Meg said the part was a good one for Barrington,' said Roger in a puzzled whisper, on an occasion when the action had stopped and an argument had broken out between the actors. 'It seems to me –'

'I've got a feeling that Stella must have been behaving better at the other rehearsals,' said Antony. 'It seems to me now that she's deliberately spoiling things for him. The same thing Amanda Chillingworth complained of. Sir Benjamin – as far as I could gather from the previous rehearsals I attended when Matthew Benbow was playing the part – is supposed to be comic but a little bit tragic, too. Brian said he wasn't going to change the interpretation, but Miss Hartley is forcing him to play it as outright comedy and that takes away a good deal from the value of the part.'

'That doesn't sound very auspicious,' said Roger, hoping that Jeremy, who was sitting not far off and who seemed to be absorbed in what was happening on stage, hadn't heard the whispered colloquy.

'I'm going to say what I believe the actors would tell us: it'll be all right on the night,' said Antony. But as the actors went back to their appointed places and took up their cues again Maitland was conscious that his companion, no less than the people more nearly concerned with the play, was now a prey to a most uncharacteristic nervousness. For the rest of the first act his attention was divided between Roger and the players, though he had to admit that to anyone else his friend would have seemed his usual unshakeable self.

It was almost ten o'clock when the first act began to draw to its close. Gilbert Bold and Lady Oldfellow were declaring their eternal love for each other, and its hopelessness, at the front of the stage, sufficiently preoccupied with each other not to notice when Sir Benjamin tiptoed ostentatiously across to take his place behind the screen. Glancing past Roger, Antony could see Jeremy Skelton's profile. The writer had made no comment during the entire performance, which must have been a considerable sacrifice for a man of his outgoing temperament. Quite obviously he did not share any qualms the other people in the theatre might be feeling. Chester Cartwright, who had subsided into a stall three rows back, had been equally silent, and Maitland took time to wonder whether either of them had heard of Stella Hartley's theory.

But the scene was proceeding. Lady Oldfellow at length agreed to the assignation her lover had suggested. It was to be a farewell meeting only, but it was obvious from Gilbert Bold's demeanour as he went off-stage that he had no intention of allowing matters to rest there. Bess entered and to a certain extent was taken into her mistress's confidence before going off again, obviously wondering what there was in all this intrigue for her. Becky came forward then, confiding her thoughts to the audience. Virtue it seemed was only skin-deep. And then from behind the screen came a clattering sound which both Antony and Roger, comparing notes later, assumed was the rapier being dropped. Almost immediately – a new touch this, they learned later, since Brian Barrington had taken over the part – the screen itself toppled over leaving the old man exposed to the audience's view. Lady Oldfellow turned with a startled cry and put her hands to her face in a gesture of horrified incredulity. And Sir Benjamin himself, hands and kerchief clasped to his stomach, staggered forward to measure his length at her feet. As he fell one hand was flung out, clutching the lace-edged handkerchief as in a death grip, and it was to be seen that the linen was stained with his life's blood.

As the curtain began to fall Brian Barrington sprang to his feet and Lady Oldfellow, in a surely unrehearsed gesture, flung her arms round his neck in an ecstasy of relief.

III

After the intermission – a nominal one only, in view of the lateness of the hour – things went along much more smoothly, and both Roger and Antony were able to relax. Amanda Chillingworth might have complained earlier at Stella Hartley's methods, but it was obvious that evening that Brian Barrington had been Stella's main target; once the character he was playing was dead there were far fewer interruptions. Even so, it was well past midnight when Jack Bashful was unmasked and the curtain came down for the last time.

Jeremy got to his feet immediately. 'I'm going backstage,' he announced. 'Are you two coming with me?'

'I don't think so,' said Maitland yawning. He consulted Roger with a glance and received a faint nod of agreement. 'The actors will be expecting you to congratulate them, Jeremy, but we'd only be in the way. So will you tell Meg we'll wait for her here?'

'With the greatest of pleasure,' said Jeremy amiably. 'What do you think about it, anyway? Is it or isn't it going to be a smash hit?'

'I see no reason why it shouldn't be,' said Roger cautiously. In view of what had been happening this was reasonable enough, though perhaps not exactly what the playwright had wanted to hear.

Antony grinned at Skelton and said, 'You'd better ask us that tomorrow. The play is fine, and from what I've always heard you can't tell anything from the dress rehearsal.'

'It's that last note that's supposed to be in Sir John's own handwriting that's the trouble,' said Jeremy gloomily. 'But it's getting late – I'd better go and tell them all how marvellous they were. I won't forget to give your message to Meg.' He left them then and made his way to the now familiar door that led backstage. Chester Cartwright, it seemed, had gone ahead of him, at any rate he wasn't to be seen when Antony looked around the empty theatre.

'Do you think . . . I'm worried about Brian, Roger,' he said, turning to his friend.

'I didn't like the way the first act went,' Roger admitted. 'But you've no need to look for a ghost to account for that. The woman's a menace.'

'Yes, I think so too. Do you really think Jeremy didn't notice? But I've been thinking, it's one thing for Stella Hartley to play up at the dress rehearsal when there's nobody looking on but us. It would be quite different for her to wreck things tomorrow deliberately. Don't you think for her own sake she'll play the role as Brian wants her to?'

'Meg says –', but he got no further. At that moment somebody started to scream . . . somebody with a good pair of lungs by the sound of it. The shrill ear-splitting sound seemed to be coming nearer and nearer. Roger was on his feet in an instant. 'That isn't Meg,' he said, 'we'd better go and see if she's all right.' The last word was spoken over his shoulder as he made for the door.

'I expect it's Stella Hartley again,' said Antony following him. 'I suppose the joker's been at it again, but you know the least thing sets her off.'

But he had spoken too hastily: it was Roberta Rowan who was doing the screaming. They reached the backstage area and by the time they came to the corridor out of which the dressing rooms led the whole cast, plus Chester and Jeremy and Meg's dresser, seemed to be assembled. Brian Barrington was shaking Roberta by the shoulders, and Joseph Weatherly was making ineffective gestures – whether to silence her or to stop this minor violence wasn't clear. 'In there,' said Roberta at last, stuttering over the words. Her teeth seemed to be chattering together. 'I went to see Meg, and then I thought I ought to congratulate Stella, too.'

'That's Stella's room!' said Mark Kenilworth. 'Where is she?' he asked looking around him.

'Go and see!' said Roberta, wrenching herself from Brian's grip and flinging herself into Weatherly's arms.

Roger was already elbowing his way through the crowd with Antony at his heels. Even so they were behind Brian Barrington and had to peer over the actor's shoulders into the dressing room. Stella Hartley was sitting at her dressing table, still wearing the sombre robe she had donned out of respect for Sir Benjamin's memory. But it was quite clear, without taking a second look, that she would never look into the mirror again.

Her red head was bowed until it rested among the array of cosmetics that lay on the table in front of her, and from her back protruded the ornate hilt of a dagger.

Friday, 13th February

I

It was five o'clock in the morning when Roger drew up outside the house in Kempenfeldt Square, for once with no difficulty in finding a parking spot. 'I don't suppose you feel any more like sleep than I do,' said Antony, preparing to alight. 'Why don't you both come in with me and we'll rustle up some breakfast. I shall probably die if I don't have a cup of coffee at least, and Jenny's bound to wake up if she hears me moving about in the kitchen.'

'That sounds like a good idea to me,' said Roger, 'if it suits you, Meg.'

'Down to the ground, darling. And we'll be as quiet as mice,' she added to Antony, 'so that neither Uncle Nick nor Vera hears us.'

That seemed on the whole a good idea. Jenny would accept a few words in explanation, knowing well enough that she would receive a more ample one later. But Sir Nicholas's demeanour, if aroused from sleep with the information that the three of them had been if not actually present at least almost on the scene of a murder, defied imagination.

As it happened they'd been allowed to leave the theatre rather earlier than the people more intimately concerned, the local Criminal Investigation Department having decided that Antony and Roger's alibis of being together in the front of the house when the murder took place were good enough in the circumstances, and as Meg's dresser had been in attendance, hers would also pass scrutiny, and it was unlikely that any of them would be able to provide information that might prove useful. But before that there had been an interminable period of waiting in the greenroom with the players, playwright, and Chester Cartwright, while enquiries, presumably, continued elsewhere.

Maitland would dearly have loved to ask questions about where everybody had been at the critical moment, but the presence of a stolid policeman in one corner of the room inhibited him. He was surprised, however, to find that all the others were quite willing to talk, not about the murder, it was true, but about the possibility of the police having finished their investigation in time for them to open the following night as planned. Roberta Rowan was herself again by now. Antony judged she wasn't normally a hysterical person, and though she demurred prettily when Joseph Weatherly pointed out that she knew Lucy Simpering's part perfectly well she gave in without argument when Barrington said briskly, 'Nonsense! Of course you'll take the part.'

Barrington was the first one called to an interview with the police, and Antony privately put down their release to his intervention. He came back to the greenroom saying quite cheerfully, 'You next, Antony, and after that they'd like to see Meg and Roger together.' And then, turning to the others, 'They won't commit themselves as to how soon they'll have finished with the theatre, but we'd better be ready in case we're able to open on time after all. So if Jeremy can arrange a room for us at his hotel to rehearse Roberta a little we'll be all set.'

Maitland's session with the police didn't take long, and Roger and Meg spent even less time with them. Meg reverted to the question of the police enquiries after Jenny had been aroused, reassured, and had come into the kitchen to help with their foraging. 'They can't write this off as an accident,' she said, 'and certainly it wasn't suicide.'

'In a way I think that's why they seemed to take so little interest.'

'That doesn't make sense, darling,' Meg protested.

'I mean because it's a serious matter, and it's going to make the headlines whether we like it or not. They'll be getting in Scotland Yard, you see if I'm not right about that.'

'I expect you are, darling, you know so much about these things,' said Meg sweetly. 'It did strike me – don't you agree with me, Roger? – that the police weren't the only people who didn't really seem to take Stella's murder seriously.'

'If you mean your colleagues,' said Roger, 'they were far more concerned with the possibility of opening on time. And I know that's tradition, but it seems pretty heartless to me. And Jeremy was no better than the rest of them.'

'I don't think he or Chester Cartwright could be expected to feel quite as the others did,' said Meg thoughtfully. 'After all, he'd only known Stella for a few weeks, while some of the others were close to her and all of us at least members of the same profession. What was really queer was that they'd none of them any idea at all that the police investigation would lead anywhere. To the arrest of one of them, perhaps. I can't make it out at all.'

'I think they just aren't prepared yet to face the fact of murder,' said Maitland. 'But as regards one of them coming under suspicion, I'm afraid that point will be brought home to them soon enough. As for me, I'm beginning to get really tired of this joker. He's been running rings around us long enough.'

'Does that mean you've an idea about Stella Hartley's murder, Antony?' asked Jenny hopefully.

'Not exactly, but I think I'll have a chat with Geoffrey Horton in the morning.' (Geoffrey was a solicitor and friend of long standing.)

'That surely means —'

'Nothing at all, love. Nothing I could explain, anyway.' Jenny looked as though she would have liked to ask some further question, but Roger distracted her attention by asking where the bread knife was kept.

'The thing I found really chilling,' said Meg, ignoring Antony's attempt at explanation, 'was Mary Russell's attitude. After all, they were supposed to be such friends. Mark Kenilworth, too. I thought he was really devoted to her, though I know some people were doubtful whether it was genuine. But Mary at least couldn't have had an ulterior motive.'

'Well, there's one thing you can be pretty certain of,' Antony assured her, 'the police will be going pretty thoroughly into everyone's relationship with everyone else. Also into their movements backstage. Some of them besides us must have alibis.'

'Roberta Rowan?' Meg hazarded.

'I can't imagine her sticking a knife into anyone, but strictly speaking she could have done it after she left your room and before she raised the alarm. I'm far from being an expert, but I'm pretty sure Stella Hartley hadn't been long dead.'

'The coffee is ready,' said Jenny with an air of relief. 'And there's one good thing,' she added, 'though of course I'm sorry about poor Stella Hartley, but even you, Meg, will agree with me that the ghost story should have been squashed once and for all. Because we can all see now where the so-called practical jokes were leading.'

165

II

Maitland waited until he was sure that Sir Nicholas and Vera would have finished breakfast before going down to report on the latest developments. 'That meant we didn't get home until about five o'clock,' he concluded. 'I hope we didn't disturb you.'

'Didn't hear a sound,' said Vera, answering for them both. She was quite safe to do so because if anything was certain in this uncertain world it was that she would have already heard if her husband's rest had been broken. 'Did you say Roger and Meg came with you?'

'Yes, but they've gone home now. I let them out myself before joining you. Meg needs some sleep, and Roger wanted to bathe and change before going to the office.' He turned his eyes from her to his uncle. 'What do you think about all this, Uncle Nick?' he asked.

'Were you expecting anything of the sort?' Sir Nicholas asked him.

'No, of course I wasn't. I could see the force of Stella Hartley's argument . . . not that Sir John Cartwright was involved, but about the way the joker's mind might be working. That was assuming it was the production itself that was being got at. If murder was being worked up to all the time I suppose you could say Stella herself was the obvious victim; any number of people might have been irritated beyond bearing by the kind of barbs she was in the habit of throwing about almost indiscriminately.'

'Almost?' asked Vera.

'Well, I think you could say it came naturally to her, but she seemed to have a special hate against Brian Barrington.'

'I gathered from several things you've said that you like the man,' said Sir Nicholas, again in a questioning tone.

'I do. But if you're going to go on to point out that he's the obvious suspect . . . he'd never have done anything to jeopardise the putting on of the play.'

'You told us, however, that the police have not said definitely that tonight's opening may not go forward.'

'No, they haven't, that'll be up to Scotland Yard, if they take over, as I'm pretty sure they will.'

166

'In any event, there is no need, I suppose, for you to be involved any further,' said Sir Nicholas in a thoughtful tone, but Antony, who knew him very well, thought that the words also contained a warning. 'You're coming into chambers, I imagine,' his uncle went on.

'Yes, for all the good it will do. The Chalmers brief wants some work, but I shall probably go to sleep over it.'

But neither of his companions seemed inclined to sympathise over his loss of a night's rest. Vera said only, 'Good thing you're not in court today,' and a few minutes later the two men left the house together.

When Jenny had said earlier that morning that the unpleasant climax to recent events would have put paid to the ghost story once and for all her husband had agreed with her, but time would have proved him wrong. Not so far as he himself was concerned, of course, or even Meg, though he wasn't quite sure about her, but as far as the rest of the players who constituted the cast of *Crabbed Age and Youth* felt about the matter. Maitland's morning coffee had just arrived when Hill announced apologetically over the telephone that a Mr Brian Barrington had arrived and would like to see him. 'Tell him to come in, and see if you can squeeze another cup out of the coffee pot,' Antony suggested.

Willett, bearing the requested refreshment, brought the visitor to Maitland's room himself. 'I hope I'm not disturbing anything important,' said Barrington as soon as he was seated in the least penitential of the chairs and the clerk had left them alone together.

'Nothing that won't wait,' said Maitland, pushing aside the Chalmers papers with something like relief. 'I think perhaps I should have been expecting you,' he added, in the diffident tone that the other man did not yet know him well enough to realise could be assumed at will.

'Nonsense,' said Barrington, in the brisk voice he used when he wanted to encourage his actors to greater efforts. 'You couldn't possibly have known I wanted to see you.'

'No,' agreed Antony doubtfully, thinking as he spoke of his uncle's reaction to the night's events. 'Anyway, what can I do for you?'

Barrington didn't answer that immediately, and even then it was obvious that the play came first in his mind. 'You know I've not been an advocate of the ghost theory,' he said, crossing his legs with an assumption of ease. 'But if the actors were jittery

167

before, they're in a state of near panic now. Except for Meg, of course.'

'I thought she was going to get some rest.'

'She can do that after lunch. I telephoned to tell her we *must* rehearse this morning because the police have agreed to our having the theatre back.'

'In time to open tonight?' asked Maitland incredulously.

'By late this afternoon. But I was saying, about Meg, I gather you've succeeded in convincing her that Stella's death explained everything in quite a natural way.'

'Yes, I think what Jenny said was that at least we could see now where everything has been heading, and naturally I agreed.'

'That's what the police think,' said Barrington rather scornfully. 'Find out who had a motive for killing Stella, and there you are! It isn't as easy as that, at least as far as the rest of them are concerned. And excepting Jeremy, of course, he's too much sense to think there's a murderously inclined ghost hanging around the theatre. Did you see the dagger she was stabbed with?' ·

'Only the handle protruding from her back,' said Antony distastefully. 'She was so obviously dead if you remember –'

'Yes, I remember quite well,' said Brian, who obviously did not relish the recollection. 'You said nothing must be touched and persuaded everyone out of the room. But the police got some expert out of bed to look at it after the doctor had finished. Some fellow from one of the museums. He said it was Elizabethan, so you see there's no earthly reason why Sir John Cartwright couldn't have had it in his possession.'

'We're getting beyond the realms of logic again,' Antony pointed out. 'Wherever he's been in the other world he couldn't possibly have had it with him.'

'The idea is, I think,' Barrington explained, and it was his turn to sound apologetic, 'that he's been wandering the earth all this time prepared to defend his honour.'

'Well, if you want to know what I think,' said Antony, 'and you might try this one on the others as it seems to me rather a good idea, if he'd been really offended by what Jeremy wrote he'd have challenged him to a duel, not played all these silly pranks.'

'Yes, that's a good suggestion, but I don't think any of them will buy it. But that wasn't what I came to see you about, Antony. You once said that it'd be easier if you were taking the case on professionally, and I said it might come to that yet. I spoke more truly than I knew.'

'What on earth do you mean?' He sounded surprised, but inwardly he was pretty sure what was coming.

'I think the police suspect me of having despatched Lucy Simpering out of this world,' said Barrington matter of factly.

'If they do,' said Maitland slowly, 'presumably they have a reason.'

'I'm asking for your help,' said Brian rather crossly.

'Yes, I realise that. I'm sorry if I didn't make myself clear. I can't possibly advise you unless I know the worst that can be said against you.'

This was obviously a new thought to Barrington, and he chewed on it for a moment in silence. 'They think I had a motive,' he said at last. 'And heaven knows, Antony, I loathed the woman but I wouldn't have killed her. There is also Chester Cartwright who saw me going into my dressing room about five minutes before Roberta found Stella and started screaming. The one I'm using, which used to be Matthew's, is next to Stella's, you know.'

'You're not going to tell me you'd been in to talk to her?'

'No, I'd been to the dressing room that used to be Edward Brome's to have a word with Mark. He'd really done extraordinarily well, taking over the part like that and I wanted to tell him so.'

'Did you see anyone else about?'

'No, I didn't even notice Chester as a matter of fact. As for my colleagues, I presume they were all fully occupied getting off their make-up.'

'Had you ever seen the dagger before?'

'No, I hadn't. And if you're going to ask me about fingerprints, I understand it wasn't the sort of design that would take them very easily.'

'I have to ask you again, Brian, what do you want me to do?'

'Keep me from being arrested,' said Barrington promptly. 'I can't afford it at the moment. We haven't an understudy left, and no one else could learn the part of Sir Benjamin in time. Besides . . . have you seen the papers?'

'They couldn't have got the story yet.'

'They could if someone had found an opportunity to phone them. If you recall, we've been trying to keep things hushed up, but they got hold of every one of the previous incidents. In any case it's only a Stop Press.' He spread out the offending journal on Maitland's desk. 'There!' he said, pointing.

It wasn't either of the newspapers that were delivered at

Kempenfeldt Square; one, in fact, that Sir Nicholas would have had some unkind words for, but with the limited space at their disposal they had certainly made the most of Stella Hartley's death and the fact that it had been the culmination of many strange happenings at the Cornmarket Theatre. 'You can imagine what the evening papers will do with it,' said Barrington gloomily. 'Every ghoul in town will be buying a ticket, hoping to see some further mayhem.'

'I thought you people liked publicity.'

'Yes of course, but don't you see this could so easily turn sour? It's all very well,' he added in a complaining tone, 'for the police to say I had a motive for killing Stella. Actually I had a very big financial motive for keeping her alive.'

'You'd better tell me,' said Maitland, 'what they think your motive is. I didn't get the impression after you'd talked to the police last night –'

'I didn't tell them anything that mattered,' said Barrington. He got up and began to pace around the room. 'They called me back later. Some kind friend had been talking, and I don't know that I ought to really blame whoever it was. They're all so full of this ghost theory that I don't think they seriously considered that one of us could get into trouble about Stella's death.'

'You still haven't told me –'

'It isn't a story I'm fond of repeating.' He came to a stop by the desk, looking down at his companion. 'All the same, Antony, I have to tell you I'd just as soon confide in you as in anybody.'

'That's very gratifying, of course,' said Maitland rather dryly, 'but if things are as bad as you fear I'm afraid it won't be able to stop there.'

'No, of course not. It started because Stella hates me,' said Brian abruptly. 'That's a very old story. We lived together for a year once when we were younger, and I was the one who broke up the partnership.'

'As a matter of fact,' Maitland told him, 'that isn't quite a new story to me. Stella told me about it when she came to see me the other night, though she implied that she was the one who ended the affair. She also told me that she'd been married twice since then, so I can't see why whatever passed between you should still rankle.'

'That's because you don't know Stella. She never forgave and she never forgot. It was a long time before our paths crossed again . . . on stage, I mean. In fact, I turned parts down several times because it would have meant playing opposite her. But then there came one that I couldn't resist, a really strong drama. An opportunity, if you like to put it that way, to pull out all the stops. And I thought, just as you said a moment ago, surely there's no need to rake over the ashes of an ancient affair like that. So I accepted, and that was when the trouble began.'

'Stella said that was the last play you acted in until you took over the part of Sir Benjamin the other day.'

'Yes, that's true.'

'You'd better tell me exactly what happened.'

'I remember that you talked to Amanda and Arthur Webb. Did Amanda say anything to you about what acting with Stella was like?'

'Yes, she had quite a lot to say. And I later observed it for myself at the rehearsals.'

'That was clever of you. It isn't too obvious except when you're actually on the stage with her. For one thing she has to be the centre of every scene she takes part in. I'm still talking about her as if she was alive, but the fact that she isn't takes some getting used to. Anyway – this is a little difficult to explain to a layman – the way your cues are given to you decides in part how you say your next lines. Something like the questions in Latin beginning with the word "num" which expect the answer, no.'

'That wouldn't do in a court of law,' said Antony. 'At least, I'd hate to have to explain it to the judge. However, I think I understand what you mean. Her fellow actors couldn't play their parts exactly as they saw them because she was giving them a not-so-gentle shove in another direction all the time.'

'She even tried her tricks on Meg, but when Meg just ignored them she got tired of that and stopped. The others, unfortunately, weren't quite so self-assured.'

'You were telling me about the last time you appeared with her.'

'So I was. I happened to be going through a bad patch myself at that moment, personally I mean, or perhaps I should say emotionally. What I needed was a smashing success to bolster me up again in my own estimation, and what I got was Stella preventing me from playing this highly dramatic role as I saw it and taking every chance she could to undermine my confidence in my own ability. You heard her from the stage the other day – that kind of thing repeated over and over can wear you down, particularly when you're trying to get into the skin of a difficult part. As it happened, the play ran for quite a while although it wasn't a smash hit, and long before it was over I realised that was it for me. I took about a year to think things out, but the theatre is in my blood: I couldn't leave it alone altogether. I was lucky in being given the chance to direct, my earlier successes seem to have been better remembered than the last fiasco, and I've hit it lucky with a number of long runs since then. But quite a lot of people know exactly how I feel about Stella, and why. In fact, I'm surprised Meg never told you.'

'Meg never gossips. But somebody else in the theatre last night knew how things were and told the police?'

'It might have been Mary Russell, but it isn't really fair to say so because I don't *know*.'

Maitland ignored this. 'I still don't see,' he said inconsequently, 'why you hired Stella for this play. I know you told me one of the backers recommended her, but surely you could have got out of it some way.'

'You're quite right, that wasn't the whole truth. I knew I wouldn't be happy until I got back into acting again and this . . . I think it was a sort of exorcism really. I suppose I shouldn't use that word in view of what's been happening and what the others believe. And because that's what Stella pretended she thought I wanted your help for in the first place.'

'But you give the impression of being a pretty self-confident person,' Maitland told him, following his own train of thought.

'That's on the surface, Antony. What I needed was to get my nerve back, to find I didn't care any longer what Stella said about me.'

'Did it work out like that?'

'No, it didn't. I still had that in mind when I took over the part of Sir Benjamin, and the scenes with the others went fine. If it hadn't been for her I could have enjoyed the part . . . I can still if you can keep the police off my back.'

'Was I right in thinking Scotland Yard would be called in?'

'You were. It was they who said we could open tonight.'

'I see. That's something I *can't* understand, but it's beside the point at the moment. You'll need a solicitor, you know. Have you got one?'

'Only a chap who handles contracts and things for me. I'm sure this sort of thing would be quite beyond him.'

'Then I think you'd better talk to Geoffrey Horton, I'll give you his address. He's a good friend of mine, and, as a matter of fact, I was talking to him earlier this morning . . . but that's also beside the point. Have you to go straight back to the rehearsal?'

'No, Jeremy's reading my part and I'm not too worried about Roberta.'

'Then I'll phone Geoffrey and see if he can see you right away.' This was done and he turned from the telephone after a short conversation to say, 'That's fixed. He'll be free in about half an hour, and his office is only a few minutes' walk from here. But before you go, have you seen the Scotland Yard detectives yet?'

'Only one of them, and he hasn't asked me any questions . . . so far. Detective Chief Inspector Conway. Oh . . . there was another chap with him but he didn't say a word so for the moment I'd forgotten his existence.'

'I know Conway,' said Maitland.

'Not an awfully jovial soul, but then you can hardly investigate a murder with a smile on your face, I suppose,' said Brian, with the air of one trying desperately to be fair.

'And it was he who agreed to your opening again tonight?' It was quite obvious Maitland still found this hard to believe.

'Yes, though I had the impression he disapproved of the whole idea.'

'He probably disapproves of theatrical performances on principle, which makes it more of a puzzle than ever.'

'I expect they'll have finished whatever it is they do at the scene of a crime, and in any case he told me Stella's dressing room would be locked,' said Barrington, unwilling to be diverted from the matter that most concerned him. 'But he's promised us access to the Cornmarket by the end of the afternoon and that's none too soon. For one thing Roberta is slimmer than Stella was so the costumes have to be altered, and we have to find her something to wear in the last act. Naturally the police have the costume Stella had on when she was killed.'

'That's good, about your having the theatre back, I mean,' said Maitland. But there was an uneasiness at the back of his mind which he would have found it hard to explain, though it was that which prompted his next remark. 'Do you think, in the midst of all the other things you have to do, you could find time to arrange a seat for Geoffrey for tonight's performance?'

'I can, of course. Does that mean –?'

'I don't know what it means,' said Maitland rather sharply. 'It's just that I think it might be a good idea to – to put him completely in the picture, as it were.'

'It's you I'm relying on,' said Barrington, ignoring this explanation.

'I haven't been exactly helpful so far,' said Antony ruefully. 'I don't see why that should give you much confidence in me.'

For some reason this protest seemed to amuse Brian Barrington. He took his time about replying. 'Before I go to see your friend, have you any other questions you want to ask me?'

'I gather you were all at the theatre most of the night,' Maitland told him. 'There must have been some talk between you and the other actors.'

'Endless talk.'

'Well then, perhaps you can tell me something about alibis, to begin with. We'll go on to theatrical gossip later; I daresay there are any number of people who disliked Stella Hartley as much as you did.'

Brian threw out his hands in a despairing gesture that reminded Antony for the first time during their private conversations that he was, after all, an actor. 'Nobody had an alibi,' he said.

'I can't believe that.'

'I take it, Antony, you're not proposing to handle Stella's death as if it were an isolated incident but are taking all the other things into consideration.'

'I don't see how we can avoid the conclusion that everything was connected.'

'I wish this chap Conway were as reasonable,' Barrington grumbled. 'To him, a murder is a murder.'

'And what about everything else? There are at least two accidents that might have been more serious than they were, even if you leave that falling block of timber out of consideration.'

'You used the word accidents and that's just what he thinks,' said Brian. 'As for the rest, publicity. Anything may be expected of a pack of actors,' he added scornfully.

'I see what you mean. But as far as we're concerned I take it your point is that, if everything is taken together, only one group of people can be suspected, and so they're the only ones whose alibis we should be concerned with.'

'That's exactly what I mean. The entire cast, to begin with, and Chester Cartwright and Jeremy Skelton too, though as they didn't really have many dealings with Stella I don't quite see where a motive would come in.'

'We'll come to motive in a minute. Taking everything together

174

I can vouch for Jeremy during the incident of the loud hailer, but for last night you say nobody had an alibi.'

'Not for the entire time between the curtain falling and Stella being found dead. Except for Meg, of course, whose dresser was with her.'

'That leads me to another point, didn't Stella Hartley have a dresser too?'

'Yes, but unlike Meg she hasn't had the same one for years, my own opinion is they wouldn't stay with her. Anyway for some reason the new one wasn't to come on duty until tonight. Mary had offered any help that might be needed, but she said that after the rehearsal Stella refused her assistance, so she went into one of the empty dressing rooms, which she's been in the habit of using as a sort of retiring room, and just waited there.'

'I see. I imagine the doctors would find it difficult to pin down the time Miss Hartley was stabbed within a minute or two, but the period during which it could have been done wasn't very long. Just tell me in a little more detail –'

'We'd all been on stage except for Roberta and Mary. I was the director at that time, not Sir Benjamin Oldfellow, and all the others, I imagine, were engaged in the same disagreeable task as I was, getting their make-up off. There are only seven characters in the play,' Barrington added unnecessarily, 'and the Cornmarket is a big theatre. We each had a dressing room of our own.'

'What about Roberta Rowan, then?'

'She was going from one room to the other telling us how wonderful she thought we all were. She came to me first of all but stayed only a moment. Then she visited Amanda and Arthur and Mark in quick succession, and spent – as you might imagine – a good deal more time with Joseph. Finally she nerved herself to have a word with Stella – I'm using her own words – and we know what she found.'

'So she was up and down the corridor a good deal, but still she didn't see anything . . . anybody, I mean.'

'No. I think that's odd, don't you?'

'If you mean that it makes me suspicious of Roberta, no, it doesn't. Anyone going to Stella Hartley's dressing room with intent to do murder would be taking more than ordinary precautions. Someone coming from one of the other rooms, say, would hesitate in the doorway before taking the plunge, and if he heard one of the other doors opening naturally he'd wait until Roberta was out of the way. The same would apply to someone

175

standing at one end of the corridor, watching for his opportunity.'

'So it would. I know if I'd been dodging around with a dagger I'd have been damned careful,' said Barrington with feeling. 'It may be significant that each member of the cast, including myself, knew that Roberta was wandering about and could take his precautions accordingly. We're both using "he" all the time,' he added. 'Do you think one of the women could have brought herself to do . . . that?'

'It sounds like a man's crime, but I say that with reservations,' Maitland told him. 'We all know what can be done if a person is driven far enough. To go back to the men, there's one you haven't mentioned . . . Edward Brome.'

'If I didn't think he was probably the last person in the world to commit murder, I'd think it suspicious the way he's haunted the theatre ever since he refused to take any further part in the play. He was standing watching in the wings through the entire rehearsal, just behind Tommy, the prompter. And in the intermission of the action they were talking together. Tommy packed up and went the moment his job was over and I don't blame him about that. Edward says he just stood where he was, thinking about the differences between his performance and the one Mark was giving in the same part. He said he was trying to decide which interpretation was the better, but I can't quite believe that. Any actor would be quite certain his own way was best.'

'You say you can't believe in Brome being a murderer, but can you honestly say you can believe such a thing about any of the people you know?'

'I suppose not. You sound as if that question had some significance,' said Barrington.

'Only to remind you that Stella Hartley is dead, and it's as certain as anything can be that someone you know killed her. I can see you don't like the reminder,' he added as Brian grimaced, 'but it will be as well to bear it in mind . . . don't you think?'

'I suppose you're right. You're right too that I don't find it a pleasant thought.'

'Let's go back to the alibis, then. We're left with the two outsiders, Jeremy Skelton and Chester Cartwright, by which I only mean the two men you've categorised as being the least likely,' said Antony. 'Unless . . . was Hugh Clinton about? I know from our point of view we didn't consider him because he has an alibi for one of the other incidents, but Conway may be

176

thinking about him.'

'I don't think he is. Hugh left with Tommy after he'd seen the stage-hands off the premises. And the lady who Meg has taught us all to call Miss Miggs had left immediately after she saw to the change of costumes for the second act.'

'Chester Cartwright, then?'

'Didn't you see him leave the auditorium?'

'No, he wasn't sitting near us. If he went before the play ended all my attention was on the stage so I wouldn't have seen him, and Roger didn't say anything about it when we talked it over later. And afterwards . . . Roger and I were just sitting waiting for Meg, you know, and I think if he'd gone backstage then we'd have seen him.'

'Well, he must have passed quite near Edward and Tommy, but if it was before the play ended, as you seem to think it must have been, they wouldn't have noticed him either.'

'He didn't tell you exactly what time he went backstage?'

'Now I come to think of it, it was while he was with the police that we were talking about alibis. When he came back Arthur asked him where he'd been before Roberta's scream. I thought it was pretty tactless myself, it's one thing to have a general discussion about a thing like that and quite another to ask a direct question. But I think Arthur had got right into the skin of the part of Richard Twells and was seeing himself as a detective by that time. Anyway Chester took it in good part, and said he'd come back to congratulate us all but had got involved with Hugh Clinton and his crew, telling them what a good job they'd done. Hugh had long gone by that time so we couldn't confirm it, but I expect it's true enough.'

'I should think so too. Nobody would tell a lie that could be as easily disproved as that one. Did he tell you he'd seen you, Brian?'

'No, he didn't mention it. It wasn't until I was called back by the police that I knew about it and that it was Chester who'd seen me. But I expect it was just in answer to a question and he never gave it a second thought, or realised that it had made the detectives think twice about me. And then, of course, there was Conway's manner this morning; between that and the questioning last night I admit I got nervous.'

'We'll hope you're wrong about that,' said Antony trusting that his tone didn't reveal his own disquiet. 'To go back to Cartwright then, the only question is what he was doing during those last five minutes after he saw you.'

'Oh, he told us that. He said he realised we'd all be busy getting make-up off and probably would rather talk to him when that was done. So he popped into one of the empty dressing rooms – there are several, you know – and used the lavatory there. He only came out when he heard Roberta's scream.'

'That only leaves Jeremy Skelton.'

'He's a friend of yours,' Barrington objected, 'and besides, you've given him an alibi for one of the earlier episodes. But I suppose,' he went on after a moment's pause, 'you wouldn't dare mention either of those things after the set down you just gave me about someone I knew having killed Stella.'

'That's right,' said Maitland smiling back at him. 'That's something you can remember if ever you're called upon to play a barrister. The last thing they want to hear is some well-meaning soul saying, "he wouldn't do a thing like that".'

'I'll remember,' Brian promised. 'But I hope –' He broke off there and added quietly, 'No, I don't want to embarrass you.'

'You hope I may make an exception in your case,' said Maitland. 'If it helps at all I'm as much inclined as the next person to let my own likes and dislikes run away with me.' He hoped the actor was satisfied with this rather equivocal statement. 'The trouble is . . . oh, well, we'll come to that in a moment. In the meantime, I know Jeremy went backstage as soon as the play was over, but I don't know what he did then.'

'Yes, I suppose we must complete the picture. He says Tommy was just leaving as he went by and they said good night to each other but Edward seemed to be in a brown study. So he didn't disturb him but went to the backstage entrance that's hidden by the screen. There's a chair there, you know, so that I don't get weary standing all the time while Meg and Joseph have that rather long scene together. And Jeremy, believe it or not, sat down there calmly and began to make a few notes of alterations he'd like to make. He told me all about this when we were together in the greenroom long before we got on to the subject of alibis. There were things he wasn't satisfied with in some of the dialogue, things he thought he could improve, but he realised of course that they'd cause us a bit of trouble at this late date. Anyway, he sat there working away until he heard the screaming, and then he joined the rest of us.'

'It's just the sort of thing I could imagine him doing,' said Maitland. 'Quite frankly, though, I should think it would sound a

178

pretty suspicious story to the police.' He was thinking of his talk with Sykes, but there was no need to go into that.

'Ah, but nobody saw *him* in the corridor outside the dressing rooms,' said Brian.

'Chester Cartwright could just as easily have gone to Stella's dressing room after you went back to your own room,' Antony pointed out.

'In that case, I think the argument will be that he wouldn't have said a word about being anywhere near there.'

'Well, if he was indeed tucked away safely out of sight, there was nothing to stop anyone else doing so.'

'And nothing to show they did. Besides, there's this motive business, that's what they're going to get on me,' said Barrington gloomily.

'Perhaps, perhaps not,' said Antony. 'In fact –'

'You don't think they have a case against me?' asked Brian eagerly.

'I think it could be made to sound pretty trivial in court,' said Maitland slowly. 'On the other hand, prosecuting counsel would have his say too, and from what you tell me, he'd have plenty of witnesses to call on. But as it stands at present, unless something else comes to light . . . there's the problem of the dagger, for instance.'

'I've never owned anything of the sort, and it certainly wasn't one of the props. You don't think I need worry?' he asked again.

'I didn't quite say that.' Antony was not too happy in the role of the messenger with bad news. 'I think if they reach a deadlock, or feel they've reached one, they may well put what they've got up to the Director of Public Prosecutions. It would depend on who dealt with the matter there really, but they've been known to bring cases on pretty slim evidence, and here they have opportunity as well as motive.'

'If they do that the play is sunk with all hands,' said Barrington despairingly.

'Wait a bit, Brian. I think you should be thinking more of yourself at this juncture. If they do bring a case, even on what I think is pretty flimsy evidence, juries have been known to be wrong. That's why I want you to see Geoffrey.'

'I see what you mean, but you won't let it come to an arrest, will you?' Barrington said confidently.

'Don't be too sure I can do anything,' Maitland warned him. 'In the meantime, have you any ideas about motive?'

'Leaving my own feelings aside, as you say I must do,' said Barrington, 'I'm inclined to think it must have been one of the cast. That is if all the things that have been happening are tied together, and I think we're agreed about that.'

'Yes we are, but spell it out for me,' Antony urged. 'Why it should have been one of the actors, I mean.'

'Because there's been a clear attempt to play upon their superstitions and their beliefs in possible supernatural intervention,' said Barrington. 'Nobody outside the profession could possibly think that would work.'

'You mean that somebody thought that even Stella Hartley's death by murder could be put down to the ghost?'

'Well, that's what they're saying now,' said Barrington. 'I told you that.'

'But nobody could think the police would buy it. Let's do the two outsiders first: Jeremy and Mr Cartwright. From the prosecution point of view now, leaving the earlier episodes aside.'

'What do you want to know?'

'Jeremy has been there most of the time while the rehearsals have been going on. I take it, though, that he didn't have any occasion to cross swords with Stella.'

'There were a few arguments in the early days. She can be pretty fussy when she wants, as I've already conveyed to you. Some of the lines had to be changed, and though this was reasonable and happens all the time he may have thought she was picking on him deliberately. He's only been involved in one theatrical production before this, after all, but even so would that constitute a motive for murder?'

'I think we may be going to have to concede something that seems to us equally feeble,' said Maitland. 'Now Jeremy has a rather strong sense of humour but not, I think, a cruel one. I could imagine him pulling a few harmless publicity stunts, but not poisoning a black cat, for instance. And certainly not arranging the accidents that befell Matthew Benbow and Edward Brome.'

'You say I mustn't acquit anyone at this stage, but why are we bothering particularly about Jeremy?' said Brian rather impatiently. 'Particularly as you can give him an alibi yourself for –'

'The police are concentrating on the murder,' Antony reminded him, 'and we're looking at it from their point of view.'

'But you just brought in the joker's activities yourself.'

'Yes, because I've good reasons to think the police may suspect that Jeremy was responsible for those, and quite frankly I don't want him to be accused of murder any more than I want the same thing to happen to you.'

'They say lightning doesn't strike in the same place twice,' said Barrington, obviously curious but concealing it as well as he could.

'So they do. Let's go on to Chester Cartwright, then.'

'Some rehearsals he attended, some he didn't. He's terribly wrapped up in the play, you know, and in his discovery. I can't see him doing anything to wreck it, and even leaving the other things aside, Stella's murder may well do that.'

'So that brings us back to the acting fraternity, and we'll include Edward Brome, Mary Russell and Roberta. Take them one at a time, Brian, and tell me what you can about their relationships with Stella.'

'All right,' said Barrington, after which there was rather a long silence. 'Characters in their order of appearance,' he said then. 'You know what I thought of her already.'

'Next, if I remember rightly, would be Meg, who is out of it. I did think at one time Stella Hartley herself might have been doing, or arranging to have done, all these things to spite you,' said Antony. 'But that's obviously out of the question now, and as Roberta Rowan is taking her part shall we go on to her?'

'Roberta's a nice little thing and far less conceited than most actors are,' said Brian, with a deprecating look as though to show that the criticism was partly self directed. 'I saw her in one or two of those experimental things and it was obvious she could act and equally obvious she could maintain the pace necessary for restoration comedy. I thought the job as understudy would be good experience for her, though of course I never foresaw she'd get the chance she'll be getting this evening.'

'How did she get on with Stella?'

'I think she tried very hard, but when she realised Stella's hostility, she effaced herself as much as possible. I think myself,' said Barrington, frowning over the thought, 'it was because Roberta looked so very young, which she is, of course. Stella can still manage that – I should say could – on stage, but she was no spring chicken and she knew it.'

'This hostility you speak of –'

'Just the usual thing, the kind of remark Stella used to delight in, cutting a person down to size is how she put it.'

'We have to consider the possibility that Roberta coveted one of the roles she was understudying for herself, and Lucy Simpering, I suppose, would be the more important of the two.'

'Of course she did, that would be only reasonable. But you're forgetting about all the other things that have been happening, Antony.'

'No, I'm not. It was obvious from the first that Stella was by far the most superstitious of all your crew. Roberta might have thought she could play on that and never have contemplated anything really drastic . . . not at the beginning.'

'If you want to know what I think –' Barrington began.

'That's exactly what I do want,' Maitland reminded him.

'Well then, I think Joseph Weatherly resented all these things on Roberta's behalf far more than she did herself. He's very much in love with her, in a completely self-effacing sort of way that isn't too common among members of our profession. There could have been some added resentment on his part because Stella so obviously would have liked Mark Kenilworth to be playing one of the male parts instead of just understudying. But I wouldn't like you to think that any of these people are guilty,' he concluded rather defiantly.

'You're being illogical again,' said Antony. '*Somebody* killed her.'

'Yes, I know, but I don't like to think about it. Not so much the matter of her death, if I must be honest, but the fact that someone I know and like – and that applies to the whole cast – must have done it.'

'Don't dwell on it for the moment,' Maitland urged him. 'You've got out of order, you know. As far as I remember it Joseph Weatherly is the last of the cast to appear.'

'You got out of order when you started talking about Stella,' Barrington retorted. 'Anyway, the cast isn't so large that there's any difficulty in remembering the whole lot of them. We may as well take Amanda and Arthur Webb together as they're husband and wife. An unfashionably devoted couple too.'

'I've heard Amanda complaining about Stella's scene-stealing propensities,' said Maitland. 'She seems to think this play gives her the opportunity to make a name for herself, which perhaps, because of Stella, might not be realised.'

'That's true enough. And again we have to say that motive might apply to Arthur too. She may be ambitious, but he's even more ambitious on her behalf. I don't think – and I may be wrong again – that he regards her with quite the selfless devotion that

Joseph lavishes on Roberta, but they're a pretty united couple just the same. And again there have been some cutting remarks from Stella about his performance that either of them might have resented. This isn't getting us very far, is it?'

Antony ignored that. 'Tell me about Mary Russell,' he invited. 'She lived with Stella Hartley as I understand it, and was her friend.'

'Yes, but she didn't like Stella's growing intimacy with Mark,' said Barrington. 'And now I come to think of it, she has about the best motive I could muster among the actors. She's never married, you know, and she's been devoted to Stella for years, positively jumped at the chance of living with her from all I hear. If Stella had been thinking of marrying again, or even of forming a relationship with Mark, I don't think either of them would have contemplated a *ménage à trois*.'

'You don't like Mary Russell, do you?'

'As a matter of fact, I do, in her own way. You keep on reminding me,' said Brian rather sulkily, 'that someone must have done it. I'm just trying to be helpful.'

'Your remarks are noted. Taking all things together, though, everything that's been happening, I don't think a woman would be my first choice.'

'Nor mine, but everyone suffered from Stella in one way or another and Mary seems to me to have a more valid motive than all Stella's pinpricks put together.'

'I have to remind you, Brian –'

'Yes, I know, I was pretty sensitive about them myself. All the same . . . that covers everybody doesn't it, except Mark Kenilworth?'

'And Edward Brome. As you pointed out he's been hanging around without apparent reason.'

'If you want to know what I think about Edward,' said Brian quite firmly, 'he was terrified of what happened but he really didn't want to give up the part. He was trying to nerve himself to tell me that he'd like to take it over again.'

'In that case, I'd rather have expected Mark to have murdered Edward,' said Antony, trying to speak lightly. 'But seriously, Brian, did he have a motive too?'

'In his own way he was devoted to Stella. Somehow any remarks she made about him were like water off a duck's back. I think he resented her growing friendship – growing intimacy, whatever you like to call it – with Mark Kenilworth just as much as Mary did.'

'Now you do surprise me,' said Antony seriously. 'That's something that never struck me. What about Mark? Was he in love with her, or in the course of falling in love with her, or was it all an act because he thought she might help him further his career?'

'I know something of his background,' said Barrington, 'though I never knew him personally until rehearsals started. He's been playing in the provinces and made a small name for himself, but he jumped at the chance of coming to the West End even as an understudy, and of course, as we were running on a tight budget and only using one for all the men there was a good chance he might appear on stage, at least occasionally, if the play ran for any time at all. I think he's ambitious, but that goes for all of us. Nobody would put up with an actor's life if he weren't. And until last night I'd have said he was also genuinely devoted to Stella, but when we were talking together – didn't you notice even before you left? – he seemed much more concerned that the play would go on as scheduled than about the fact that she was dead.'

'If he was play-acting – about being in love, I mean – and she was growing deadly serious,' said Maitland, thinking it out as he went on, 'might that not have given him a motive? The only way of getting out of her clutches?'

'That would be true enough if her death were the only thing that had happened,' Barrington reminded him.

'Yes, I know what you mean, but it might have been an afterthought. Supposing he was trying to frighten somebody out of the cast, as Edward Brome was frightened, and then later it occurred to him to make use of the general belief in Sir John Cartwright's ghost to get rid of a woman who had become a succubus.'

'Well, it's ingenious, of course. Oh, lord, Antony,' said Brian Barrington ruefully, 'I can't believe it of any one of them.'

'You'd better leave me to worry about that,' said Antony. 'And Geoffrey, of course. Which reminds me, it's about time you were getting round to his place.'

'I suppose so,' said Barrington resignedly, 'though there doesn't seem to be much point – you've practically wrung me dry of information.'

'Well, I'm afraid you'll find that Geoffrey will want the bare facts at least of what's been happening all over again,' Antony told him.

'But why? I mean, it's your help I want, not his.'

'These things have to be dealt with in form. Besides, you'll find the police will think it much more natural if they do want to talk to you again if you call on Geoffrey to hold your hand rather than on me.'

'But —'

'Don't borrow trouble, Brian. What time does the curtain go up?'

'Seven-thirty on the first night.'

'I was wondering whether I could get a word with all these people we've been talking about.'

'Not before they go on,' said Barrington quickly. 'There are a thousand things to see to and I don't want them upset.'

'No, I understand that. Afterwards, perhaps?'

'We'll be having a rather sober party in the greenroom. Mary said it would be dishonouring Stella's memory for us all to appear in a public place, but I thought Roberta deserved a welcome to the cast, so we compromised on that. Why don't you come, and bring Mrs Maitland too, if you like. Roger will be coming with Meg.'

'Not the press? I could hardly ask my questions with them around.'

'Not the press,' agreed Brian unsmiling.

'All right, I'll come, though I can't answer for Jenny. She may go home with Uncle Nick and Vera. It's a good suggestion of yours, though, it may help to give me an idea.'

Brian Barrington was on his feet. 'I've got the feeling, for all your denials, Antony, that you've got an idea already,' he said. 'And if you have one I wish to goodness you'd pass it on to Conway. I don't want him standing in the wings with a warrant when I come off tonight.'

III

No sooner had Barrington gone, leaving a cold cup of coffee behind him, than the phone on Antony's desk rang again. 'Detective Chief Inspector Conway to see you, Mr Maitland,' Hill announced. 'He's been waiting for nearly half an hour,' he added ominously.

Antony had realised for some time that this was inevitable, and greeted the news with mixed feelings. The detective was not one of his favourite people, but on the other hand he might very well succeed in obtaining more information than he gave. 'You'd better send him in,' he said, and went to the door of his office to open it in an insincere parade of welcome.

Conway was a sharp featured man with an acid tongue and little if any sense of humour. He was accompanied by another plain-clothes detective, unknown to Maitland, whom he introduced as Detective Sergeant Porterhouse. Conway's manner was stiff but correct, and he waited until they were all seated again before saying rather abruptly, 'I came to ask you some questions, Mr Maitland, but I see you've already acquired a client for yourself in this affair of Stella Hartley's murder.'

'I gather you saw Mr Barrington as he left,' said Antony. 'I think I may say he's a friend of mine, Chief Inspector, and unless the position is very different from what I understand it to be there's no question yet of his needing representation by counsel.'

'Are you denying that he was consulting you?'

'No, why should I? What happened last night was naturally shocking to Miss Hartley's colleagues, and I think you'll agree bewildering to a layman. But I believe you had some questions for me.'

'I certainly have! Would it be too much to ask you to go back to the beginning and tell me why you were in the theatre last night?'

If I tell you, will you believe me? Antony wondered. He paused long enough to note that Conway's never-too-certain temper was beginning to rise. 'I was ghost hunting,' he said.

'I've already heard enough about that damned ghost from the cast of the play,' said Conway. So far as Maitland could remember that was the first time he had ever heard the detective come even within a hair's breadth of swearing. 'Don't tell me you believe in that fairy story.'

Maitland couldn't resist it. 'Surely you know, Chief Inspector,' he said earnestly, 'that there are some very well attested instances –'

'Which have nothing to do with the present matter,' said Conway in a dampening tone.

'When did you get a chance to talk to the theatre people anyway?'

'They were rehearsing at Mr Skelton's hotel. I was round there myself first thing,' Conway told him, and then looked as if he regretted having provided even so much information.

'In that case you have no need to hear the story from me,' Antony pointed out.

'Mr Maitland, you know perfectly well I have to get a statement from you.'

'And you want me to go back to the beginning,' said Antony slowly. 'The beginning, I suppose, was when Mr Chester Cartwright approached Jeremy Skelton, asking him to write a play based on an outline he had discovered in the handwriting of Sir John Cartwright, and I first heard of that from Mrs Farrell ... Margaret Hamilton. I'm sure you already knew Sir John Cartwright's name, but if by any chance you aren't familiar with it already, Meg would be able to fill you in about him much better than I can.'

'She did,' said Conway. This time his smile had a reminiscent quality that Antony found less offensive than his usual manner.

'Then you know all about him, and won't want to hear that part of the story again. Meg naturally has been present at all the rehearsals, and I myself have attended a number of them.'

'I think, however, that there was a special reason for that.'

'Yes, there was. Right from the beginning queer things have been happening in the theatre.'

'Tell me about them.'

'It started at the party Mr Skelton gave before the rehearsals began. That had a publicity angle, the party, I mean, and the press was there in the person of the drama critics of four of the Sunday papers.'

'That must have pleased you,' said Conway in a thoughtful tone.

'It didn't, but except for one small brush I managed to avoid them pretty well. I think you probably know that theatrical people have a reputation for being superstitious.'

'Yes, I've heard that, but didn't know till this morning how true it is.'

'I expect they all talked at once,' said Antony sympathetically, 'but Brian Barrington has a different angle. He takes omens as being lucky for him if they are reversed. That's why he insisted on Friday the thirteenth for the opening, and on Jeremy holding his party on a Friday. Anyway, before it was over this black cat walked in. Stella Hartley was cooing over it, thinking, of course, that it was bringing good luck, and it died in her arms. There was a fuss about that, I can tell you. Brian Barrington saved the day by saying that for him the episode portended good luck – a live

187

black cat would have been the worst thing imaginable, and as he was so intimately concerned with the production what was good for him was good for the rest of them, too.'

'And what did you conclude from all that?'

'I admit the first thing that crossed my mind was that it might be part of the publicity, but I dismissed that idea when the poor thing died. It was much more likely that it was a stray that had wandered in and its time had come. The party was at Mr Skelton's hotel, as I expect he told you, and he made enquiries among all the staff. Nobody had seen the cat arrive, nobody knew how it had got into the room even, and I don't know what happened to the corpse. It was only very much later that I began to think that it had been poisoned, and constituted the first shot in the campaign that started almost as soon as the rehearsals did.'

'As you say, too late to worry about that now,' Conway agreed philosophically. 'In any case, who opened the door to let it in at that particular moment? I understand all the people who might possibly have had a motive were in the room at the time.'

'A waiter, I imagine, who had been bribed to introduce it into the room just when the joker thought the poison was ready to work. I daresay you could find out –'

'Really, Mr Maitland, I've no intention of wasting my time in such a way,' said Conway, outraged. 'What happened next?' he added in a more conciliatory tone.

'You must have heard all this from Meg, and I only got it at second hand from her. The first part anyway.'

'All the same –' Conway paused there, obviously waiting for him to continue, and went on when he didn't reply immediately, 'I know you're a friend of the Farrells, but I want to understand exactly how you came to be mixed up in what was happening.'

'All right, if you insist.' He thought for a moment. 'The second thing – always supposing the cat really was the first – was some writing in lipstick on Meg's mirror that said *This is no play of mine.* I think, but I'm not sure, that started the cast talking straight away about ghosts. Can't I interest you in Sir John Cartwright's ghost, Chief Inspector?'

'No, Mr Maitland, you can *not*, but I should be interested in the reactions of all these people.'

'Well, so far as I know them I'll come to them later. The next thing wasn't particularly sinister, rather a tiresome practical joke. Somebody substituted flour for Stella's face powder, she got it all over her face before she noticed it, I gather, and wasn't a bit pleased.'

'Did it occur to you at this point that a dead set was being made at Miss Hartley?'

'I thought about it naturally enough – though you must remember no one could have known she'd have called the cat to her – and came to the conclusion that this particular joke had been aimed at her because she was by far the most superstitious one of all of them and would spread alarm and despondency most effectively. The next thing was pretty general, anyway, . . . a single magpie flew into the theatre. That was a pretty queer thing to happen, you must admit. And when next day a quotation from *Macbeth* appeared, done in spray paint on the wall of the greenroom, the demoralisation was complete. Only part of the quotation was given, and I can't remember that accurately, but I bet any of the actors could have given you the whole thing.'

'Mr Weatherly did; the Sergeant has it written down in his notebook,' Conway agreed. 'The Scottish play, they all seemed to call it. And all this you heard at second hand?'

'That's what I told you. But it was at that point that Mr Barrington thought it would be a good idea if I attended a rehearsal or two to see if I could come to some conclusion about what was happening. I've a suspicion Meg was at the back of that idea. Barrington didn't believe in the ghost himself and as he is superstitious backwards none of the things that had happened worried him particularly, except that the evidence of ill-will on somebody's part was disturbing, but he was worried about the effect on his cast. I must stress, Chief Inspector, that I went along purely as a matter of friendship. I didn't know him well but I liked what I'd seen of him, and Meg – who knew him much better – liked him, too. I've a great respect for her judgement.'

'I'll remember that,' said Conway, with the air of one making a concession. 'So you went to the theatre?'

'Yes, the next day.'

'I think, Mr Maitland, that means you had some theory about all this.'

'Certainly I had. I thought the jokes were purely a matter of publicity, but from that it seemed to follow that one of the people with most at stake in the play's success was perpetrating them.'

'And who would those people be?'

'Well, the backers of the play, of course, but they had no access to the theatre and wouldn't have known their way around. One of the people most nearly concerned was Mr Barrington himself,

189

whom I dismissed from consideration because he'd have known quite well the effect these events would have on his cast and the likelihood of their falling to pieces in consequence. There was also Jeremy Skelton –'

'Another old friend of yours,' said Conway pensively.

'Certainly, Chief Inspector, I've known him a long time,' said Antony rather sharply. 'And at that stage I did dwell on him for a moment, because there's no denying, he *has* a sense of humour. But it isn't a distorted one and I didn't think he could have been responsible. To put it more clearly, he hasn't a spiteful bone in his body. The remaining person was Mr Chester Cartwright, and there I thought I had something. The other two men have established reputations; he stood to gain more than either of them in prestige from the play's success and was most in need of the financial gain it might bring him. Unfortunately, the next thing that happened convinced me that I'd been wrong. A block of wood fell from the flies on to the stage. It didn't hurt anybody, but there's no denying that someone might have been badly injured or even killed by it. It seemed quite evident to me then that the object was to wreck the play itself, which would have been detrimental to any of the three men I've mentioned.'

Conway gave him rather a hard look. 'But you didn't suggest that the police should be called in?'

'I did, as a matter of fact, but Mr Barrington said that would be the wrong kind of publicity. And if you think a moment you'll see he was right, Chief Inspector, when he added that they'd put it down as an accident, and the rest of the things as practical jokes, which is exactly what happened later when Edward Brome was hurt.'

'And what do you put them down to, Mr Maitland?'

'I think everything was connected, even Stella Hartley's murder.'

'Now there I can't agree with you.'

'In that case I don't see why you want to hear the rest of this saga.'

'Because if the matter comes to trial all this will certainly be brought out by the defence. And if you think it's relevant, Mr Maitland, I don't see why you should object to telling me. Perhaps you can convert me to your point of view.'

Antony laughed. 'I consider that very unlikely,' he said. 'But I never said I minded going over the various incidents. The next thing was a hollow voice echoing through the theatre. Another

190

Shakespearean quotation, though not from *Macbeth* this time. However, it did have some ominous qualities. Have you got a note of that one, too?'

'Sergeant Porterhouse has.'

'It was quite impossible to tell where the voice was coming from. Afterwards we searched the theatre and Barrington found a loud hailer at the back of the dress circle. But would you believe it, even that didn't convince the rest of them that a ghost wasn't involved? I think it was Stella Hartley who said something about Sir John's having to work with what came to hand. No, that was later. *Then* she said Barrington had put the loud hailer there himself to convince the others that there was no supernatural agency involved.' He paused, eyeing Conway more closely for a moment. 'You've heard about all this before, Chief Inspector,' he said. 'Hasn't it occurred to you to put some enquiries in hand as to who might have purchased that instrument?'

'Mr Skelton also suggested that might be done,' said Conway, 'but I can't see that it's any part of the murder investigation. If I'd been you at that stage I'd have been more interested in where the magpie came from.'

'I was, but I talked to Barrington about it and found that most of the people involved have places in the country as well as a *pied à terre* in town, for when they're working. Jeremy Skelton is an exception to that, of course. At least, he and Anne live in the country but it's too far away to be called a weekend place.'

'Does this apply to Mark Kenilworth and Roberta Rowan, who at that stage were merely understudies?' Conway enquired.

'Mark Kenilworth, I believe, has spent weekends with Stella Hartley and Mary Russell. Roberta Rowan's home – her parents' home, I mean – is in Sussex. I've no idea how easy or difficult it might be to catch the bird. Difficult, I should think.'

'Not at all,' said Porterhouse, looking up suddenly from his notebook and surprising Maitland by the unexpectedness of his intervention. 'You need a net and some twigs to prop it up to make a snare, and if you wanted to attract a magpie, anything glittering would do. I've done it often as a boy . . . not with magpies, of course. But it does take patience.'

'Thank you, Sergeant,' said Conway rather repressively.

Antony was eyeing Porterhouse with a new respect. 'I'm glad to have that cleared up,' he said. 'The next day the first really serious thing happened, and this time the police were told. You'll have heard all about it from your local people. Edward Brome nearly got himself gassed in his dressing room . . . I mean he *was* gassed, but fortunately didn't die. I have to admit I'd done all I could think of by that time and come to the conclusion that someone had a grievance against one of the three men I mentioned . . . Brian Barrington, Chester Cartwright or Jeremy Skelton. But I thought it was probably against Barrington, because the other two weren't so well known to the players.'

'That was just two or three times you attended rehearsals?'

'Yes, I have my own work to get on with, and once the police had been called in it seemed to be more their job than mine. Oddly enough, things seemed to quieten down after that, but then Meg told me one evening that the costumes had been slashed and the wardrobe mistress was in a terrible state about it. And the next thing was that one of the trap-doors on the stage fell in when Matthew Benbow was standing on it and he broke his leg. The bolt had been partly sawed through, but it can't have been aimed particularly at him – any one of the cast might have been standing on it when the accident happened. And I keep on using that word,' he corrected himself, 'but I don't believe for a moment it was anything but deliberate. Barrington said he knew exactly what the police would say if he called them in again, and it turned out he was right.'

'So the understudy, Mark Kenilworth, came into his own?'

'No, he'd already taken over Edward Brome's part. I'm sure you must have been told by somebody, Chief Inspector, that Brome refused to return to the play after what happened to him, though oddly enough he continued to attend most of the rehearsals. It was Brian Barrington who took over the part of Sir Benjamin Oldfellow, in addition to directing. And that's just about everything, except for the note that was found yesterday morning and said to be in Sir John's own writing. Have you had an opportunity of comparing them, Chief Inspector?'

'Mr Barrington showed me a book with a sample of the way Cartwright wrote, and there's certainly a similarity. But forgery is not an unknown art, Mr Maitland.'

'That's just my point. Do you still insist all these things are unconnected with Stella Hartley's death?'

'A series of practical jokes for publicity purposes,' said Conway, who had obviously quite made up his mind. 'And three accidents that might have happened at any time.'

'There were no fingerprints on the gas tap,' said Antony, 'except the thumbprint I left when I turned it off. Benbow and I

192

had been talking, you know, and we found Brome together.'

'I learned as much from the divisional detectives,' Conway told him.

'I thought as much. And if that wasn't enough, someone had used a saw on the bolt of the trap-door.'

'A careless workman,' said Conway. 'And in the first instance, perhaps, an overzealous cleaner. I really can't take all this seriously, Mr Maitland.'

'Then I don't quite understand why you wanted it all repeated,' Antony retorted.

'I've explained that once. Besides, I may not be interested in the events themselves but I am interested in your reaction to them. And you haven't told me yet why you were in the theatre at the dress rehearsal.'

'Because Stella Hartley came to see us one evening. My wife, Jenny, was there, of course, as well as Meg and Roger Farrell. Yes, I thought that would make you sit up,' he added with some satisfaction.

'Mrs Farrell – Miss Hamilton – made no mention of the fact.'

'She wouldn't, unless you asked her a direct question. Meg hates gossip.'

'An admirable trait, but one that should be set aside in a murder investigation,' said Conway coldly.

'I don't suppose she thought it was important,' said Antony in a soothing tone that he knew would infuriate the detective. 'And there wasn't anything in it really. Stella was a firm believer in the ghost theory and she'd got it into her head that the next thing to happen would be that Brian Barrington would really be stabbed behind the screen when that part of the play was reached. Has someone explained that the character he's playing is killed at the end of the first act?'

'Mr Skelton . . . at great length. But are you telling me you took her seriously?'

'Not really, but she said it was dramatically the obvious thing to happen next,' said Maitland slowly. 'I did promise her I'd warn Barrington to be on his guard.'

'Against the ghost of Sir John Cartwright?' said Conway, with a rather sour smile.

'You forget, Chief Inspector, she thought that even though he was a spirit he had to make do with whatever material things came to hand. But the way I looked at it, if she'd thought of that, someone with a dramatic turn of mind might have done so too. So

I spoke to Brian Barrington, but the warning was unnecessary, as you now know. Is there anything else I can tell you?'

'About last night. About the attitude of the various people to the practical jokes. And about the relationship between Brian Barrington and Stella Hartley.'

'On the first two points I'll be glad to oblige you, Chief Inspector,' Antony told him. 'Of the last I know nothing except what I've been told . . . nothing of my own knowledge.'

It was only too obvious that Conway didn't like the reply, but he contented himself by saying, 'The other two questions, then.'

'About last night. What Stella Hartley had said to us had some influence on me, I'll admit, it gave me a feeling that something might be going to happen and that's why I went, and why Roger attended too, though we both of us realised there was nothing much to be done if someone was really intent upon mischief. We sat in the front row of the stalls for the whole of the performance, which was rather long as I understand is almost inevitable at a dress rehearsal. After they'd finished we stayed where we were, waiting for Meg, while Jeremy Skelton went behind the scenes to congratulate the actors on their performance.'

'During the rehearsal did anything happen that might be material to my enquiry?'

'There were some signs of strain among the cast. I don't think that was anything to be surprised at. Nothing at all that might be material, as you put it.' (Stella Hartley's influence on the way Brian Barrington had played his part was an impression only, Antony told himself, not a fact.)

Conway gave him another of his hard looks. 'And then Miss Rowan screamed and you also went behind the scenes?' he said.

'The noise had attracted everybody, and there was a great deal of confusion. Roberta was pointing and Roger and I reached the door of Miss Hartley's dressing room just behind Brian Barrington. It was only too obvious, after a very brief examination, that she was dead, so I cleared everyone out and left things as they were for you people.'

'That was thoughtful of you.' The sarcasm in the detective's tone bothered Maitland not at all, it was so very characteristic. 'But as it seems I'm not going to get any help from you on the factual plane, perhaps you'll go on to my second question.'

'I should have thought what I've just told you was fact,' Antony protested. 'But about the attitude of the various people concerned to what you call the practical jokes – though I don't know why I should blame you for that because it's what we've all been doing all along – there's nothing much I can say except that the actors believed in Sir John Cartwright's ghost. All of them, I think, though some of the men were a bit chary about saying so. And Brian Barrington didn't, but at the time of most of the incidents he was directing, not acting.'

'Not exactly helpful, Mr Maitland.'

'I didn't think it would be,' said Antony cheerfully.

'Does some more detailed information about the people I'm dealing with come within the bounds you've set yourself?' Conway asked with exaggerated patience. 'And I shouldn't have to tell you of all people, Mr Maitland, why I ask you that.'

'You want to know the kind of witnesses they'll make,' said Antony, apparently enlightened, but in reality wondering who had informed the police about Brian's relationship with the dead woman.

'You're exactly right, and I think it very astute of you,' said Conway. (Sarcasm again, and perhaps this time he had asked for it.) 'There is also the fact that the discovery of the practical joker's identity might have provided a motive for Miss Hartley's murder if she had been the one to make it. But I gather you don't agree with me about that possibility.'

'I considered it, but Stella was so convinced about the ghost that it seemed very unlikely. Besides, the whole string of affairs seems to me more like a – like a relentless progression.'

Conway smiled bleakly. 'Something in the nature of a Greek tragedy,' he commented. 'I don't agree with you about that, but I have to admit I've also discarded my own tentative theory in favour of a simpler one. All the same, I'd still like to know –'

'Very well, then, I'll tell you as far as I remember, though I don't think it will take you any further than what I've said already. Of the two Webbs – her stage name is Chillingworth – Amanda believes firmly in the ghost, and Arthur wouldn't commit himself when he spoke to me about it, but I rather think he's come round to that idea since. Mr Barrington – I told you this – doesn't believe in ghosts, though he's superstitious, and he certainly doesn't believe in Sir John, or anyone else from the spirit world, returning to haunt us. As for Mr Cartwright, he's quite certain that the events were of a malicious nature, not supernatural, and that they were directed against Brian Barrington. Matthew Benbow . . . this isn't strictly relevant, do you still want to hear it?'

'You may as well tell me.'

'He thinks Sir John's ghost probably was responsible for everything that happened. Of course I haven't talked to him since Stella's death. He says Sir John Cartwright would have no need to know the theatre intimately – what ghost would? – and he certainly would have known how the actors would be affected by what was being done. As for Edward Brome, though I haven't spoken to him about this specific point, I'm quite sure he thinks his accident – as you're pleased to call it – was part of a campaign by Sir John Cartwright to stop the play from being put on. Stella Hartley was very vocal on the subject, quite convinced, and Mary Russell echoed her. Roberta Rowan kept her own counsel, and – as in the case of Joseph Weatherly and Mark Kenilworth – I can only tell you Barrington's opinion that *all* the actors were affected by the ghost hunting.'

'And Miss Hamilton . . . Mrs Farrell?' Conway seemed unable to decide on which form of address would be more correct in the circumstances.

'As far as I could be sure about her attitude, she resisted the idea at first, was brought round to it gradually, and now has dropped it altogether. But even about her I can't be *sure*.'

'I have known occasions –' Conway broke off there, and when he went on, it was with a change of course. 'Mr Barrington, you think, is the only one of the actors who doesn't believe in ghosts?' he asked.

'So far as I know.'

'Doesn't it strike you, Mr Maitland, that if your theory is correct and all the events are connected – not that I believe it for a moment – one of the actors must be responsible? Neither Mr Skelton nor Mr Cartwright would have such a good idea of the effect all these things would have on them.'

That was exactly what Brian Barrington had said to him, but Maitland wasn't prepared to agree, though how far this was due to his ambivalent feelings towards Conway he wouldn't have liked to say. 'I don't think I'd go quite as far as that,' he said cautiously.

'I understand. You have some theory of your own, and I'd be interested to hear what it is.'

Antony laughed, and just for the moment was genuinely amused. 'I told you about my earlier theories, which I've since discarded, since they were private ones. Nothing would induce me to – to theorise ahead of my data, as my uncle is fond of saying, about Stella Hartley's murder, even for your edification, Chief Inspector.'

'Knowing you, Mr Maitland, that makes me wonder whether you have some information up your sleeve that you're saving to spring on the prosecution at the trial.'

Maitland was suddenly very still. 'Is that your next move, Chief Inspector? An arrest?' Conway made no attempt to reply, and after a moment Antony went on. 'It was a surprise to me that you released the theatre in time for tonight's opening.'

'I should say that was my own business, wouldn't you?'

'You must allow me to take an intelligent interest in the situation, however. Tell me, why did you jump to the conclusion that Brian Barrington was consulting me as a client, rather than as a friend with more experience in police matters than he has.'

'That should be obvious,' said Conway stiffly.

'Not to me. If you're implying he's a suspect,' Antony added, deliberately provocative now, 'that just won't wash.'

'Won't it, Mr Maitland, won't it? Opportunity –'

'In common with half a dozen other people.'

'– and motive –'

'Still not enough, Chief Inspector.'

'– and the fact that the victim had scrawled his initials – B.B., which seems to be what his colleagues always call him – in lipstick across a copy of her script for the play. Something you didn't notice, Mr Maitland, the paper was partly hidden by her hair . . . for which I suppose we should be truly thankful.'

'I see. Still not proof,' he added after a moment, 'but enough, I suppose, to excuse your apparent jumping to conclusions.' He caught Porterhouse's eye as he spoke and if he hadn't been so worried could have hardly kept his face straight when that rather solemn young man winked at him.

'It seems I'm wasting my time,' Conway said, getting to his feet. 'But I should warn you, Mr Maitland, if Mr Barrington is not your client and you are trying to conceal anything from me –'

'On the contrary,' he said, following the other man's example and coming to his feet. 'If I were to confuse the issue with guesswork you might have something to complain of. But there's one more thing you might tell me . . . has anything been found out about the dagger?'

Conway took his time about answering but when the reply came it didn't seem worth the hesitation. 'No,' he said. 'It's definitely Elizabethan, but nobody admits to having seen it before.'

'And you're letting the company have the theatre back this evening?'

'That's two questions, Mr Maitland, one of which I've answered already?'

'Why.' asked Antony bluntly.

'If I had my way –' Conway started angrily but broke off in time to avoid what Antony was sure would have been another indiscretion. 'It was considered expedient,' he answered primly and started for the door. Antony hoped he didn't hear Sergeant Porterhouse's muttered, 'Orders from on high,' as he closed his notebook and got up to follow his superior officer.

IV

The moment he was quite sure the two detectives must have left the premises Antony was down the corridor like a flash and burst unceremoniously into his uncle's room. Fortunately Sir Nicholas was alone, but as Maitland closed the door and began to advance towards the desk he sat back in his chair, removed the rather intimidating glasses he wore for reading, and looked the younger man slowly up and down.

'I'm aware, Antony, that we have recently suffered an invasion by two members of the police force – your old friend Conway, I believe, being the senior of the two – but that is hardly an excuse for your bursting in here like a maniac. Supposing I had been in conference, or did you trouble to ascertain from Mallory that I wasn't?'

'No, Uncle Nick, I didn't. I'm sorry, of course I should have done so. And Conway's no friend of mine,' he added rather ruefully.

'I'm quite aware of that.'

'I wanted to talk to you, you see.'

'That also is self-evident. It concerns, I imagine, Stella Hartley's murder, and Barrington's visit to you earlier this morning.'

'If Conway hadn't been waiting I'd have talked to you about that right away, even though it didn't seem quite so urgent then as it does now.'

'All the same I think it would be advisable to take things in

198

order. I presume the matter is not so pressing that you can't do that. I may find your story more comprehensible that way,' said Sir Nicholas, not sounding particularly hopeful.

'All right, Sir, I'll do my best. The thing is, Brian Barrington thinks the police suspect him – well Conway confirmed that, and not only by implication.'

'How did you induce him to do that, I wonder?'

'It isn't really difficult to get Conway's goat.' Maitland was too preoccupied with his story to notice the look of pain that crossed his uncle's face. 'But I'm getting ahead of my story. I mean, Brian didn't know then what I know now, but he was worried enough to want my help.'

'Did you agree to his request?' asked Sir Nicholas, rather as though the answer held no particular interest for him.

'I sent him to see Geoffrey, that was the best I could think of. But first I got him to tell me why he thought he was their chief suspect, which was because of his relationship with Stella Hartley. And I'm sorry, Uncle Nick, I'll have to jump here to my talk with Conway. They're treating the murder as an isolated incident, nothing to do with what has been going on all through rehearsals.'

'I think that was only to be expected, though from what you told me about your talk with Sykes I should rather have thought they would be looking more closely at Jeremy Skelton.'

'Yes, but they wouldn't find the vestige of a motive for him to have killed her.'

'They can't build a case on motive alone,' Sir Nicholas pointed out.

'No, of course not. This brings me to the thing Conway must be kicking himself now for having told me. I didn't see it when I saw her but they discovered a piece of paper when they moved her – her script, actually – with the letters "B.B." scrawled on it in lipstick. You may not know but that's what most of Barrington's friends call him.'

'An accusation from the grave,' said Sir Nicholas sepulchrally. 'It means she didn't die immediately, but there are a great many cases on record when a person stabbed in the back did a good deal more than that before finally succumbing.'

'If she wrote it.'

'I'm beginning to feel you're not being altogether frank with me, Antony. Do you or do you not think Barrington guilty?'

'I don't know, Uncle Nick. I don't think so, even in the face of this new evidence, but I –'

'Are you trying to tell me that you've developed a theory about what happened?'

'Yes, I have,' said Antony defensively. He hesitated a moment and then added, 'That's what's worrying me.'

'If you're wondering whether you should have spoken of it to Conway you know as well as I do, Antony, that you should have done nothing of the kind. Save it for the trial if there is one, which from what you've told me sounds very likely.'

'I know that's the right thing to do in most cases, and that's why I wanted to consult you. Because in this particular instance it may be different. At the moment Brian's main concern is for the play. It would take too long to explain just at the moment, but it isn't only a matter of financial success but because he's getting back his nerve as an actor again, and that's terribly important to him. If he's arrested, *Crabbed Age and Youth* won't open . . . it isn't just a whim, he's really serious about it. So that raises the question, what ought I to do?'

'As it seems likely that Barrington will be arrested in any event –'

It was never a good idea to interrupt Sir Nicholas, but at the moment Maitland was too worked up to consider the possible dangers. 'I know that put baldly like this it sounds as though there was no problem, but what bothers me is the fact that the police are allowing them to open tonight.'

'Are they indeed? I've been taking it for granted that the first night would have been postponed.'

'Well, it isn't going to be and . . . Uncle Nick, you'll say I've been consorting too much with members of the acting profession, but I've got a horrible feeling that someone's sense of the dramatic is at the bottom of this decision to let the play open.'

'Now I should never have suspected that Chief Inspector Conway would have a flair for drama.'

'I don't mean Conway, I don't think it's his decision at all. I think it's the Assistant Commissioner, Sir Alfred Godalming.'

'But what has all this to do with the play's opening tonight?'

'Everything, Uncle Nick. Just imagine, one performance and then the arrest of one of the leading actors. The trial would be bound to cause a sensation, and as they know I was trying to help Barrington about what they choose to call the practical jokes they must have been pretty sure, even before Conway saw him here, that I'd be asked to take the defence. I don't for a moment believe that Conway suspects me of trying to get my client off by any improper means – he doesn't like me but he knows me too well for that. But Sir Alfred Godalming's a different matter as we both know. He'd think, the affair having become a *cause célèbre*, that I'd be frantic to win it, and there'd be a very good chance of catching me out trying to rig the evidence, or something like that.'

'That's a very pretty picture, Antony,' said Sir Nicholas thoughtfully. 'Unfortunately, I'm bound to say that in this case you may well be right. You're expecting then that the performance will go on as scheduled this evening –'

'Conway confirmed that.'

'– and that Barrington will be arrested more or less as he comes off stage.'

'That's exactly it, Uncle Nick. And even if I manage to persuade the court of his innocence, which won't be easy in view of his attitude towards the play . . . you see my problem, don't you?'

'Certainly I do. If you talk to Conway and don't convince him – or even if you do convince him, and Sir Alfred is still stubborn – you may have thrown away a good strategy that could have been used in court. I think you ought to leave it up to Barrington.'

'Jenny and I have been asked to the party after the play tonight. It's being held at the theatre rather than in a public place because of Stella's death. I also wanted to ask you whether you'd come along instead of Jenny. I know you'd be welcome.'

'Why?' asked Sir Nicholas.

Correctly interpreting this as being a query into his own motives, Maitland replied promptly, 'For moral support, of course And Geoffrey will be there, too, and I hope by then he'll have the answer to some enquiries I asked him earlier to put in hand on my behalf.'

'Very well, I'll come. Though I've little hope,' said Sir Nicholas, tartly, 'of being able to restrain you from any foolishness you may have in mind.'

'You advised me to ask Brian how he'd like to deal with the matter,' Maitland reminded him.

'So I did. And in the meantime, I think we might adjourn this meeting in favour of luncheon, over which you can explain to me this theory of yours, and why the man who seems likely to become your client had a very good motive for wishing Stella Hartley dead.'

V

Everyone has heard of the first night of *Crabbed Age and Youth*, how every ghoul in London clamoured for tickets as Brian Barrington had predicted and all the serious theatre-goers besides. Not that there was much room to accommodate latecomers, the bookings had already been heavy.

Roger had won what amounted to a running battle with Sir Nicholas over the last few weeks (though amicably enough conducted) as to who should pay for their transportation that evening. A hired limousine seemed the only practical way of getting to and from the theatre, so it called for him first in Chelsea, and then came on to pick up the Kempenfeldt Square party. Meg, of course, was already at the theatre, though Roger reported that she had had a couple of hours' sleep at home that afternoon.

The first people they encountered on arriving at the theatre were Jeremy and Anne Skelton. Jeremy's mood that evening was a complex one. One moment he was elated, and the next quite sure that the whole thing would be a dismal failure. And then again he would remember Stella Hartley and pull a long face. Anne was her usual quiet self, and gravitated almost immediately to Jenny's side, while Vera, though her hair was already escaping from confinement, looked her usual imperturbable self. Roger, too, never one to show his feelings, seemed no more on edge than was usual with him on a first night, but Sir Nicholas – to the casual eye a little bored with all the fuss – kept eyeing his nephew as though he were a ticking time bomb. Which wasn't a bad analogy, Antony thought. He was nervous himself and trying hard not to show it, and he had a very strong feeling that before the evening was over anything at all might happen, and none of it pleasant. He had already informed his uncle that Brian Barrington had proved extremely elusive that afternoon, so he hadn't been able to ascertain his wishes. 'So we'll just have to hope I'm wrong about what the police mean to do,' he had said, but when even Sir Nicholas had agreed with his forecast he hadn't very much real hope about that.

Their seating had been arranged about eleven rows back and well to the side, where they would be nowhere near the press contingent. Jeremy insisted on sitting next to the aisle. 'If I can't bear it,' he said, 'I may have to get up and go and walk about in the corridor.'

'Go to one of the bars, you mean,' Anne corrected him gently. Jeremy grinned at her and made no reply, but Maitland himself was pretty certain that one of the five bars at the Cornmarket Theatre would be Skelton's objective if things seemed to be going badly.

The playbills were purchased and admired; paper and print that succeeded in looking old fashioned without being at the same time illegible. 'Seems strange,' said Vera, looking down at the list of names, 'to think of one of these old plays being made into a murder mystery.'

'That isn't quite right, my dear,' her husband informed her. 'The play is by Mr Skelton, it's only the idea that comes from the seventeenth century. Have you heard when Mr Cartwright proposes to produce that document, Antony?'

'No, but I think he means to do it as soon as the play is launched.'

'Jeremy's seen it,' said Anne rather quickly.

'I didn't say he hadn't, my dear,' said Sir Nicholas equably. 'No need to sound defensive.'

'Well, some people think he may have made the whole thing up,' said Anne. 'But Jeremy's certain it's absolutely authentic, Sir Nicholas, and so is Mr Barrington, of course.'

'Where's Cartwright, by the way?' asked Antony. 'I thought he might be sitting with us.'

Roger had obviously been looking around him, and it was he who answered the question. 'He's over there just behind the row of press men. Do you see that white-haired man sitting next to him? They're in deep conversation, and I think he must be Dean Fineberg from one of the American universities. Mcg told me earlier today he'd be here, and she thinks there's a job in the offing.'

'But the choice of seats was probably not gratuitous.'

'No. I think,' said Jeremy smiling, 'that he wanted to eavesdrop on anything the critics might say. A forlorn hope, I imagine, because I don't think any of them would give away his own ideas to another. I only hope,' he added, voicing an idea that was obviously very much at the forefront of his mind, 'that they don't go back to their offices and write a series of vitriolic reviews.'

'I don't think you've anything to worry about on that score,' said Antony, then hoped he hadn't stressed the last words too much, so that the whole party would become infected with his own nervousness. 'It's a funny thing,' he added thoughtfully, 'that I feel almost as caught up in this play's success as you do, Jeremy.'

Contrary to his expectations, after the difficulties of the dress rehearsal and all that had happened since then, the curtain went up within two minutes of the appointed time. If Brian Barrington was nervous, as he must have been, there was no sign of it; Meg was her usual magnificent self, and Roberta Rowan – when her turn came – played up manfully. (Though once Jeremy was heard to mutter, 'She's giving Brian the wrong cue.') But all was well, Barrington was far too old a hand at this sort of thing to be put off by a minor detail like that. He was probably improvising, but the audience couldn't know it, and he brought his speech around smoothly again to a point that Roberta recognised.

After that the first act went from strength to strength. Sir Benjamin died as dramatically as anyone could have wished, and Lady Oldfellow's horror was plain for all to see. Jeremy Skelton, who in spite of his forebodings was still in his seat, leaned across and whispered to Antony, 'There's a bottle of champagne with your name on it in the Edmund Kean bar. I'll leave you to it because I know these press fellows . . . there's no hope of my escaping them, but you may as well do so.'

The champagne was waiting for them quite safely and the rest of the party found a quiet corner where they could partake of it in peace. Anne, also a fugitive from the press, had already seen something of the play, as had Roger; but to Sir Nicholas and Vera and Jenny it was completely new, even though they knew something of the plot, and Maitland tried to concentrate on listening to their comments, rather than on his own anxieties.

'Never have thought a contemporary could have written it,' Vera declared, 'even with this outline of the plot you talked about.'

Sir Nicholas turned to Anne. 'Your husband is certainly to be congratulated, my dear. He's done an extraordinarily good job.'

'Doesn't it shock you at all, Vera?' Jenny asked, teasing her.

'Why should it? A bawdy lot, all of them,' said Vera. 'The play had to reflect that or it wouldn't have been true to the period. That's right, isn't it, Nicholas?'

'Certainly it is.' There was some further discussion of the various performances, with particular reference to Meg's, and if Antony was more silent than usual none of them commented on it. He was wondering if he'd really been right in his theory about the police's intentions, or if he had spoiled his uncle's evening for him unnecessarily by telling him what he thought. In any case there was no help for it now, and no immediate cause for alarm. Who lived might learn. They went back to their places just in time for the second act curtain to go up.

And now it was Arthur Webb's turn to dominate the proceedings in his role of Richard Twells, manservant turned detective. As he watched, Antony's admiration for the actors grew. Whether they had cared for Stella Hartley or not, each one of them must have been affected to a greater or lesser degree by her death, but here they all were: Lady Oldfellow, Bess Brownlees, Lucy Simpering, Gilbert Bold, and Jack Bashful exposed at last as the villain of the piece. 'Very proper, the most unlikely person,' Maitland heard Vera mutter as the curtain came down.

Jeremy Skelton had come back to his own seat not long after the curtain rose for the second act and had remained there quietly ever since. Now, as the applause rose to a positive tumult, he whispered something to Anne and then left them to disappear behind the scenes. Sure enough there were hopeful cries of 'Author,' rising to quite a clamour, and he joined the actors in taking his bows and even made a short speech at the end, raising his hands to quiet the tumult and giving most of the credit for the evening's success to his illustrious colleague, Sir John Cartwright, so that it occurred to Antony for a moment that this might be in the nature of a belated attempt to appease the dead. After that there was renewed applause, but eventually the curtain came down for the last time, the house lights went up and the audience began to disperse.

The fact that Sir Nicholas would attend the party in Jenny's place had already been arranged. She and Vera were to go home in the limousine, which would then come back and wait for the rest of the party, which by then would have had Meg added to its number. Roger and Anne went ahead towards the door that led backstage, with Maitland and his uncle following. Antony looked back from the doorway, but by then Jenny and Vera were lost in the crowd.

Behind the scenes all was confusion and Anne began to look a little bewildered. 'They lost a friend,' she said, turning a little so that all her companions could hear her. 'Don't they care at all?'

'Though Meg would never admit it, Stella wasn't altogether a likeable person,' said Roger carefully. 'Anyway, I think they're all so excited they've forgotten all about her for the moment.' And this seemed to be true enough. Even Mary Russell, who must have considered herself in some way bereaved, was flushed with the success of the evening, Roberta Rowan was crying openly, and Weatherly had his arms around her so that Antony was reminded vividly of the last embrace on stage between Lady Oldfellow and Gilbert Bold, newly released from suspicion of having caused the old man's death. Lady Oldfellow herself, in the person of Meg, left the group of actors and came to tuck her hand under her husband's arm, shattering the illusion. She too looked pleased and excited, while as for Brian Barrington he was frankly elated and had probably forgotten all about the police's suspicions, for the moment at least.

'And it's all your doing,' he said, grabbing Jeremy's hand and shaking it violently. 'You and all these wonderful, wonderful people.' He calmed down a little while Antony introduced him to Sir Nicholas, but then took Antony's arm and pulled him to one side.

'You see I can do it,' he said. 'I'm back in my proper place and I'm damned well going to stay there.'

'Yes, I can see you are,' said Antony. 'It was a wonderful evening.'

'It will run,' Barrington prophesied. 'And don't think for a moment Stella's death has anything to do with it. It will run because people will want to come for the right reasons, because it's a good play and we're acting it well and everyone will have a thoroughly good time. Oh, there's Chester who started it all. Come over here, Chester, I was afraid you weren't going to be able to drag yourself away from your friends to join the party.'

'I think,' said Cartwright carefully, 'that it went over well. I didn't hear any comments from the press men, but I did from the audience round about me and they were most enthusiastic.' As he paused, Barrington took the opportunity of introducing him to Sir Nicholas, the only member of the party so far unknown to him. 'And what did you think, Sir Nicholas, coming to it completely fresh?' Chester asked.

'A great and well-deserved success,' said Sir Nicholas.

Perhaps Anne thought this praise too moderate because she

206

proceeded to amplify it. 'Everybody near me was talking about it too, praising it, and I thought the applause would never stop.'

'All right, then.' Barrington was suddenly authoritative. 'Time to simmer down. We've got to get our make-up off, I'm not really one hundred and fifty,' he added to Sir Nicholas, 'but I had to keep it on for the curtain calls. So will you, Chester, and you, Jeremy, take our guests to the greenroom? We'll be with you as soon as we can.' He turned to move away and all of a sudden there was a sound, unexpected by all of them except Antony and perhaps Sir Nicholas, from the direction of the stage door . . . heavy footfalls and the doorkeeper's voice raised in unavailing protest. Antony was immediately convinced that he was about to be proved right, and had a moment almost of panic because he had been unable to speak to Brian and find out his wishes. A moment later Detective Chief Inspector Conway, followed by Detective Sergeant Porterhouse and two uniformed constables, came into sight.

Barrington said quite casually, 'Oh, there you are, Chief Inspector. Were you in the audience, and did you enjoy the play?'

'I'm not here to discuss the performance,' said Conway, 'and as a matter of fact I was not among the audience. I'm afraid my errand is a little more serious than you seem to think. Perhaps Sergeant Porterhouse and I could talk to you alone, Mr Barrington.'

Even in his state of euphoria Barrington couldn't mistake the ominous nature of these words. He looked at the detective in silence for a moment, and then turned a look of obvious appeal to Antony.

Maitland in his turn glanced rather desperately at Sir Nicholas, but got only a stony look in return. He was in no doubt at all from Conway's manner that an arrest was imminent, as he had feared, and for all the thought he had given the subject he'd been quite unable to reach a decision whether to let matters take their course or to try desperately to save the day – and the play from disaster. But Uncle Nick was giving him no help at all. He'd back him up, as Antony well knew, whatever he decided, but he wasn't going to make the decision for him. 'I think, Chief Inspector,' he said, forcing his tone to a mildness that he didn't feel, 'that perhaps we'd better talk a little before we take any drastic action.' As he spoke he remembered Brian's parting words to him that morning, and took what comfort he could from them. 'If you'd ask all these people to wait a while in case they're

207

needed we could use the greenroom. I should like my uncle – you know Sir Nicholas Harding, of course – to join us, and Mr Barrington should have his solicitor present.'

'Are you trying to delay matters, Mr Maitland?' asked Conway rather sourly.

'Far from it, Chief Inspector. Just trying to keep you from making a terrible blunder.' He went on rather quickly before Conway could raise any further objection. 'If you'll go back into the auditorium through the door we used, Roger, you'll find Geoffrey Horton waiting there. Please ask him to join us.'

Roger departed on his errand. Conway was frowning. 'You seem to have been expecting our arrival, Mr Maitland,' he said, making the words a question.

'Well, you see,' said Antony, almost apologetically, 'there was this odd business of your allowing the company to have the theatre back so quickly. So I put two and two together –'

Conway was still scowling at him, and decided to finish that sentence himself. 'And decided to confide in me after all,' he said. There was no friendliness in his tone.

Antony said a silent prayer that he was doing the right thing. 'I think in the circumstances,' he said, 'in fairness to Mr Barrington –' He let that sentence trail away into silence and then started again, but that too was to be an uncompleted remark. 'I think I can convince you –'

'Are you adding mindreading to your other attributes?' The people around them, so noisily excited a moment before, were silent now.

'Call it what you like,' Antony retorted. 'I admit I consulted my crystal ball about your intentions,' he went on airily, 'but I wouldn't say your approach was exactly subtle, would you?'

'Perhaps not. Perhaps I didn't feel that subtlety was necessary.'

'Antony –' said Barrington and was silent again. Maitland gave him a look he hoped was reassuring and was relieved – insofar as he was capable of feeling such an emotion just then – when Roger came back with Geoffrey Horton in tow.

'Chief Inspector Conway seems to have some questions for your client, Geoffrey,' he said, 'and he's very kindly agreed to my sitting in on the session, and Uncle Nick, too.'

'I gave no such permission,' said Conway stiffly.

'No, but you're going to, aren't you? You want to hear what I have to say because you think it may be useful later,' said

Maitland shrewdly, and went on without waiting for a reply. 'Will you lead the way, Brian? I expect you want Sergeant Porterhouse with you, Chief Inspector, but if your other men go, one to the stage door and the other to the door into the body of the theatre, that would ensure that everybody stayed put.'

'For once I find myself in agreement with you, my dear boy. That seems to me to be a very good idea,' said Sir Nicholas, making his presence felt for the first time. For some reason, perhaps because of this, Conway took Maitland's sudden fit of incisiveness with surprising calm.

'Very well,' he said. He spoke briefly to his men and even more briefly to the rest of the assembly and turned to follow Brian Barrington. 'Now, Mr Maitland!' he said, turning to Antony as soon as the six men were alone with the door closed behind them.

'Just a minute,' Barrington interrupted as Maitland was about to reply. 'Can you tell me what all this means, Antony? Am I going to be arrested?'

'Not if I can prevent it,' said Maitland firmly, 'though I admit it seems at the moment to be the general idea. I'm right about that, aren't I, Chief Inspector?'

'Perfectly right, Mr Maitland.'

'Have you spoken to Mr Kenilworth?'

'Naturally, he was one of the first people I questioned.'

'And?'

'He confirmed that your client had indeed visited him in his dressing room for a few minutes, but he was extremely vague about the time. I'm afraid this evidence won't be of much use to the defence,' said Conway with a note of satisfaction in his voice. 'And if you're about to point out that our case is circumstantial, may I remind you that in a case of murder, it is very rarely otherwise? In view of –'

'Yes, I know all about that,' Antony interrupted him impatiently. 'However –'

'However,' said Conway, picking up the word. 'You seem very sure of yourself all of a sudden. I'm willing to hear what you have to say, as long as you don't take too much time about it.'

Whatever that portended it was certainly not capitulation. More like the spider and the fly, Antony thought, an apt analogy in view of his own fears. 'First of all,' he said, 'I'd like you to think what could be done in court with this idea of yours that none of the original incidents in the theatre had anything whatever to do with Stella Hartley's murder.'

'That has naturally been considered,' said Conway, at his most austere.

Maitland disregarded this and went on as though there had been no interruption. 'The prosecution wouldn't have a hope of keeping an account of what went on during the rehearsals out of the evidence; and even if they did everybody in the country has read about the ghost of Sir John Cartwright during the past few weeks. I doubt if you could find a jury of twelve people anywhere in the country who haven't.'

'That may be true, but –'

'You're going to tell me that has nothing to do with the case, and that the jury will be told to disregard everything that happened except the murder. I'll admit that, but imagine yourself in the jury room while they were considering their verdict.'

'If all you're going to do is point out some hypothetical difficulties the prosecution may have,' said Conway coldly, 'you're wasting your time. And mine, which I happen to consider more important. If you really have anything material to say –'

'I have,' said Antony. 'But I'd like you first to consider the matter as it would appear to an unbiased person.'

'I came into this case with a completely open mind.' Conway was practically rigid with indignation now.

'Yes, Chief Inspector, I'm sure you did,' said Maitland soothingly. 'I also think you'd have preferred more time to – to pursue your enquiries, if you hadn't been jockeyed by one of your superior officers into making a rather premature arrest.' (Uncle Nick was probably swooning at the liberties he was taking with the English language, but he'd no time to worry about that.)

'I'm quite ready to take full responsibility for my actions,' Conway told him.

'Nobody's blaming you,' said Antony kindly. And went on quickly, to avoid what promised to be an explosion of some magnitude, 'I've had it pointed out to me several times that only a member of the acting fraternity would have known exactly how all these things would affect the rest of the cast.'

'I mentioned it to you myself,' said Conway, obviously not yet in the mood to forgive and forget.

'So you did, and you deduced from that that as far as the practical jokes went one of the actors must be guilty. I dispute that. I think that anyone as superstitious as these people proved to be would have been afraid of calling down Sir John

210

Cartwright's curse on himself or herself by acting that way.'

'That may be true,' Conway conceded, 'but it has nothing to do with the case against Mr Barrington.'

'It has everything to do with it. Because all this can be argued in court, Chief Inspector, I think it would pay you to listen to what I have to say.'

'I've already said I will,' Conway snapped.

'All right, then. I think all the things that have been happening, the things that it pleases you to describe as practical jokes and accidents, have been done with one reason in mind . . . to try to stop the play being put on. Why should any member of the cast wish for that particular outcome? Why should the director have desired it? He was under no compulsion to take the play, to go to considerable trouble, as I believe he did, to get backing for it.'

'I suppose this is leading up to some conclusion, Mr Maitland. Are you going to tell us what it is?'

'I'm sure you realise by now that nothing can stop me,' said Antony, but if he thought a touch of humour would soften Conway's austerity he was mistaken. 'Sergeant Porterhouse has a note of all the incidents,' he went on. 'They started quietly enough, though the idea that the play might be haunted was very quickly implanted. And all the time they were increasing in desperation as the person concerned realised that without some overt violence the production wasn't going to be stopped. He'd underestimated the resilience of the company. I don't think for a moment that murder was contemplated in the beginning, but apart from Edward Brome none of the cast was deterred from the parts they were playing; all the obstacles arose only to be overcome. I think the murder of Stella Hartley was the last frantic attempt to get things stopped, and certainly in the ordinary way the police investigation would have prevented the play from opening on time. Perhaps, in view of the various things that have come to light, from opening at all.'

'You make a good case, Mr Maitland,' said Conway. He still sounded far from cordial, but a little doubt had crept into his voice.

'As I said, if you go ahead and serve your warrant, all this will be argued in court. Now with your permission, Chief Inspector, there are two people I should like to join us, I think they may be able to help.' He paused only a moment, not long enough for Conway to agree or disagree. 'Would you be kind enough,

211

Sergeant Porterhouse, to ask Mr Skelton and Mr Cartwright to come in?'

Brian Barrington was staring at Maitland as though he suspected him of having gone mad. Porterhouse got up in silence and went out. Conway said, almost viciously, 'You take a good deal on yourself, Mr Maitland,' but then his eyes turned to Sir Nicholas, a silent spectator, and whatever further comments he might have been about to make remained unuttered.

VI

Porterhouse returned surprisingly quickly with his charges, too quickly really for Maitland's taste. He'd brought the matter so far and there was no going back now, but he was realising fully for the first time the difficulties that lay ahead in the course he had mapped out for himself. He had persuaded Sir Nicholas to attend because he felt his presence might go some way towards persuading Conway to listen to him, and if things went wrong now his uncle would have a good deal to say about the matter. But he wouldn't lose any sleep about that, it was something that could be dealt with when the time came. His thoughts were all for his duty to Brian Barrington, who, strictly speaking, was not his client but towards whom he felt as much sense of responsibility as if a brief had been offered and accepted. If he had had time to consult him . . . the decision had been entirely his own. And if it proved to be the wrong one, as suddenly seemed most likely, he thought it would haunt him for the rest of his life; in a lighter mood he would have added, like Sir John Cartwright's restless spirit, but just now he had no feeling for humour in the situation.

Jeremy Skelton came in first with his usual rather springy stride and a worried look in Barrington's direction. 'Is everything all right?' he asked. 'I rather thought –'

Brian essayed a grin, though a rather half-hearted one. 'You thought you'd see me standing here already with gyves upon my wrists,' he said lightly. As he was still in costume and full make-up – though he had taken his wig off, which gave him a rather odd, unbalanced appearance – Antony realised that this was the only possible way of putting it for one of the actor's temperament, even in what must be his present state of uncertainty.

212

'Well –' said Jeremy, and broke off there, uncertain how to proceed. He looked around him until his eyes came to rest on Maitland's face. 'What's all this about, Antony?' he asked. 'They've gone to take their make-up off now, but everyone's worried to death out there.'

'This won't take very long,' said Antony. 'Chief Inspector Conway has been kind enough to allow me to ask you a couple of questions.' He half expected the detective to contradict him, but Conway was strangely silent. Ominously so, Antony thought. He's giving me enough rope . . .

'There's formality for you,' said Jeremy. 'What are these questions, then?'

'Just a minute.' Maitland's eyes went past him to Chester Cartwright, who had followed Skelton into the room. The man was in a blaze of excitement, there could be no doubt about that, the general concern didn't seem to have touched him at all. Perhaps he had already reached some satisfactory arrangement with his theatre companion of that evening, so that the continued running of the play didn't matter to him. Or perhaps . . .

'It all worked out far better than you expected, didn't it, Mr Cartwright?' Antony asked.

For a moment he thought he was going to get an immediate agreement, but Chester pulled himself up on the point of speech. 'In view of what has happened that seems rather a tactless comment,' he said, rather primly.

'Yes, so it does,' said Maitland almost meekly. 'Jeremy, do you mind telling us what Mr Cartwright said when you first showed him your play written from Sir John Cartwright's outline?'

'A lot's happened since then,' Skelton pointed out, obviously puzzled by the question.

'Indeed it has, that's the whole point really. Do you mind answering me?'

'Of course not. He was mad as fire at first.'

'Perhaps you'd explain that to us a little more fully. It's the first the Chief Inspector has heard of it.'

Jeremy was obviously puzzled, but he turned a little to include Conway in his remarks. 'I could see his point in a way,' he said generously. 'The outline of the plot said that Sir Benjamin Oldfellow died of poison somewhere off-stage, so the only drama it was possible to wring out of his death was someone coming in to tell Lady Oldfellow about it. But here was the old boy saying "stap me vitals" at every possible turn, it was just too much of a temptation to make him die that way. Dramatic irony, I suppose you'd call it.' (If I hear that phrase once more! thought Antony.) 'And it did add to the suspense to have him dying on stage, Chester saw that later.'

'I think,' Maitland prompted him, 'that wasn't quite all that Mr Cartwright took exception to.'

'No, there was also the fact that I decided on the modern two-act format, but that wasn't really very important except that some of the climaxes in the action had to be arranged differently. Also Sir John had stipulated several changes of scene, but I knew it would save expense and make it easier to get backers if the action was contained in one set only.'

'For which I was very grateful,' Brian put in. 'Chester saw the point too when I explained it to him.'

'Yes, Mr Cartwright changed his mind, or said he did,' said Maitland, 'and took every available opportunity of repeating the statement. We all thought – at least I did, and I expect other people's reactions were much the same – that the prospect of fame and fortune through a successful production had changed his perspective.'

Conway came forward with the air of one who could be silent no longer. 'Mr Maitland,' he said sternly. 'If you're trying to make a point I think you must make it now without further equivocation. But I should warn you –'

'Yes, I know we're not in court and that nothing I say is privileged,' said Antony with a touch of impatience. 'All the same,' he added thoughtfully, 'I suppose I should be grateful for the reminder.' He turned back to Chester again, but if he'd expected a wary look to have replaced the one of exultation, he was quite mistaken. The man was clearly still on top of the world, and Antony's qualms returned in full force. (Shall I be defending Brian, or shall I be fully occupied fighting an action for slander?) But his voice was steady enough when he spoke again. 'I think, Mr Cartwright, that you're in love with the outline of the play and couldn't bear to see the smallest change in it. What Sir John Cartwright had written down was sacred ... or should I be saying what you had composed on his behalf?'

'Nothing of the sort. I told you I found it in my aunt's attic after she died, and when you imply that some human agency was responsible for the things that happened I think you're forgetting the last note in Sir John's own handwriting.'

'Copies of which you'd had before you for years, so that if

214

anyone could be supposed to have been able to produce a fair facsimile it would have been you,' Antony pointed out. 'Besides, I thought you didn't believe in ghosts. But about the outline, it doesn't matter either way, whether you wrote it or whether you didn't. It became something of an obsession with you. You're your aunt's sole heir aren't you, and inherited her property as well as everything else?'

'That's true, but I don't see what business it is of yours.'

'We'll come to that,' said Maitland quickly, seeing that Conway was growing even more restless. 'I'm going to suggest to you, Mr Cartwright, that you thought it expedient to change your announced opinion about the play, but that you continued to hate the changes as much as ever. You thought you could ensure that it never reached opening night by playing tricks in the theatre. I'm not suggesting that you wanted to hurt anybody when you started, but the actors were tougher than you thought and it was clear you had to take more desperate action. Edward Brome was injured, and then Matthew Benbow, and still the production was going on.'

'From all I'd read, and from all I've heard, they should have been terrified to come near the place by that time,' said Chester unexpectedly. 'A haunted theatre –'

'Yes, you were believing in it yourself by that time – weren't you? – even though you didn't admit it. Your great, great, great uncle – how many generations have passed since his death? – wouldn't have approved at all of Jeremy Skelton's play, would he?'

'Of course he wouldn't! There was this perfectly good idea and he dared to change it.' He broke off and a cunning look came into his eyes and he spent a moment looking round the assembled company as though trying to assess their reaction to what had been said. 'That isn't an admission of guilt,' he told them. 'I couldn't help what happened.'

'I'm beginning to think that's true,' said Antony, and a little regret had crept into his voice. 'You're obsessed by the outline just as it was written, and as you became more desperate you began not to care who got hurt.'

'Why should I care? What my uncle thought about what was going on was all that mattered.'

Jeremy Skelton was looking at him wonderingly. 'I never realised you still felt like this, Chester,' he said.

'Of course I did! You explained your reasons speciously

enough, and then Barrington came along with his offer of backing. What could I do but seem to go along with you? I didn't believe for a moment that *he* was satisfied. So I did what I could.'

He was smiling now, a secretive smile that Maitland felt had a chilling quality. 'This morning when the police said the play could go on I thought I'd failed, but I don't think I have after all,' Chester added, with a triumphant look in Barrington's direction.

'If you mean that you think the police came here to arrest Brian, you may be wrong about that,' said Maitland, with another silent prayer that Conway wouldn't contradict him. 'So there's no earthly reason why there shouldn't be more performances. You saw how enthusiastic the audience was tonight. It may run for years!'

'They can't do that! It's an insult to Sir John, a parody of what he intended.'

'Mr Cartwright!' Conway could contain himself no longer. 'Are you admitting to being the perpetrator of the practical jokes?'

'No, of course I'm not!'

'I think that the time has come for me to hand over the floor to Mr Horton, Chief Inspector,' said Antony. 'If you'll allow me, of course.'

'As Mr Horton is, I presume, Mr Barrington's solicitor,' said Conway, 'he has rather more right to be heard than you have.'

'I knew you'd see it my way,' said Antony, rather as though the detective had agreed enthusiastically to his suggestion. 'You know what I want you to tell us, Geoffrey.'

If Horton, who took his professional duties seriously, had any dislike for the position his friend had manoeuvred him into he gave no sign. In fact if any of those present had been a mindreader he would have seen that the solicitor's main worry at the moment was whether he was going to have to act for Antony Maitland when Cartwright brought charges of slander. 'You phoned me this morning with a rather urgent request for enquiries to be made in Haslemere,' he said.

'That's where Mr Cartwright's aunt lived,' Antony explained to Conway, who didn't look particularly grateful for the information.

'I got a firm of enquiry agents on to it right away,' Geoffrey went on as though there'd been no interruption. 'Old Miss Cartwright was quite well known in the town, as anyone with a reputation for eccentricity is likely to be. If she had lived right out in the country . . . but as it was, the aviary she kept on her porch caused a little comment.'

'I set all the birds free after she died,' said Chester.

'Among the birds she kept there,' said Geoffrey, still unmoved, 'was a magpie that was a particular pet of hers. I have the report here,' he added, 'if you wish to see it, Chief Inspector. As well as the information I've already given you. It also mentions that she had a reputation for never throwing anything away.'

'Then it is only right that I should warn you, Mr Cartwright,' said Conway, 'that if Mr Benbow and Mr Brome wish to lay charges you may find yourself in a difficult position.'

'Bringing the bird up to town and turning it loose in the theatre isn't the same thing as turning on gas taps or sawing through the trap-door bolt,' said Chester a little wildly.

At that moment Maitland felt the first glimmer of hope that perhaps, after all, things would go as he wished.

'Are we to believe then that there were two practical jokers?' asked Conway rather sardonically. But he certainly wasn't ready yet to concede defeat. 'However, Mr Maitland, this is all very interesting but it isn't getting us any nearer to Stella Hartley's murderer.'

'Are you still insisting that wasn't connected to the other things? It was the logical conclusion, the final stroke that was going to make the production impossible. Only it didn't work, did it, Mr Cartwright?'

'Brian killed her,' said Chester sullenly. 'Why else should she have written "B.B." down as she was dying?'

'How did you know that?' Conway's tone was like a whiplash, but both Cartwright and Maitland ignored him.

'I think you of all people in the room know that isn't true,' said Antony, speaking almost gently now. 'I think your sole purpose was to protect Sir John Cartwright's memory, as you thought. It wouldn't have mattered who you killed, but Stella was about the most unpopular member of the cast, and you knew all about Brian's dislike of her. On your own admission you were in the dressing room corridor –'

'I saw Brian there,' said Cartwright viciously.

'For the moment we're considering *your* actions, Mr Cartwright. What do you think prompted me to ask Mr Horton to make enquiries about the magpie in your home town of all places?'

'I'm sure I don't know.'

217

'I'd written you off as a suspect until I heard exactly what had killed Miss Hartley,' Antony told him. 'What else did you find in your aunt's attic?'

There was an odd silence in the room, except when Sir Nicholas caught his breath, and Jeremy Skelton muttered to himself, 'The dagger, of course!' To Antony the pause seemed to grow into an eternity, and then Chester Cartwright suddenly took a step forward, thrust his face to within a foot of his own, and began to speak.

'It had to be an Elizabethan weapon,' he said. 'Sir John insisted on that. And there was the dagger ready to hand in Aunt's attic. You were quite right . . . she never threw anything away. But it all turned out for the best, didn't it? The play went on this evening, but when the police have arrested him' – he jerked his head in Barrington's direction – 'I don't think there's another company in the English-speaking world would touch it. It had one performance, but I think my uncle allowed that for my sake, though I assure you my own concerns were the last things in my mind. Dean Fineberg arrived today and was in the theatre with me this evening, and I sign a contract with his university tomorrow morning. It's one of the most prestigious in the United States,' he boasted.

'Do you really think so?' asked Maitland sadly. There was relief in having got his way, but there was regret as well. He looked at Conway. 'What do you think, Chief Inspector?' he asked. 'Will Mr Cartwright be signing that contract or not?'

VII

So the party was held after all, though belatedly and with everyone in a rather sober mood. They were all too conscious of the gap in their numbers once the police had left with Chester Cartwright in custody. Nothing could quite dim Brian Barrington's relief, and he expressed his thanks so often and so vehemently that Antony was finally driven to saying almost crossly, 'If you don't stop that, Brian, I'll go straight home.' So Barrington grinned at him and went to talk instead to Roberta Rowan and Joseph Weatherly. The report of what had happened had gone like wildfire through the room and gained a little with every telling.

218

Geoffrey had attended the party too, because he was staying the night with the Maitlands, but he obviously felt himself very much an outsider, and they were all relieved when Meg expressed a wish to go home early, 'Because with one thing and another, darlings, I really do feel rather tired.'

When they got back to Kempenfeldt Square Roger told the limousine to wait. 'Meg and I won't stay long,' he assured the others, 'but I'm damned if I'm going to be left out of the final explanation. As for the extra time for the car, Meg can pay for that. She's obviously going to be coining money for the next year or so.'

Jenny and Vera had waited for them in the study, and that was where they all congregated. For their benefit, as well as for Roger and Meg's, who had heard only the inflated version of the story that had been going the rounds at the party, Antony (after a brief skirmish with his uncle, who, he said, could have told everything there was to tell just as well) capitulated so far as to explain what had happened to change Conway's mind about executing his warrant.

'Hadn't much to go on,' Vera said gruffly when he had finished. 'Dangerous. And you knew all about it, Nicholas. I wonder you let him do it.'

'My dear Vera, have you ever known me to have the slightest influence over my nephew's actions?' asked Sir Nicholas, rather unfairly. 'You can't hold me responsible for what he did. If this man Cartwright hadn't lost his nerve he might easily have brought a suit for slander, but I pointed that out to Antony even though I knew perfectly well he never has the slightest regard for his own interests, and after that I washed my hands of the whole affair.'

'You didn't at all, Uncle Nick, you went with him,' said Jenny.

'I was taking a chance and it came off,' Antony said. (And I hope none of you ever know how much I was afraid it wouldn't.)

'Never mind that,' said Roger pacifically.

And, 'Tell us how you worked it all out, darling,' Meg implored, almost in the same breath. 'The last time we talked about it you had quite made up your mind that Chester Cartwright was out of the running.'

'Uncle Nick's heard all this once,' Antony protested.

'Won't mind hearing it again,' said Vera. 'Your story,' she added firmly when she saw that Antony was still hesitating.

'All right, then,' said Maitland, resigned. 'It was the dagger

219

that made me rethink the whole thing and realise that it didn't have to be one of the actors. The press had been informed about the incidents . . . anybody could have done that, but I'm inclined to think it must have been Chester himself. And it wasn't absolutely certain that the person who turned on the gas knew that Brome had no sense of smell. But the weapon . . . how many people have such a thing lying about their homes? Unless it was concealed – and why should it have been? – somebody would have known about it. And if it had been bought especially for the purpose it could have easily been traced. Anybody who reads Jeremy Skelton's stories would have known that,' he added with a smile.

'That's perfectly true,' said Roger, anxious now to hear the rest of the story. 'And so?'

'And so I thought about Aunt Cartwright's attic,' said Antony. 'You see it seemed the one place it might have come from, with not a soul able to identify it except Chester himself. When I asked you to put that enquiry in motion, Geoffrey, all I thought was that we might learn she was an eccentric old lady who hoarded useless things. The aviary and the magpie were just a bit of luck; I thought Sergeant Porterhouse must have been right about how the bird was trapped . . . I've told you all, I think, about his rather ingenious theory. So then I realised that none of my ideas about motive might be exactly right, but if Chester Cartwright had held by his first opinion of the play he might have behaved exactly as I described tonight.'

'But if he hadn't confessed?' asked Sir Nicholas rather dryly.

'You don't need to remind me. He'd have had an excellent chance of suing me for slander and getting away with it, but worse than that I should have let Brian Barrington down by revealing a potential defence to the police, who would certainly have passed it on to the prosecution.' He took time to catch Jenny's eye and smiled at her reassuringly. 'The odd thing was, Chester was in such a state of euphoria that even when he admitted what he'd done he still seemed to think his object had been achieved, that Conway would go ahead and arrest Barrington, and that no company of actors in the future would touch the play with a ten-foot pole because they'd think it had a curse on it.'

Sir Nicholas permitted himself a slight shudder at this mode of expression. 'He'll be found unfit to plead,' he said, 'unless he sobers up by the time they reach the police station and makes a completely sane statement denying the whole thing. And if you want my opinion, Antony, this obsession of his has gone too far. It's almost as though he's possessed with Sir John Cartwright's spirit, and I think myself he'll go on talking in the same vein until the police are thoroughly sick of him.'

'I rather think you're right,' said Roger thoughtfully. 'But what about your friend, Sir Alfred Godalming? If I understood you, you think he was behind the decision to arrest Barrington at that particular time.'

'As things turned out there was no way Conway could have executed the warrant,' Antony told him, 'and if Uncle Nick's right and Chester Cartwright's as mad as a hatter –'

'That is not what I said,' Sir Nicholas murmured.

'– I imagine there's no question but that the police will be satisfied they've got the right man. Sir Alfred won't like it, of course, and I don't suppose it will endear me to him, but there's nothing he can do about it and I'm more glad than I can say that Barrington won't be brought to trial.'

'It'll do you out of a brief, darling,' Meg pointed out.

'So it will. I should have thought of that,' said Antony, smiling at her. 'Still, I shouldn't have liked the play to be stopped dead in its tracks, would you? And for some reason I feel almost as strongly as you do about that.'

It was already very late and the party broke up soon after that. Upstairs the spare-room bed was made up already, and Geoffrey left them almost immediately. After he had gone neither Antony nor Jenny had a word to say until they were safely in the bedroom with the door closed behind them. The bed was turned down but Jenny ignored its invitation and sat down in her favourite chair and kicked off her shoes. 'It might be a good idea to switch on the fire,' she said. After a moment, 'Antony –' she added, and broke off.

Antony was just getting up from his knees. He had obeyed her about the fire, but privately he thought that it was not merely the cold of the night that was making her feel chilly. 'Are you too going to tell me I was taking a chance?' he asked, with a humorous inflection in his voice.

'No, I wasn't thinking about that, and as a matter of fact I don't want to,' she added candidly. 'I think what worried you most is that you might have been doing Brian a bad turn by taking the line you did, but you know you can't expect us – Uncle Nick, Vera and me – to look at it in exactly that light. I'm thinking mainly about that wretched man, Godalming, and I don't somehow think Chief Inspector Conway will be properly grateful to you for putting him on the right track.'

'I don't suppose I'm ever going to form a beautiful friendship with either of those two,' Antony admitted, 'but just at the moment that doesn't worry me overmuch. That was a rather grim party, though, after everything was over,' he went on, reverting to the thought that was uppermost in his mind. 'Looking back I think everyone behaved rather well, when you think that all the people concerned with the play must have been relieved it wasn't one of their number who was under arrest.'

'You're blaming yourself, aren't you?' asked Jenny. 'And there's no need for that, somebody had to do it.'

'Yes, but why me?' There was no need, thank heaven, to explain things in detail to Jenny.

'Because of Meg, I suppose, in the beginning,' said Jenny literally, 'and because you liked Brian Barrington and believed what he told you.'

'Liking is no reason for believing people,' Antony told her, 'as you must have heard me say a thousand times.'

'Well then, because you can see further through a brick wall than most people,' said Jenny. He made no direct answer but stretched out his left hand to her, and when she took it pulled her to her feet so that she was standing very near to him. Without her shoes he had to bend his head a little further than usual to kiss her. 'If you don't like thinking about poor Mr Cartwright,' Jenny added a little breathlessly a moment later, 'think about Brian Barrington instead.'

Saturday, 14th February

The morning papers had reviews of the play, but no hint of the sensational events that had followed. The ghost story was rehashed again, which was only to be expected, but the comments on the play itself were unusually unanimous ... everyone seemed to have liked it, even those of the critics who can never resist qualifying their approval in some way.

'I think we're all set for a long run,' said Meg, coming in with her husband at teatime. 'Where's Geoffrey?' she added, looking round as though she expected to see the solicitor hiding in a corner of the room.

'He went home after breakfast,' Antony told her. 'For which for once I was truly thankful, he did nothing but lecture me all through the meal.'

'Can you wonder?' asked Roger, who felt it was safe to be amused by the events of the previous evening now that they were safely behind them. 'And I think Meg's quite right about the play. The telephone doesn't seem to have stopped ringing all the morning. We didn't wait for the reviews last night, but of course the rest of them had already seen them. Barrington says they couldn't be better.'

'I daresay he's right,' said Antony, but he sounded preoccupied. 'Have you seen the evening papers, by the way?'

'No, is there something more about it?'

'Not about the play. About Stella Hartley's murder. Chester Cartwright is under arrest, and they'll be bringing him up in the Magistrates' Court on Monday. I imagine he'll be remanded for a medical report.'

'Do you agree with Uncle Nick that he'll be found unfit to stand trial?' Meg asked.

'Yes, I do, and I hope we're both right because I'm sure it's what ought to happen.' He smiled faintly, but without any very real amusement. 'It will certainly turn out like that unless he stops talking nineteen to the dozen,' he added, 'and seeming not to realise the consequences to himself of what he's done.'

'There's another item that ought to interest Jeremy particularly when he sees it,' Roger told him.

'What's that?'

'Cartwright's cottage – the one he inherited from his aunt – burned down during the night. Nobody seems to know what caused the fire, but I don't suppose he cares much about that now one way or the other,' said Roger practically. Meg, however, was not prepared to dispose of the subject so easily.

'Do you think he could have done it himself?' she asked.

'I'm not in the mood for making any more guesses,' said Antony, but went on to contradict himself. 'It's quite possible, I imagine, that if he lighted a long enough candle and set it among some shavings before he came up to town it would have done the trick, besides supplying a sort of alibi. I think he's probably mad enough not to have thought anyone would suspect him. But if it *was* arson, that raises rather an interesting question.'

'I can give you the answer to part of it,' Roger told him. 'The famous outline of Sir John Cartwright's idea for a play was burned to ashes with the rest of the contents. There was some hope, according to the account I read, that it might have been protected by the sheets of glass that were supposed to preserve it, but apparently the heat of the fire was too intense. Chester's friend Dean Fineberg, who had hoped to save something out of the wreckage by getting his hands on it, is apparently fit to be tied. He's been talking to the press about the great loss to our cultural heritage.'

Jenny was staring at her husband in dismay. 'Oh, Antony!' she said, as tragically as Meg herself might have done. 'That was the one mystery left . . . whether Chester Cartwright wrote the thing himself, I mean. And now we shall never know!'